Deception always has a price tag.

No matter how small the lie, no matter how worthy the motive. And often one fib led to another. If he had to do it all over…

The sound of horse's hooves approaching interrupted his thoughts. A sleek chestnut galloped closer, the rider a woman with a blond ponytail, her face flushed as she passed him and stopped near the horse barn.

He recognized her immediately.

Abby.

She expertly dismounted and stroked the mare's head with a loving gesture. She laughed and the sound carried to where Jesse stood.

He remembered that laugh, musical and lighthearted. She'd laughed often back then; he wondered if she did now. Seeing her, even briefly, brought memories rushing back. Did she remember him with fondness, with pain—or at all?

From this distance, she looked the same, but maybe, up close, she'd changed as much as he had.

Dear Reader,

It's that time of year again—back to school! And even if you've left your classroom days far behind you, if you're like me, September brings with it the quest for everything new, especially books! We at Silhouette Special Edition are happy to fulfill that jones, beginning with *Home on the Ranch* by Allison Leigh, another in her bestselling MEN OF THE DOUBLE-C series. Though the Buchanans and the Days had been at odds for years, a single Buchanan rancher—Cage— would do anything to help his daughter learn to walk again, including hiring the only reliable physical therapist around. Even if her last name did happen to be Day....

Next, THE PARKS EMPIRE continues with Judy Duarte's *The Rich Man's Son,* in which a wealthy Parks scion, suffering from amnesia, winds up living the country life with a single mother and her baby boy. And a man passing through town notices more than the *passing* resemblance between himself and newly adopted infant of the local diner waitress, in *The Baby They Both Loved* by Nikki Benjamin. In *A Father's Sacrifice* by Karen Sandler, a man determined to do the right thing insists that the mother of his child marry him, and finds love in the bargain. And a woman's search for the truth about her late father leads her into the arms of a handsome cowboy determined to give her the life her dad had always wanted for her, in *A Texas Tale* by Judith Lyons. Last, a man with a new face revisits the ranch—and the woman—that used to be his. Only, the woman he'd always loved was no longer alone. Now she was accompanied by a five-year-old girl...with very familiar blue eyes....

Enjoy, and come back next month for six complex and satisfying romances, all from Silhouette Special Edition!

Gail Chasan
Senior Editor

Please address questions and book requests to:
Silhouette Reader Service
U.S.: 3010 Walden Ave., P.O. Box 1325, Buffalo, NY 14269
Canadian: P.O. Box 609, Fort Erie, Ont. L2A 5X3

Her Kind of Cowboy

PAT WARREN

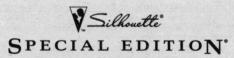

SPECIAL EDITION

Published by Silhouette Books

America's Publisher of Contemporary Romance

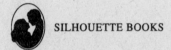

SILHOUETTE BOOKS

ISBN 0-373-24638-2

HER KIND OF COWBOY

This edition published by arrangement with Harlequin Books S.A.

® and TM are trademarks of Harlequin Books S.A., used under license.
Trademarks indicated with ® are registered in the United States Patent
and Trademark Office, the Canadian Trade Marks Office and in other
countries.

Visit Silhouette Books at www.eHarlequin.com

Printed in U.S.A.

Books by Pat Warren

Silhouette Special Edition

With This Ring #375
Final Verdict #410
Look Homeward, Love #442
Summer Shadows #458
The Evolution of Adam #480
Build Me a Dream #514
The Long Road Home #548
The Lyon and the Lamb #582
My First Love, My Last #610
Winter Wishes #632
Till I Loved You #659
An Uncommon Love #678
Under Sunny Skies #731
That Hathaway Woman #758
Simply Unforgettable #797
This I Ask of You #815
On Her Own #841
A Bride for Hunter #893
Nobody's Child #974
A Home for Hannah #1048
Keeping Kate #1060
Daddy's Home #1157
Stranded on the Ranch #1199
Daddy by Surprise #1301
Doctor and the Debutante #1337
My Very Own Millionaire #1456
Dakota Bride #1463
A Mother's Secret #1548
Her Kind of Cowboy #1638

*Reunion

Silhouette Romance

Season of the Heart #553

Silhouette Intimate Moments

Perfect Strangers #288
Only the Lonely #605
Michael's House #737
Stand-In Father #855
The Lawman and the Lady #1025
The Way We Wed #1070

Silhouette Books

Montana Mavericks
Outlaw Lovers #6

PAT WARREN,

mother of four, lives in Arizona with her travel agent husband and a lazy white cat. She's a former newspaper columnist whose lifelong dream was to become a novelist. A strong romantic streak, a sense of humor and a keen interest in developing relationships led her to try romance novels, with which she feels very much at home.

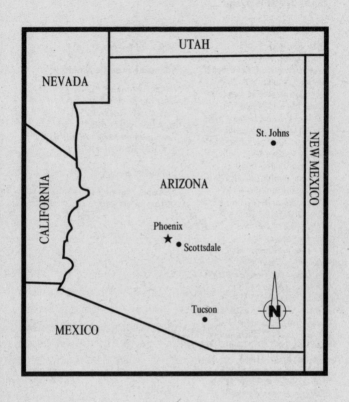

Prologue

Where was he?

Abby Martin paced under the big old cottonwood tree beside the stream on her parents' cattle ranch. The hot August sun had finally set about two hours ago, around seven o'clock, but the heat lingered. She scarcely noticed as she paced impatiently on the scraggly grass. He should have been with her by now.

Where was Jesse?

Her father had hired the tall, handsome ranch hand two months ago, just before she'd come home for summer vacation from Arizona State. The moment she'd laid eyes on him, she'd fallen hopelessly in love. Though they'd never spoken the words out loud, Abby was certain that Jesse felt the same by the way he'd look at her, hold her, kiss her. Then he'd whisper in her ear to meet him by the stream beneath *their* tree or sometimes in the hayloft. And he'd make tender love with her.

In the hazy moonlight, Abby squinted in the direction of

the outbuildings surrounding the main house, but she saw no sign of anyone on horseback heading her way. She hated sneaking around, but her mother was so against either of her two daughters having anything to do with the ranch hands. Jesse had told her that he wasn't just a cowboy, that he couldn't tell her more right now, but he had plans for the future. Big plans. Abby was sure she was a big part of those plans. When the time was right and they could be open and up-front about their feelings for each other, she'd tell her parents. She was certain they'd care for Jesse once they got to know him.

Thrusting nervous hands through her long blond hair, she readjusted her ponytail, then stopped, listening hard. Yes, there it was, the sound of a horse's hooves coming closer. In moments, Jesse came into view, his black hair ruffling in the evening breeze. As it did each time she saw him, Abby's heart skipped several beats. She watched him swing off his mount and tie the reins to a tree branch near the spot where her mare stood.

He wasn't smiling as he usually was, causing an anxious chill to race along her spine. But he rushed over and took her in his arms, holding her close. Yet so attuned was Abby to his moods that she knew instantly that something was wrong.

"What is it?" she asked, a sudden sense of foreboding causing her voice to tremble.

Jesse eased back reluctantly. "I have to leave right away for California. A family emergency. My father's had a heart attack." His brow creased with concern. He lifted a hand and caressed her face. "I'll be back as soon as I can."

"I'm so sorry about your father." He'd rarely mentioned his family. Of course, he had to go. Abby knew that. But oh, she hated the thought of his leaving. "You've been working since sunup. You *are* going to fly rather than drive, right?"

Distracted and anxious to be on his way, he shook his head. "No flights out till late tomorrow morning. I can be there before then if I drive straight through." Seeing the distress in her eyes, Jesse felt torn. He owed her an explanation, but there wasn't time. As soon as his father was out of danger, he'd return and explain everything. "Don't worry. I'll be fine."

Bending to her, Jesse pulled Abby close and gave her a hard kiss, then leaped up onto the black stallion.

Suddenly unsure of his feelings for her, Abby gazed up at him. "You will come back, won't you?"

"Yes, as soon as I can." Adjusting the reins, he turned the horse and rode off.

Abby watched him ride out of sight. "Remember me...." she murmured, as if in prayer.

Chapter One

He was going back. Back to face his past, to make amends, to right a wrong. And to revisit a lost love.

The hot summer wind whipped at his hair through the open windows of his Bronco. An outdoorsman through and through, Jesse Calder rarely engaged the air-conditioning, preferring the scent of the rich earth and of growing things. He'd passed Arizona's Painted Desert a while back, heading south and deep into cattle country.

He'd passed tall, stately ponderosa pines, juniper and spruce, piñon and fir trees, most growing thick and wild. Now the land stretched as far as he could see, acres of cotton on one side and on the other, grasslands where cattle grazed under the watchful eye of cowboys on horseback. He could see cactus and brush and chaparral, so different from his native California.

Déjà vu. Jesse felt an uneasy familiarity on the last leg of the long drive from his home on the Triple C ranch in northern California to St. Johns, Arizona, near the state's eastern border with New Mexico. This journey was very different from the first time he'd driven the same route six years ago. Then, he'd been twenty-five, high on life, driving his new red sports car with the top down. In perfect health and doing what he loved, he'd felt that the world was his oyster.

Amazing how quickly your life, your whole attitude could change, Jesse thought as he glanced at the Little Colorado River paralleling the highway. It was early June, just as it had been on his first trip, but that was pretty much where the similarity ended. Desert summer heat shimmered in waves from the pavement.

Not much traffic on Route 180 in late afternoon, so he put on the cruise control and breathed in the pungent smell of leather and livestock. Like his twin brother, Jake, ranching was in Jesse's blood. It was the life he'd been born into and, more importantly, the life he'd chosen, during good times and bad.

And there had been plenty of bad.

Maybe things went wrong six years ago because of the deception, slight though it was, Jesse thought, a frown wrinkling his brow. His father, Cameron Calder, had decided that the time had come for the Triple C horse ranch to diversify, to add cattle or sheep, if it were to remain competitive and the finest ranch in the western states. That decision had changed Jesse's life.

Cam had sent Jake to Montana to study sheep and Jesse to Arizona for the summer to learn all about cattle ranching. His father wanted no preferential treatment for his sons, so because the Calder name was already well-known throughout the west, Cam insisted his sons use an alias, a practice not uncommon in ranching circles. For that summer, he'd used the name Jesse Hunter.

Running a hand over his short beard, Jesse remembered that neither he nor Jake had been enthusiastic about a summer away or the deception. Still, they hadn't wanted to go against their father's wishes, not after he'd raised them single-handedly after their mother abandoned the family when the twins were only two.

Vern Martin, the owner of the Arizona cattle ranch where Jesse had wound up, hadn't been all that taken with Jesse Hunter at first, figuring he was a drifter who spent all his money on fast cars and fun times, a ladies' man with a questionable future. As the mother of two young daughters, Joyce Martin had been even less welcoming. But Vern needed help and Jesse was strong, plus he'd had ranching experience. Vern hired him.

Jesse was no stranger to hard work, having pulled his own weight on the Triple C since boyhood. The men on the Martin ranch worked from sunrise till sunset under the hot Arizona sun, he recalled as he drove along in his white Bronco. The vehicle was indicative of his change in maturity from his red convertible days. He'd worked without complaint, knowing that was what Cam expected of his son. He'd bunked with the rest of the hands, asked questions, listened and learned. He'd quickly earned the respect of the men as well as Vern Martin. There'd been precious little time left over for fun, even if he'd had the energy for it.

Until Abby Martin came home from college for the summer.

She was quite simply the most beautiful girl Jesse had ever seen, with long blond hair and huge green eyes. At nineteen, Abby rode like a pro and usually dressed casually in jeans and well-worn boots. She knew her way around the

ranch and worked her favorite horses under the watchful
eye of Casey Henderson, the ranch manager.

Her sister, Lindsay, two years older, rarely left the main
house without full makeup and a designer outfit. She seldom
spoke to the hired help, but Abby knew most of the men by
name and was friendly to all. Secretly, Lindsay liked to flirt,
but when one of the men reacted, she'd run off. She'd come
on to Jesse almost immediately, but to her annoyance, he
hadn't responded.

Because he'd had eyes only for Abby right from the start.
And she for him. Soon they were meeting away from pry-
ing eyes despite Joyce Martin's constant surveillance. They
spent many wonderful hours together, but things had come
to a head before Jesse could tell Abby the truth about who
he really was. He'd gotten a phone call that Cam had had a
heart attack and Jesse's only thought had been to rush to his
father's side. He'd promised Abby he'd be back to explain
everything, only then, the unthinkable happened.

Fifty miles from home, the drunken driver of a pickup
had slammed into Jesse's convertible head-on and changed
his future. Spotting Curly's Market just ahead, Jesse slowed,
then exited the highway and turned into the asphalt parking lot. The summer he'd lived in this area, he'd often
stopped on his evenings off at Curly's to pick up inciden-
tals and his favorite M&M'S.

Stepping out, Jesse stretched, then rolled his shoulders.
Since the accident, sitting in one position too long made his
six-two frame stiff, his muscles tight. Walking through the
door, he wondered if Curly would recognize him; he'd often
lingered to chat with the old ranch hand turned shopkeeper.
Physically, Jesse knew he looked different after numerous
surgeries. And there was the beard he'd grown to hide some

of the facial scars and the slight limp that showed up when he was tired.

More important, he knew he was a different man inside than he'd been six years ago. There'd been a restlessness in him back then, a desire to see and do everything, to live life to the fullest. He was more settled now, more introspective, more at peace with who and what he was. A near-death experience, more than a week in a coma, months of physical therapy rebuilding his battered body and nearly a year recovering could change a person greatly.

Pushing open the screen door, Jesse let his eyes adjust from bright sunlight to the dim interior. Foodstuffs in cans and cartons were stacked on shelves along three walls, and a refrigerated section held milk and soft drinks. In the back were tools and jeans and work shirts piled on tables. In the middle of the sagging wood floor were bins of flour, sugar, rice and small barrels of penny candy. Two overhead fans tried their best to move the hot air around. He inhaled the scent of cinnamon, dust and the hot chili peppers that hung in clusters from the low ceiling. The store was empty except for Curly, who stood behind the short counter by the register, his white hair as curly as ever. No one seemed to remember his real name.

Jesse nodded to the owner, then wandered the aisles. He came to the conclusion that hardly a thing had changed in the market in six years, which somehow cheered him. Nice to know that, in an ever-changing world, some things stayed the same.

He grabbed a frosty root beer and a couple of packages of M&M'S, then strolled back to the register.

"That be all?" Curly asked as he rang up the sale.

"Right." Jesse laid several bills on the counter. "Kind of quiet today."

"It's the rodeo down Springerville way. They have one every year 'bout this time." He handed Jesse his change. "You new around here or just passing through?"

"I'm on my way to the Martin ranch. They're having trouble with a stallion and…"

"Yeah, yeah. Remus. Got burned in that fire a while back. I heard you was coming. From California, right?"

"Right." Jesse remembered how quickly news spread around the tight-knit ranching community. Looking full face at the man, he tried to spot a flicker of recognition in the shopkeeper's curious brown eyes before holding out his hand. "Jesse Calder."

Curly wiped his stained fingers on his pants before shaking hands. "I heard about your daddy. Heard he can talk to horses and they listen." Looking skeptical, Curly leaned back against the wall. "Damned if I can figure how that can be done. Horse whispering, they call it, right? And now you do that, too?"

"Something like that." Jesse flipped open the tab on his root beer.

Curly watched the young stranger take a long drink. "Mind if I stop by the Martins and watch? I'd sure like to see that."

"If it's okay with the Martins, it's fine with me." The man didn't have a clue who he was, Jesse decided as he climbed back behind the wheel.

Settling the can in the cup holder, he started the engine, wondering if the Martins or Casey would figure out his identity. Then he wondered if it wouldn't be better if they didn't recognize him. Six years ago, he hadn't called Vern Martin to explain why he wasn't coming back, to say nothing of how they'd react if they learned he'd used a phony name.

Back on the highway, Jesse frowned. He was aware that deceptions always have a price tag. No matter how small, no matter how worthy the motive, the deception erases all credibility, all trust. And often one lie leads to another. If he had it to do over…

He'd wanted to explain, at least to Abby, who'd been so loving and sweet. Though it had been cut short, they'd had a special time that summer. As soon as he'd been released from the hospital, he'd called the Martin ranch, hoping Abby would pick up. Only Lindsay had answered and said that Abby wasn't there. When he'd asked if she'd gone back to college, Lindsay in a smug tone had told him that Abby had gotten married and moved away. That had surprised him. Only weeks before, she'd been meeting him, holding him, making love with him.

Jesse had asked to speak to Vern so he could explain why he hadn't returned, but Lindsay wouldn't allow him to get in another word. In no uncertain terms, she told him he was *persona non grata* at the Martins, ordering him to quit calling and to stay away.

Somewhat shocked, Jesse had hung up. He knew that Abby had had no way to reach him, not knowing his real name. Yet he had trouble imagining that she'd met someone in such a short time and gotten married. That didn't seem in character for the girl he'd known. Maybe she wasn't the person he'd thought she was, after all.

Even as a youngster, Cam had often remarked that Jesse was stubborn. As his health had improved, he'd wanted to go to the Martins, to explain to Vern that an accident had kept him from returning, that he wasn't the sort who'd leave someone high and dry without a damn good reason. And he'd wanted to hear from Abby's own lips that she was happy with this new guy. But Cam and Jake, very aware he was still weak, still not up to par, had talked him out of the trip.

It hadn't been easy, trying to forget Abby. During his slow healing, the hours of exercises, memories of their time together haunted him. He'd begun to think he was falling in love with her and she with him before he'd left. They'd had a lot in common—their love of ranching and horses and even children. Abby had told him she wanted to be a teacher. They'd lie in each other's arms on the grassy hillside and talk for hours, once almost till dawn. Who knows where their feelings would have taken them if fate hadn't intervened? Yet now, he knew he had to put her out of his mind because she belonged to another man. It seemed to Jesse that their time together hadn't meant as much to her as it had to him if she could so easily, so quickly marry another.

It had been a fluke, the Martins hearing about Jesse Calder and his work with traumatized horses. Casey, the Martin ranch foreman, had called and all but begged him to take a look at Remus. Despite his family's cautious warnings, he'd decided to go, to see for himself. Especially because Casey had said that Remus belonged to the youngest Martin daughter.

But now, spotting the arched entrance to the Martin ranch just ahead, Jesse couldn't help wondering if he'd made the right decision as his stomach muscles tightened.

Before he'd made the decision to go, he'd looked into just what kind of operation the Martins had. After all, his last visit had been six years ago and he'd been concentrating on cattle, not horses. He'd learned that the ranch had been in the Martin family since 1880 and currently consisted of more than one-thousand acres with fifteen-hundred Brahman cross cows, nine-hundred head mother cows, six-hundred head yearlings and eighteen bulls. They raised their own native grass and hay, about two-thousand tons yearly. They had forty saddle and workhorses and a staff of about thirty including Casey, the manager, and Carmalita, the cook.

At first glance, Jesse could see a few changes since he'd last set foot on Martin soil. Sporting a fresh coat of white paint and new green shutters, the big house, as everyone called the owners' three-story home, stood off to the right from the entrance and down a ways. On the grass in front was the same old cottonwood tree and around the perimeter of the wide porch were flowers that he remembered Joyce Martin planted and pruned herself.

A short distance from the big house was a new small building decorated in a rainbow of colors. Jesse couldn't imagine what that was used for.

He parked the Bronco and stepped out. His back hurt like the devil after the hours sitting behind the wheel, a legacy from his accident. He'd been given pain pills, which he didn't take because they made him fuzzy-headed. A generous shot of Scotch when the pain got really bad helped more than the pills and tasted better.

Jesse removed his sunglasses, hooked them on his shirt pocket and glanced to the left. Two rustic cabins with wide porches running along the front of each sat side by side, just as before. The first one looked empty, but he remembered the second was where Casey lived. Strolling past the cabins, he saw what he'd been looking for adjacent to what looked like a brand new horse barn: a freshly built round pen he'd told Casey he'd need to work with their stallion.

He walked over, propped a booted foot on the lowest

rung and leaned onto the white fencing. His practiced eye noticed every detail; the swing gate at one end that opened to the barn's far door and the patted-down dirt floor, free of grass and stones.

"So, what do you think?" a raspy voice asked from behind him. "That round enough for you?"

Jesse turned. Casey Henderson still looked like a fireplug with his short, stocky body, his ruddy face and the red suspenders he was never without. A black patch covered his left eye, a souvenir from his rodeo days. His right eye searched the younger man's face intently.

"Yes, sir, the pen's just fine." He held out his hand. "Jesse Calder." For a fleeting instant, he thought he saw a flash of recognition or perhaps just suspicion on the manager's tanned face.

But Casey's grip was strong and brief as he introduced himself, then whipped a red kerchief out of the back pocket of his worn jeans. "Still can't figure why you had to have a *round* pen." Removing his black hat, he ran the kerchief over his sweaty, nearly bald pate.

"You'll see when I start to work with Remus," Jesse told him.

Casey motioned with his chin toward the large aluminum horse barn gleaming in the hot sun. "Let's go see him then. You think you can help Remus?" he asked as they walked.

"We'll find out," Jesse answered noncommittally as he fell in step with Casey. Working with damaged horses, both with his father and alone, he'd learned that most responded well to their methods, given enough time. But there were a few too badly traumatized to ever be helped. "What happened to him?" On the phone, the ranch manager had been fairly vague.

"Well, it's a sad story, really." Casey waved to a group of

men strolling to the mess hall across the wide drive from the barn. Beyond that was the bunkhouse for the single men and a couple of small cabins for the married ones.

"Martins' youngest daughter, Abby, ran across Remus three or four years ago. She teaches a little preschool class and she was picking up one of the kids over on Pickerel Lane. Seems the family across the street from where she stopped had moved away and abandoned Remus. He was wandering around a messy corral, half-starved. Abby's got a real soft heart so she looked into it. Seems he'd been abused for quite a while."

At the mention of Abby, Jesse's interest accelerated. He well remembered how much she'd loved horses. He also wasn't surprised she was working with children since she'd talked about doing just that all those years ago. She and her husband must live close by.

They reached the barn door where Casey paused, squinting up at the sun. "Naturally, she talked Vern into bringing the stallion here and she nursed him back to health. She tamed him, too. He became real gentle."

Three or four years ago, Jesse noted. Had Abby and her husband lived here with the Martins back then? He wondered if he dare ask Casey without giving himself away. If they learned who he was, so be it, but he'd hoped to buy a little time first, perhaps get a chance to talk with Abby and explain.

"Then along came that damn fire." Casey adjusted his big hat that all but engulfed his head, his eyes downcast. "It was my fault. One really cold night last February, I put a space heater in next to Remus's stall on account of his end of the barn was the original from before the building was redone and there was no heat. Don't know what happened, but somehow the heater fell over and started a fire. By the time me and the boys saw the blaze, poor Remus was wild, screaming, burns along his left side. We got him sedated, got the vet. He's pretty much healed now, but he don't trust no one, not even Abby. Won't let anyone touch him, much less ride him. Vern wanted to put him down, but Abby wouldn't let him. Then we read about your work."

Casey stuffed the kerchief back into his pocket. "I'd be right grateful if you could fix him. And Abby would be, too."

Jesse had seen the same kind of guilt before and knew it was a heavy load to carry. "I'll try, but I want you to know I don't do it for the owner. I do it for the horse. If he won't let anyone near him, like you say, he's unhappy and afraid. *That's* what needs fixing."

"Any way you call it, just fix him." Casey shoved open the heavy sliding door.

Jesse decided to take a chance. "So then Abby lives here and still has an interest in Remus?" When Casey turned and settled his one piercing eye on his face, trying to read him, Jesse shrugged. "I'd heard she married and moved away."

The older man studied him for a long moment before answering. "She did, but that was a while ago. Her husband died so she came back." Again Casey aimed his chin in the direction just beyond the big house. "That there's her schoolhouse for the little ones around here, before they go to regular school. Started out small but she's got about a dozen of 'em now, coming and going. But she's still mighty interested in Remus."

A widow. That was one he hadn't thought of. Jesse followed Casey into the barn and along the concrete walk with horse stalls on both sides. He noticed that the dividers were in good repair, the hay fresh and the lighting dim. He remembered that the Martins had run a clean operation. Half a dozen workhorses were in their stalls.

"Most of the horses are still out, but they'll be coming in soon, 'cept for the overnighters," Casey explained. He greeted two cowboys by name as they walked by.

A partition separated the main building from a much smaller area at the far end. Jesse slowed as he moved within sight of a single stall where a black horse stood perfectly still watching their approach.

"That's our Remus," Casey said, standing aside.

The stallion's right side, Jesse noted, looked perfectly normal. But as he silently stepped closer, he saw the damaged hide that started on his face and ran along his left flank, leaving a large section mottled and scarred. The wound appeared healed. The real trauma was inside Remus's brain.

Gauging his mood, Jesse took one step closer and talked to him, his voice low and soothing. The horse's ears, revealing his emotions, were suddenly split, one forward and one back, displaying concern at this newcomer, trying to figure him out. Again Jesse said a few words, but when he stepped closer, Remus's ears pinned back in an angry, aggressive response just before he reared up on his back legs, blowing out through his nose, his eyes going wild. Jesse retreated to join Casey who was looking very skeptical.

"See what I mean? Ornery cuss. Doesn't seem to like you, either."

"It's about the reaction I expected, given all he's been through. I'll start with him in the morning."

"You're not afraid to get in that round pen with all that dangerous horseflesh?" Casey asked as they walked away.

"I have to gain his trust first in order to work with him."

"Maybe we need to get the vet to give him a shot, calm him down before you start."

"No, I don't want him sedated. I'll just need a light cotton line once you open the door and let him into the pen."

Casey shook his head as they left the barn. "All right, it's your funeral." He turned to close the double doors, then remembered something. "Hold on a minute." He disappeared inside.

Jesse shoved his hands in his back pockets and glanced toward the huge cattle barn next door, recalling that it was divided into sections for milk cows, the calving stalls, the insemination area. Now in the summer, most of the cattle were out to pasture, the cowboys who watched them drifting in staggered groups to chow down. Through the wide mess hall windows, he saw about half a dozen men seated at long tables. The Martin ranch seemed shorthanded, which was not usual during the busy summer season.

The sound of a horse's hooves approaching from the range interrupted his thoughts. A sleek chestnut galloped closer, the rider a woman with a blond ponytail, her face flushed as she passed him and smoothly slowed to a stop at the far door to the horse barn. He recognized Abby immediately as she expertly dismounted and moved to the chestnut's head to stroke the mare with a loving gesture. A tall man with bandy legs came out of the barn and took the mare's reins from her, probably to cool her down. He said something to Abby and she laughed, the sound carrying to where Jesse stood.

He remembered that laugh, musical and lighthearted. She'd laughed often back then; he wondered if she did now. Seeing her even briefly brought memories of their time together rushing back. Did she remember them with fondness or pain, or at all? How long ago had her husband died and how? From this distance, she looked the same, but maybe, up close, she'd changed as much as he had.

Casey came out, closed the doors and followed Jesse's gaze. "That's Abby, the youngest daughter. I'll let you settle in first, then take you to meet her and Vern tomorrow." He nodded toward the mess hall. "Hope you're hungry. Our Carmalita's the most popular gal on the ranch 'cause she cooks like an angel." He led the way to the long one-story building.

Tugging his gaze from Abby, Jesse followed.

"Vern had the cabin next to mine near the big house fixed up for you. Figured you might like some privacy, you know."

"Very thoughtful of him." Only how would Vern Martin feel if and when he learned of Jesse's past deception?

Inside, Casey introduced Jesse to the men still eating, explaining why he was there. Several had heard about the Calder methods and expressed curiosity and skepticism, but Jesse didn't say much, just that they should wait to make up their minds after he had a chance to work with Remus.

But it was when Casey took him over to Carmalita that Jesse had his first nervous moment. Six years ago, he'd spent some time talking with the dark-haired, dark-eyed woman who'd worked as cook for the Martins for twenty years, ever since her husband had been killed in an accident on the ranch. Vern had told her she had a lifetime job and a retirement when she chose to quit, but at fifty, she showed no signs of slowing down.

A dish towel draped over her shoulder, one small hand buried in a pot holder, she stirred something deliciously fragrant in a big pot on the large stove in the back room, her dark eyes looking Jesse over as closely as she might a chicken she was choosing for dinner. He noticed that she still favored peasant blouses with her long black skirt and the large gold hoop earrings he remembered. He met her gaze silently as Casey explained who he was.

Finally, she put down the spoon. "You look familiar. You got a brother?"

"Yes. His name's Jake and we're twins."

"Mm-hmm. It's the eyes, those blue eyes. He ever been here?"

"I don't think so," Jesse answered honestly.

"I knew another Jesse once," she continued. At last, she shook her head. "Anyhow, welcome. Go help yourself."

Relieved, Jesse thanked her and walked with Casey to the heavy buffet table laden with food. He hadn't realized how hungry he was until he'd smelled the barbecued chicken. He took a plate, filled it and sat down at the nearest table where Casey joined him. Most of the men were finished and gone, only a few lingering over coffee.

Jesse ate silently, wondering just when Carmalita's memory would put two and two together. He noticed that Casey had been quiet since they'd left the kitchen. Although Jesse hadn't had very much to do with Casey back when he'd worked the ranch, he'd known the manager to be honest and intelligent. Probably only a matter of time before someone would challenge Jesse. He'd known from the start that might happen and also known that he'd admit everything and hope they'd understand. Especially Abby.

He searched his mind for a subject to distract Casey. "Is Vern Martin a hands-on rancher or does he leave most of the decisions up to you?"

Casey finished a piece of chicken before answering. "Fairly hands-on, I'd say. I've been working here going on thirty years, when old man Martin was still alive. That man worked like a horse, day in and day out. Vern, he don't work that hard, but he knows what's going on in every corner of this ranch. He talks over stuff with me, but he's the final say-so." He slathered butter on an ear of corn.

"And his wife?" Years ago, Jesse had found Mrs. Martin to be prickly, condescending and critical, but maybe she'd mellowed.

"Joyce, she keeps the books. She don't go out much. Got a bad back."

Jesse could relate. "There's another daughter, right?" He'd been wondering where stuck-up Lindsay had wound up.

Casey wiped his hands on a napkin. "That one, she's not a bit like her sister. Got herself engaged 'bout six months ago. Fellow from San Francisco, real nice. He stayed with us awhile, seemed to like it here. But something happened and they broke it off."

But Jesse really wanted to hear about Abby. "So the younger sister moved back home after her husband died and she teaches kids in the little schoolhouse," he said, thinking aloud. At least Abby had realized part of her dream. "Was her husband from around here?"

Leaning back, Casey looked at Jesse, as if debating how much to tell. "She met him at college, down in Tucson. Weren't married but a month when he up and drowned in a boating accident. Abby came home on account of she was going to have a baby." He shook his head. "Those girls are twenty-six and twenty-eight and still living under their daddy's roof. Joyce is happy about that, but Vern, he'd like a couple of son-in-laws to take over the ranch one day." He stood and adjusted his suspenders. "Trouble is, we don't always get what we want, right? I'm going to get more iced tea. Want a refill?"

"No, thanks." Jesse tossed his napkin onto his empty plate, then sat back thinking over what he'd just learned. Abby had never so much as mentioned anyone at college. Must have been a whirlwind romance. Or did she marry him on the rebound when Jesse didn't return? No, they'd never discussed marriage or even love. Still, she hadn't struck him as the type who'd quickly move into another relationship. Well, he'd likely find out soon enough.

Rising, he cleared his plate and walked outside while Casey stopped to talk to Carmalita. The sun was just sinking beyond the far horizon, bathing the hillside in oranges and yellows. At home in California, the sun usually set beyond the mountains surrounding the Triple C, nothing at all the way it did here. Jesse had never seen more beautiful sunsets than in Arizona.

Turning toward the house he was to occupy for a while, he noticed two little girls playing with a brown puppy in front of his porch. They had to be four or five, one very blond, the other with a dark braid down her back. Smiling, he walked toward them. As soon as the puppy spotted Jesse, he ran forward, all big feet and pink tongue, then rolled over onto his back, inviting a belly rub. Jesse squatted down and obliged the little guy as the two girls came rushing over.

"What's his name?"

"Spike," they both answered.

"Whose puppy is he?" Jesse asked as the little dog squirmed in ecstasy.

"Hers," said the blond child, indicating her friend. "I'm Grace and she's Katie. What's your name?"

Pleasantly surprised that she wasn't the least bit shy, he

smiled at her as she plunked herself down in the grass. Katie sat down close to her friend, obviously a little bashful. "Jesse. Where do you girls live?" he asked, thinking the two must be holdovers from the little schoolhouse.

Grace pointed toward the big house. "I live over there and Katie lives in town but she's staying over 'cause her mom's sick. Where do you live?"

He couldn't help but be taken by the precocious little girl with the big blue eyes. "I guess I'll be living over there for a while." He pointed to the cabin Casey had said was his.

Before he could get in another question, he saw from the corner of his eye that someone was running toward them. Standing up, Jesse recognized Joyce Martin as she stopped in the middle of the drive and called both girls by name, urging them to go to her immediately. Thinking to introduce himself, Jesse took a step closer, but Joyce sent him a warning glance before hustling the girls inside.

Casey came alongside. "I see you've met Mrs. Martin."

His tone told Jesse that the woman wasn't one of Casey's favorites either. "Not exactly. Is she always that friendly?"

"Pretty much," he answered, chuckling. "She's over-protective of her family. Guess she's got her reasons." He pulled a ring of keys from his pocket. "Why don't you go get your bag and I'll show you through your cabin?"

"Okay." Jesse had parked his Bronco in the wide apron by the big house and decided to move it nearer the cabin. As he got behind the wheel, he glanced up to the second-story window that he remembered used to be Abby's room.

She was standing there, holding back the sheer curtains on both sides, watching him. Too far away to read her expression, he stared back for several long seconds, then pulled his gaze away and parked the Bronco by the cabin.

Stepping out, he saw that she hadn't moved, her head still turned toward him.

Right then, he'd have given a lot to know what she was thinking.

Chapter Two

Abby Martin stood looking out her bedroom window watching the new hire follow Casey into the cabin. She waited until the lights went on and the door closed. Oddly uneasy and not quite sure why, she pulled the sheers over the window and picked up her hairbrush.

Dad had told her all about Jesse Calder, the man from California who'd had great success in working with traumatized horses. Apparently his father had learned from the teachings of Monty Roberts, the original horse whisperer who'd taught himself to communicate with horses starting years ago when he was a child.

At first, she'd been skeptical, worried a stranger might set Remus back even further. But Casey had researched the Calders and learned that they were not only legitimate, but owners of one of the largest horse ranches in the west. The ranchers they'd contacted who'd used Jesse's services had nothing but praise for him and his methods. Casey had convinced her and Dad, and they'd invited the man to visit to see what he could do.

Abby pulled her long blond hair free of the band and began brushing. She was aware that one thing that had bothered her was the name. Jesse. The mere sound brought memories, sad ones, from a time she'd worked so hard to forget. Then, just when she'd convinced herself that there really was nothing to a name, a man named Jesse had shown up today.

Undoubtedly, her mind was playing tricks on her. But when she'd seen him walk over and get into the Bronco just now, then sit and gaze up at her, she'd felt something eerily familiar. Of course, she was being paranoid. He was tall and lean, like that other Jesse, but more muscular. And he had a beard, but then, any man could grow one. Then there was the limp. Not pronounced, but he walked slowly and carefully, as if denying he had a problem. She couldn't see the color of his eyes from this distance, but, even if they were the same, all manner of people had blue eyes.

Bending over, she brushed her hair vigorously, as if she could brush away the errant thoughts. Foolish mind, conjuring up images of a man who'd pretended to care, then left her with a mere moment's notice. That had been Jesse Hunter, not Jesse Calder. She would have to keep that in mind. She would make an effort not to prejudge and to give him a chance to help Remus.

As she heard four little feet scampering up the steps amidst giggles, she straightened and smiled. Bath time, she thought as she left her room to meet the girls.

Casey stood near the round pen, but back a ways so as not to distract Remus. It was seven in the morning and Jesse Calder had released the stallion from the barn half an hour ago. He'd moved inside, closed the gate and stood there quietly, not moving, a light cotton line coiled and hanging from one shoulder.

Casey waited, gazing from Remus to Calder and back, wondering when the man was going to do something. But he just stood there while the horse snuffled and snorted, first pawing the ground, then trotting around the pen nervously. Finally, Remus stopped near the center of the circle and made eye contact with the man standing so silently, each taking the other's measure, it seemed.

Behind him, Casey heard quiet footsteps and glanced back to see Vern Martin arrive and stop alongside him. The two men studied both stallion and trainer for long minutes until Vern spoke.

"What's he doing?" he whispered, not wanting to spook the horse.

"Damned if I know," Casey answered softly. "He's been standing there thirty minutes or more, staring him down. At this rate, he'll be here till Christmas."

"You're the one said this Calder fellow could work miracles," Vern reminded him.

"That's what I heard, from more than one rancher. But like they said, you got to be patient and let him do it his way."

A tall man with silver-blond hair thinning on top and a nervous twitch beneath his sharp blue eyes, Vern was not a patient man. He watched for another few minutes, then shook his head. "Well, I can't stand here all day. I've got work to do."

"Yeah, me, too." But Casey was obviously reluctant to leave.

"I'll meet Calder later," the rancher said. He clapped his manager on the shoulder. "Let me know if anything happens." Settling his white Stetson on his head, he walked away.

Casey's curiosity kept him rooted to the spot. Another ten minutes and he saw Jesse walk slowly forward until he was in the center, the stallion backing farther away with each step. Then Jesse did an odd thing. He turned his back on the horse and just stood there as if he hadn't a care in the world. Casey watched him take in several deep breaths as if to relax himself.

"Braver man than me," Casey whispered to himself, having seen Remus thrash about in his stall when anyone came too close, those strong legs like lethal weapons.

Clearly, Remus didn't know what to make of this newcomer who seemed unafraid. He resumed circling the pen, round and round, over and over. Still, Jesse didn't move.

Suddenly, the stallion stopped about ten feet behind the man, his ears sharply forward, showing his interest. Slowly, he moved toward Jesse as Casey held his breath. Closer, closer. Near enough that Jesse *had* to feel the stallion's warm breath on his neck. Then the horse stopped. After a few moments, his head leaned closer and he appeared to be sniffing Jesse's scent. The trainer let him, not moving a muscle.

Just then, the double steel doors to the barn slid open with a loud thud and two ranch hands walked out leading their mounts, talking loudly. Remus jerked back, startled, the spell broken. He rushed away from Jesse, stopping on the far side of the pen.

Frowning, Jesse walked to the gate and let himself out.

Casey went up to him, wanting an explanation. "I hope you don't mind me asking, but exactly what was it you were doing in there?"

Jesse recoiled the cotton line into a tighter circle. "Mostly just letting him get familiar with my scent, in a non-threatening way." He glanced toward the men who'd left the barn. "Do you suppose you could ask the guys to use the doors on the other side for a while?"

"Yeah, sure." Casey shuffled his scuffed boots, still not satisfied. "Okay, so now he knows your scent. What's next? You going back in there?"

Turning to study the stallion, Jesse shook his head. "Not right now. Later this afternoon."

"Why was it you turned your back on him? He could've hurt you bad."

Jesse allowed himself a small smile. "I doubt that. Horses are flight animals, not fight animals. They won't attack unless they're attacked first. I was just standing there, no threat to him. He was making all the moves."

"Yeah, but when you going to *do* something? I mean how long is this going to take, you think?"

Jesse shrugged. "That depends on Remus. He's in charge of the timetable. I've got to get him to trust me before I can help him. No one can predict how long that will take." With his peripheral vision, he'd seen Vern Martin watching for a short time. "Mr. Martin in a hurry for results? Because if he is, you've got the wrong trainer."

"No, no. I was just wondering." Casey hoisted up his jeans a notch. "You just take your time, son." He started walking away, then stopped. "If you need anything, just ask."

"I will. Thanks." With one final glance at Remus, Jesse strolled thoughtfully toward his cabin.

No matter how many times he'd worked with damaged horses, especially on their owner's turf, he always had to justify his methods. Everyone expected a quick fix, as if he had a magic wand. This sort of thing took time. Humans didn't get over a trauma overnight, so why would they think horses would? It wouldn't be until they began to see results that they'd finally come around. However, he was used to the re-action so he didn't take it personally.

At his porch, he heard voices across the wide driveway and turned to see over a dozen children in front of the rain-bow-hued schoolhouse playing ring-around-a-rosie in groups of four, led by Abby who was clapping in time to the music from a boom box set under the tree. Jesse sat down on the top step to watch.

It was obvious that the kids were different ages, from tod-dlers of around two to six and seven-year-olds. He spotted Grace and Katie, both with braided hair today. With the reg-ular schools on summer vacation, there were probably more kids than usual. Yet they all seemed orderly and well behaved despite a few of the younger ones falling down as they twirled around, giggling. Abby had them well in hand.

She had on white shorts today and a loose-fitting pink shirt, her golden hair pulled back in its usual ponytail. The years seemed to vanish as Jesse watched her, thinking she hardly looked a day over the nineteen she'd been when he'd first seen her six years ago down by the big cottonwood tree alongside the stream. She'd been dancing at twilight with an imaginary partner, arms stretched as if holding him, hum-ming a slow tune. Her naturalness, her fresh beauty, had blown him away.

"All fall down!" the children yelled out, then dropped to the ground, laughing. Jesse watched Abby pick up the small-est child—a boy who'd probably barely turned two wearing blue overalls at least a size too big for him—swing him around, then kiss his dark curls before setting him down with the others. She seemed totally at ease with the children, in her element, enjoying them. Jesse felt an unexpected jolt of envy and wondered at its source.

A young girl who looked to be of high-school age came out of the big house carrying a pitcher of red liquid and paper cups. Probably a local teenager helping Abby for the summer, Jesse thought as they both herded the children into the little house. Squinting, he made out the sign above the door. Miss Abby's Preschool. It would seem Abby's dreams had come true.

He was about to go in when he heard a low, throaty bark, a shuffle of feet followed by a distinctive whine from the direction of the mess hall. Glancing down the walkway, he saw a big old hound dog headed his way, running in that comical way he remembered.

"Jughead," Jesse said as the cocoa-brown mixed breed barreled up the steps and into his arms, nearly knocking him over. "How've you been, boy?" he asked as the dog proceeded to lick his face.

He'd forgotten about Jughead, the ranch dog that had been a youngster during Jesse's first visit. Though he'd been friendly to all, Jughead had had a special affinity for Jesse, following him everywhere, even sleeping near his bunk. Missing his own Border collie back home, he'd spent some of his off hours trying to teach Jug some tricks. Like retrieving sticks thrown, or rolling over on command. He'd never learned any. The silly dog couldn't even swim, always hanging back at the water's edge, too scared to go in. But he'd been so loyal, so needy of affection since most of the men thought he was too dumb to bother with, that Jesse had sort of adopted him.

And now here he was, proving that dogs never forget.

Looking around, Jesse wondered if anyone still here from
back then would remember Jug's devotion to Jesse and figure out his identity. "I think I met one of your sons," he told
Jughead, remembering the brown puppy named Spike. With
a final fond scratch behind the dog's ears, Jesse rose to go
inside. He opened the cabin door and Jug scooted in before
he could stop him. It wasn't until he turned that he noticed
Abby standing in her schoolhouse doorway, watching him
with a thoughtful look on her face.

Resigned to the fact that sooner or later, the truth would
come out as it usually did, Jesse followed the dog inside.

Early afternoon and there were half a dozen men lingering behind the horse barn to watch Jesse work with Remus.
The word had spread and curiosity had been aroused. Casey
had told everyone to use the other door and he'd warned all
who came to watch that they had to be quiet. Curly from the
store leaned against the barn wall and shaded his face from
the hot sun by tipping his hat lower.

Even Vern was there, Casey noted. He'd taken the rancher
to meet Jesse just before lunch and heard Vern ask the trainer
to explain his methods. Lord knows the boy had tried. He'd
said things like "silent communication with horses is far
stronger than the spoken word," and "the horse is an intelligent animal and should be in unison with man, not against
him," and finally "man should cause a horse to *want* to per-
form to his wishes." Neither Vern nor Casey had understood
half of what he'd said or meant.

A sudden movement caught Casey's eye and he noticed
Abby slip into the shadows of the barn to watch.

Now Jesse had the simple cotton line around Remus's
neck and had him circling the pen while he stood in the cen-

ter holding the rope's end. Round and round Remus went, slowly at first, up to a trot, then slowing down again. Patient as Job, Jesse held the line and steered him, changing directions now and again. After half an hour or so, the men began drifting away, murmuring their disappointment at a show that didn't pan out. Soon after, shaking his head, Vern strolled off, too. Only Casey remained.

And Abby, who stood silently watching from the shadows, sure he couldn't see her.

She didn't know who interested her more, the man or the stallion. She decided there was an uncanny resemblance of this Jesse to the other, but they weren't the same. This man was infinitely patient, with gentle moves, his gaze focused. The Jesse she'd known had been like a live wire, jumping onto his horse and riding bareback, racing with the wind, eager and enthusiastic. Much like she'd been back then. She doubted that that Jesse could have mellowed this much.

But her heart wasn't convinced, reacting to seeing this man as if the two were the same. The beard camouflaged the lower half of his face, but it looked as if Jesse Calder also had a square chin hinting at stubbornness. The other Jesse had worn his thick, black hair longer, down to the collar of the denim shirts he'd preferred. This man also wore denim, the sleeves rolled up on muscular arms. And he had on sunglasses, rarely worn by anyone else on the ranch.

Remus looked better than she'd seen him in months. He marched around the pen and didn't seem to mind the man holding the rope. But he never took his eyes from Jesse, still distrusting, still skittish. Abby knew it would take time getting through to Remus, if at all. This man seemed their only hope. She hated to give up on the stallion, on anyone.

She should go, Abby thought, yet she stood rooted to the spot. She'd left Susie, her teenage assistant, in charge at the little schoolhouse reading a story to the older ones while the younger ones napped. But Abby didn't like to be away too long. She was about to leave when she saw Jesse step closer to Remus. Immediately, the stallion skittered away. Jesse widened the loop and yanked the line from the horse's neck, then left the pen.

Abby stayed hidden, but Casey walked over to him. "So, was it a good day?"

Jesse knew he was trying the man's patience. "Yes, I'd say so."

"Don't you get tired, standing out there for hours?"

"Not as tired as Remus is. He's the one running. I'm just standing there holding the line."

"So you figure you taught him something today?"

"Sure. He's familiar with my scent, knows I'm not really afraid of him and he knows I'm patient. A good day's work."

"Uh-huh," Casey answered, sounding unconvinced.

Jesse smiled. "I know you don't see it yet, but you will."

"I sure hope so."

"Listen, I was wondering, is there a horse I could ride once in a while? I usually ride every day at home." The doctors had also told him he had to stay active, to not let his muscles tighten from nonuse. He'd equipped a gym at the Triple C and did strengthening exercises daily. Already he was thinking that helping Remus was going to take a while so he'd have to improvise.

"Sure 'nuff," Casey told him. "Domino's good. Six-year-old quarter horse, black with white markings in the second stall. You'll find saddles in the tack room. Help yourself."

"Thanks." Checking his watch, Jesse saw that it was still

several hours till the dinner bell. Exercise was what he needed, he decided as he walked to the barn.

Abby watched him go. She wished she could take the time to follow him, to see how he rode. The way a person rode a horse was distinctive and often revealing to the practiced eye. No two people rode quite the same way.

Maybe another day, she'd catch up to him, to check him out on horseback and up close. Just to put to rest the vague uneasiness she'd felt since he'd arrived.

Jesse finished cooling down Domino after his ride and left the barn. He'd run across several of the men cutting and clearing dead tree branches and had stopped to help out. Fatigue poured over him like a sudden spring shower. He ached, like he'd known he would, especially his back, but it was nothing a long, hot shower couldn't fix.

Removing his hat, Jesse wiped his damp face on his shirtsleeve as he headed for his cabin. A cold drink would hit the spot, preferably a frosty beer. He'd have to get over to Curly's and stock a six-pack in his small fridge.

Man, it sure was hot! More accustomed to the cooler summers of California, the change was a little hard to get used to. He didn't think the desert heat had bothered him as much the last time he was here. Another few days and he'd acclimate and…

Jesse stopped short when he noticed a long-legged woman in shorts and a tight top, her auburn hair short and windblown, sitting on the top step of his cabin. She was attractive without question, but in his opinion, she wasn't even in Abby's league. He recognized Lindsay and remembered that he wasn't supposed to know her.

She smiled as she watched him come closer. When he

stopped and propped one boot on the bottom step, her lazy brown-eyed gaze swept over him, head to toe, very slowly. "Hi," she finally said. "I'm Lindsay Martin."

"Hi, yourself," Jesse answered cautiously. He vividly remembered the night six years ago when she'd come to his cabin looking for an easy seduction. Her eyes had blazed when he'd politely but firmly turned her down.

"If you're the new horse trainer, I have an invitation for you."

"Is that right?" He couldn't help wondering if she'd recognize his voice or maybe his eyes. Lindsay was smart, but he'd long suspected she also had a mean streak.

"Mm-hmm," she purred. "Are you Jesse Calder?"

"One and the same." He saw her smile widen as she uncrossed her spectacular legs and rose to her full height of about five-eight. Jesse had to admit she had a build that could make strong men weak, and she damn well knew it. And used it to her advantage, he'd wager. Unless she'd changed, which it didn't appear she had.

"We'd like you to come to dinner at the big house," she said as she slowly descended the stairs. "In about an hour?"

It was not something Jesse wanted to do, to face all the Martins around a dinner table, wondering who would figure out his identity first. He'd wanted to talk with Abby, but alone, not surrounded by her family. This charade had gone on long enough. He needed to clear the air, first with Abby, then the Martins. Yet right now, he saw no easy way out. Rejecting his host's offer probably wouldn't sit well with Vern.

Lindsay was alongside him now, waiting for his answer, her heavy cologne swirling around him. He was stuck and he knew it.

"Thanks. I'll be there."

Slowly she trailed a long red fingernail along his arm from shoulder to wrist. "See you then, sugar."

Jesse watched Lindsay walk across the road in that undulating way he remembered. He couldn't help wondering what her fiancé had been like and what had happened that they'd called off the wedding. Maybe the guy had gotten tired of Lindsay's obvious flirtatious ways.

Sighing, he ran up the steps and went inside to take his shower.

Vern himself opened the door and greeted Jesse as an equal, no doubt due to his father's reputation. The big house was old and home to third generation Martins, but looked as if it had been renovated not long ago. Jesse hadn't been inside on his last visit, so he had no comparison. He thought the place was typical of many working ranch homes—spacious, red tile floors, western decor, big, comfortable furniture.

He smelled apple pie and heard sounds coming from the kitchen in back, but he saw no one except Vern who hustled him into his den and poured him two fingers of whiskey, neat, in an old-fashioned glass. Jesse preferred Scotch but beggars couldn't be choosers and his back, even after a long shower, was still hurting.

Vern freshened his own drink. "Real nice to have another man in the house," he said, motioning Jesse to twin leather chairs facing a stone fireplace large enough to roast a couple of pigs in. Sitting back, Vern took a generous swig of his drink, then sighed audibly. "Best part of the day, don't you agree?"

Jesse didn't necessarily agree, but he tossed back the whiskey and hoped it would dull the pain in his back. "I like your house," he said honestly, glancing around Vern's masculine retreat. "Built much better than they do these days."

"You got that right." Vern narrowed his blue eyes and studied the younger man. "Did you know I met your dad some years ago?"

"No, sir, I didn't."

"Sure did. At a rodeo in Colorado. We were both a lot younger back then." He chuckled. "I regret not keeping in touch with Cam through the years. You look like him, you know."

"So I've been told." Had Vern Martin asked him over for a reason or was he just longing for some male companionship? Jesse wondered.

"How's he doing these days?"

"Good. He had a heart attack a while back, but he's doing real well."

"You have a brother, don't you? I always envied Cam with two sons." He took a sip of his drink, then coughed into his fist. "I love my girls, but sometimes it's hard living in a house full of women." Vern paused, looking thoughtful. "How's the Triple C doing?"

Was that inquiry Vern's hidden agenda in asking Jesse over? he wondered. "Doing very well. Arabian market fell through, as you know, but quarter horses are going strong."

"You breed and train, right?"

"Yes, and board horses, give riding lessons. A few years back, we added cattle. Diversification, my father believes, is the key to survival. Of course, we don't have nearly the herd you have. We allocate about eighteen acres to cattle, have about three-hundred head cross cows. And we grow our own grass and hay."

Vern nodded in agreement. "Ranching's a tough business, some years worse than others. Good help is hard to find."

Studying the man, Jesse could see worry lines by his eyes and his color wasn't good.

Vern cleared his throat. "I found out I've got a bit of a heart problem, too." He glanced toward the open door. "Don't want the family to know. I'm thinking I'd be better off selling. You wouldn't know of anyone looking, would you?"

"Not offhand, but I can check with Dad."

"Yeah, that'd be good. And let's keep this between you and me. No use worrying the others." He downed the rest of his drink.

They heard footsteps just before Grace came scurrying into the den. "I'm supposed to tell you dinner's ready." She looked at Jesse. "Oh, hi. You're the man who fixes horses, right?"

"You could say that," Jesse answered, smiling.

"Okay, we're coming, honey." Vern stood as the child ran back out. "That's my granddaughter, Grace. Pretty as a picture, isn't she? Looks just like her mother."

So this was the baby Abby had come home to have. "She's cute."

"Sure is."

So Abby was raising a fatherless child. He knew all about how difficult it was to raise children alone, like his own father had had to do.

"Casey tells me that Abby's husband died," Jesse threw out, hoping Vern would elaborate.

"Yeah. Devil's own luck." He set down his empty glass. "We never even got to know him, you know. They met at college and eloped over a weekend. They were supposed to come here at semester's end. Joyce was planning a recep-

tion, but two weeks later, he fell off a boat and drowned."
He shook his head. "Our girls haven't had much luck with
men. Lindsay almost got married a while back, but something happened between them and the wedding never took
place. I have two beautiful, bright marriageable girls and not
a suitable man in sight. What I need is a good, strong ranch
man who could take over for me." Vern sighed heavily. "And
they're scarcer than hen's teeth."

Jesse wondered for the hundredth time how different
things might have been had that truck not hit his convertible. He'd have seen to his father's health, come back and
probably married Abby.

"You married?" Vern asked suddenly.

"No, sir." He hated to hand this poor guy yet another disappointment by revealing his past. He'd have to do it soon,
but not right now. First, he had to talk with Abby. Alone.

Abby was having trouble eating. Seated across the din-
ing room table from Jesse Calder, she kept looking at him
from under her lowered lashes. Up close, he was even more
like Jesse Hunter with those piercing blue eyes that seemed
to look right through her. She noticed a small scar above his
left eyebrow and wondered what had happened.

He was fairly quiet, answering Dad's questions, evading
Lindsay's overtures, trying not to notice that Mom wasn't
very friendly. Her mother hadn't wanted to invite him to dinner, but Dad had insisted, for no apparent reason. However,
Joyce had put on a great dinner, her famous roast pork with
vegetables, but Abby might as well have been chewing saw-
dust.

Studying him, she didn't think he had much of an appe-
tite, either. He'd turned down Dad's offer of wine as she had.

The only one drinking was Lindsay, now on her second glass.

Keeping up with the conversation, Jesse managed to study the Martin clan, one by one. Joyce had her auburn hair up in some sort of twist that added to her stern look. She wore a navy-blue dress with a little white collar and matching shoes. All that for a weekday meal with someone she didn't know yet. Or did she dress so formally every night?

Vern had on his usual jeans and checkered shirt, the line on his forehead showing just where his hat usually sat. Having said his piece in the den, he was quiet. Lindsay wore a low-cut blouse and a short leather skirt, her eyes bright from the wine she seemed overly fond of. Grace looked cute in a T-shirt and shorts that matched her cornflower-blue eyes. She wasn't much of an eater but she loved to chatter, bombarding him with questions.

But it was Abby who held his attention. She'd brushed out her blond hair and let it hang past her shoulders, making him remember the times he'd thrust his fingers through the silky thickness. Her incredible green eyes rarely met his and when they did, she quickly looked away. Had she figured out his identity yet?

Jesse didn't smile much, Abby couldn't help noticing, except when he talked to Grace who'd insisted on sitting next to him. He answered her questions patiently and didn't talk down to her. He had nice hands, she decided, his fingers lean and strong. She rather liked the beard, but it was his eyes that disturbed her, that deep blue.

So like the other Jesse's.

"Tell me, Mr. Calder," Joyce Martin asked, her first comment to him that didn't involve serving the food, "is your mother involved in ranching with your father?"

"No. My mother's gone."

"Oh, I'm sorry." Joyce managed to sound sympathetic. "When did she die?"

Jesse set down his fork and looked at her. "I'm not sure she did. She left my father, my twin brother and me when Jake and I were only two. From what I've heard, she wasn't fond of the ranch. Dad got full custody of us." He turned to Abby across from him. "It's not easy, raising kids alone."

Abby saw compassion on his face, but she didn't want him thinking of her as the pitiful widow. "It's not like that here. I have a lot of help from my family."

"You're lucky. My brother has a two-year-old son who lives with us. The three of us take care of him."

"And his mother?" Joyce wanted to know.

"It was a messy divorce. Jake has custody."

Joyce raised a questioning brow. "Three men raising a child alone? I don't know."

"No offense, ma'am," Jesse answered, "but some women don't make good mothers."

Apparently, Joyce decided to drop the matter as she glanced around the table and saw that everyone was finished. She rose. "You all sit still and I'll bring in some pie."

Jesse saw Abby rise to help her mother as he spoke to his hostess. "Thanks, Mrs. Martin," he said, "but I couldn't eat another bite. The dinner was delicious."

Halfway out of the room, her arms full of plates, Joyce glanced over her shoulder. "Well, all right, if you're sure."

As Abby moved to clear his side of the table, Jesse caught

her attention. "I'd like to show you what I'm doing with your horse, if you've got a minute."

"You don't mean tonight?" Lindsay interrupted. "It's nearly dark. I thought we might go out by the highway, the three of us. There's this new little club that opened up—"

"Not me, not tonight, but thanks," Jesse told her. He turned back to Abby expectantly.

She made her decision quickly, before she could change her mind. Perhaps if she talked with this man, she'd get it in her head that he had nothing to do with that other Jesse. "I'd like to see your progress with Remus. I don't often have time during the day. I'll meet you as soon as I finish helping Mom."

"Great. I'll let Remus out into the pen."

Grace jumped down. "Can I go, too, Mommy?"

"No, sweetie, not this time." The little girl followed her mother into the kitchen.

Lindsay flounced out of the room, but Jesse didn't have time to worry about her. He had to talk to Abby, to convince her he hadn't meant to leave the way he had.

"Thank you, Mr. Martin." He reached to shake hands with his host who appeared half-drunk.

"Sure, sure." Vern didn't notice the offered hand as he busily poured himself more wine.

Jesse saw himself out.

Abby leaned on the top board of Remus's specially built pen and watched Jesse with her horse. He'd turned on the outside lights and she could clearly see that he was holding a rope lightly coiled at his side. Jesse walked closer to the stallion, using the rope as a threat, as if he intended to lasso him with it. Remus danced out of range, his twitching tail revealing his discontent at this evening invasion.

Over and over, Jesse crowded him, closer and closer, and each time, the stallion would back away. Abby drew in a nervous breath as Remus reared back, pawing the air, but Jesse moved quickly out of harm's way. She couldn't help wondering if he'd ever gotten hurt working with wounded horses.

After a few more encounters, Jesse stopped, speaking softly to the horse, then left the pen and joined her by the fence.

"You have a way with horses," she told him, knowing there were plenty of men who'd never get in a pen with a horse like Remus.

Jesse hung the coiled rope on a post. "And you have a way with children." He motioned toward the little schoolhouse. "That's a lot of kids to keep in line."

"I've always liked children." She glanced at Remus standing at the far end, watching them warily. "I'm curious. Why a round pen?"

Jesse shrugged. "It's going to sound obvious and silly, but often when you work a horse and he wants to escape, he heads for one of the corners and you have to tug and coax him away. In a round pen, there's nowhere to hide. And I don't have to butt heads with him over it."

"That makes sense."

There was precious little moonlight, which was why he'd hit the lights. Turning, Jesse leaned his back against the rail and looked her over. She was wearing a soft-blue shirt over tan slacks and her hair was hanging loose around her shoulders. Her eyes were that incredible cornflower blue that he remembered so well. Like he remembered how they'd darken when he'd touched her, loved her.

He jerked his attention back to the horse. "Casey tells me

Remus had been mistreated when you found him. How'd you get him over that?"

"It wasn't easy. That was why I was so upset when he got burned. He's already been through so much." She scooched up and sat on the top railing, her feet on the second rung. "Mostly I was just gentle with him, helping his wounds to heal, letting him get to know me and realize I was no threat to him. His previous owner, a big, burly man, made a contest out of it, demanding dominance to satisfy his own ego, so his neighbors told me. Then he abandoned him and moved on."

"Some people should never own horses. Common sense isn't as common as you might think." He smiled at her. "You may have a career as a horse whisperer."

"Mmm, I doubt that. I saw you work Remus earlier this afternoon. I've never seen such patience."

"That's what it takes. You've got to stand steady. If you move fast or demonstrate too much energy, the horse will bolt. I've learned to stop, breathe slowly and deeply, to visibly relax so he can see that. Horses are attuned to instincts as much as voice and actions. He instinctively knows that if I'm relaxed, I'm no danger to him. Even tonight, although I pressed him with the rope, I didn't capture him with it."

Abby was listening on two different levels: the first, all about Remus, the second the struggle inside her about the familiarity of this man. His voice had the same timber as the old Jesse. How could that be?

She cleared her throat. "So now he's used to your scent and knows you're no threat. What is the next step?"

"To get him to allow my touch, to learn some simple commands and follow them."

"He's pretty high-spirited."

"That's fine and you want some of that. But he also has to learn to interact with people and other horses."

A light breeze shifted a lock of Abby's hair and settled it on her cheek. Jesse's hand half raised to brush it back when he stopped himself. He hadn't the right to touch her, not yet. Maybe not ever.

Now that he had her here, he searched his mind about how best to tell her the truth. Before he could speak, Abby interrupted his nervous thoughts.

"How do you go about breaking a horse? For years I've watched how they do it here and I'm not real happy with their methods."

Jesse took a step closer to where she sat, inhaling her soft floral scent. "The original horse whisperer, the man who taught my father, and then later Dad taught me, didn't believe in *breaking* horses. He called it starting them or joining up, as the horse joins with man. That sort of communication results in the horse voluntarily cooperating."

She wondered if his short beard would feel soft or prickly, then chided herself for her roving thoughts. "We have this mare that absolutely won't take the bit, won't cooperate at all. Dad got her from a friend in a trade. No one can seem to get through to her. I don't suppose you'd want to give it a try?" Then she quickly thought better of the request. "Oh, but, I shouldn't ask since that's not why you're here."

"I'd like to try. I can't work with Remus all day. You work a little, then let him rest and remember what he's learned. Then go back and try again." He smiled up at her. "Keep in mind, though, that I'm not a magician."

"Absolutely. I just wondered if there was a better way. I

hate the idea of dominating any animal, making him give up his will to suit ours. It seems wrong."

"I think it is. Along the way, the owner gets frustrated, which can cause him to hurt the horse he's trying to grind down into submission. The male ego is the cause of most horse cruelty."

She smiled down at him. "And as a man, you don't have a problem admitting that?"

"No, because I'm not one of those men."

"I'm glad you explained things to me." She had no reason to linger and should probably go in.

Jesse held out his hand to help her down.

Feet on the ground, her eyes went to his big hand that all but swallowed hers. Suddenly, her heart picked up a beat as something familiar caught her eye.

There on his thumb was an *X*, a scar she remembered. Jesse Hunter had told her he'd gotten cut on a barbed wire fence when he was only ten, leaving a clear scar in the shape of an *X*. How could two men with the same first name have so similar a scar?

Still gripping his hand, Abby's eyes rose to his, questions swimming in them. "This scar…it can't be! But it is. You and Jesse Hunter, you're one and the same!"

Disbelief and shock had her trembling as the truth slammed into her. "Oh, God!"

Chapter Three

"Please, Abby, I can explain." He raised a hand to touch her, but she stepped back out of reach.

"Explain? You lied to me six years ago when you said you'd come back and explain why you left." Her voice was trembling and she fought to control it. "Why? I want to know why." And why now, when she'd just about stopped thinking of him daily.

Jesse wondered if the truth would really make her feel better. He had to try. "Sometimes my name can be an obstacle in getting to know someone. I was trying to get experience working with cattle because my father wanted to add cows to the ranch, to diversify."

"Why couldn't you just be honest and say that? My father would have…"

"…never hired me if he'd known I was a Calder. I needed to be anonymous, to be just one of the men so I could learn from the ground up." Jesse scraped a hand over his beard, searching for the right words. "I never meant to hurt anyone, least of all you."

Angry, hurt, breathing hard, Abby just stared at him, as a variety of emotions bombarded her. She waited. There had to be more.

He shuffled his feet, wondering why he'd thought this would be easier than it was turning out to be. "That summer, my brother went to a ranch in Montana to learn all about sheep because Dad didn't know if he wanted to add cattle or sheep. He used the name Hunter, too."

"Did he romance a girl there, too? Did he lie to her, then leave her hanging?" Her eyes struggling with tears, she stared into his, daring him to contradict her. Jesse had lied about his name. What else had he lied about?

The sound of male laughter floated out of the open door of the barn. "Please, I have a lot more to tell you. Could we walk a ways?" He honestly hadn't realized the depth of her hurt. Did his leaving send her into the arms of another man, the one she'd so hastily married?

Abby shook her head, edged away from him. "You're a little late with your explanations. Six years too late." She needed to get away before the tears burning her eyes fell and let him see just how badly he'd upset her. Again.

"Abby, I always knew you to be fair. I'm asking you to walk with me, to hear me out. Fifteen minutes. Is that too much to ask?" He'd never begged before, but he had to make her see.

She could give him that much. A part of her wanted to hear the rest. "All right. Fifteen minutes." She checked her watch. "It's more than you deserve."

They began to walk away from the round pen and the barn, down a jagged path toward the stream that snaked through the ranch. The smell of mesquite peppered the air with its pungent aroma, mingling with the scent of wild honeysuckle. The heat of the day was at half power with the retreat of the sun and a light breeze cooled things down. The hoot of an owl echoed from a distance as night birds twittered in the trees.

A perfect night for an imperfect couple.

Jesse touched her elbow to guide her toward a large rock alongside a weeping willow at the water's edge, but she jerked away. At the rock, she turned to look at him. "I thought you wanted to talk. You've already wasted several minutes."

He faced her, gauging his words. She was actually going to hold him to a time limit. Beneath the hurt in her eyes, he saw anger and hoped he could erase it. "I lied about my name, but that was all I lied about, Abby. I never lied about how I felt about you. I fully intended to return and tell you who I really was after I'd made sure my father had survived his heart attack. But about fifty miles from home, a drunken driver in a pickup hit my convertible head-on."

Her eyes widened at this news, but she stood silent.

He could have told her about how they'd had to rebuild his nose, about his clavicle broken in two places, his collapsed lung, the removal of his spleen, the four surgeries on his leg that would never be exactly the same and the crushed vertebrae in his back that would likely give him pain for the rest of his life. He could have, but he chose not to. The last thing he wanted was her pity.

"Ironically, I wound up in the same hospital as my dad, only he got to go home before me. I was pretty badly banged up, in a coma for over a week, then months of healing and physical therapy."

She didn't want to feel sympathy for him, but she couldn't

help it. Months recovering from a head-on collision. And she'd had no idea. "Why didn't you call me?"

"I couldn't for the first few weeks, but I phoned as soon as I was able. I talked to Lindsay. She told me you'd gotten married and moved away."

Abby shifted her eyes to the stars in the cloudless sky, studying them as if the answers were spelled out there. "I tried finding you. I called every Hunter family in northern California. I checked on the Internet on a link for traveling ranch hands. Naturally, I came up empty-handed." She wrapped her arms around herself, as if to ward off a chill even though it was quite warm.

"I'm sorry, really sorry, Abby. I even sent you two letters."

Frowning, she turned back to him. "Here, at the ranch?"

"One here and one to the university even though they told me you'd quit. I was hoping they'd forward it. But I guess you'd already gotten married. They both came back marked 'not at this address.'" He dared to touch her arm, needing the contact. His skin was cool and she didn't pull away this time. "Your husband, this Tom Price that Casey told me about, you must have met him when you went back to the university soon after I left, right?"

"Something like that." Abby moved away from the rock, away from his touch, turning her back to him. "You'd hurt me. I felt so alone and…"

"…and you married him on the rebound?" Perhaps that was a presumptuous assumption, but after they'd been so close, Jesse couldn't believe she'd tumble into love that quickly.

She didn't answer him. She didn't have to. "Then you had to go through his death. Were you with him when he drowned? Did you come back here after that?"

Abby didn't want to go into the details. "I came back

home because I was pregnant with Grace." Finally, she slowly turned around. "What exactly did Lindsay say to you? Do you remember?"

"Oh, yeah. She told me I wasn't welcome around here, not to phone or send mail or come by ever again."

"I…I guess she was trying to protect me."

"From me? Why? I didn't think your family even knew we were seeing one another."

"Mom and Dad didn't, but Lindsay's enterprising. She probably saw us leaving to meet down by the river or maybe in the hayloft." No, she didn't want to think about those times. "Listen, I understand why you couldn't come right back, but I still don't see why you lied about your name. That's…that's…"

"That's the way it's done in ranching circles, Abby."

"But it's dishonest. It's like spying to pick up another rancher's secrets."

Jesse shook his head. "What secrets? Ranching is ranching. I wasn't running around taking notes and jotting things down. I was trying to see if we could handle raising cattle much as your father does here. To see if cattle would fit in with our herd."

He didn't think he'd done anything wrong, and maybe he hadn't. *All in the eyes of the beholder,* Abby thought. She rubbed at a spot over her left eye where a headache was forming. "Well, that's all well and good, but I'm sorry. I can't trust you, Jesse. And if my father should find out, he'd feel as betrayed as I do."

"I think you're wrong. I'm not ashamed of what I did, not any of it. I'll go to your father right now and tell him everything and…"

"No! No, don't do that. He's got enough problems right

now. You may have noticed at dinner that he's distracted and worried."

Jesse frowned. "What kind of problems is he having?" Vern had confided in him, but he wondered if Abby knew.

"I'm not sure. He won't talk about it, but I think it has to do with money. He's lost several good men. Don't tell him about this right now. I don't want to add to his worries."

"All right." He stepped closer, took both her hands. "What about us, Abby? Do you forgive me?" When she hesitated, he went on. "We were close once. I've missed you." He saw the wariness in her eyes and knew he'd put it there.

She wasn't without her own secrets, her own deception. She had no reason not to forgive him. How could she continue to blame him when he'd been in that terrible accident? But she certainly wasn't about to fall under his spell again. Once you've been burned, it would be stupid to stick your hand back in the fire.

"Yes, I forgive you." Gently, she removed his hand. "But that's as far as it goes, Jesse. You're here to help Remus and nothing more. There is no *us* anymore. Good night." Turning on her heel, she started walking back, then shifted into a run.

Jesse watched her go. Had he made any headway today? Hard to tell. When he'd known Abby six years ago, she'd been a soft-spoken girl, sweet-tempered and gentle. This Abby was a woman who'd buried a husband, had a child, started a business and knew her own mind.

He smiled as he walked slowly to his cabin. He rather liked the new version.

Abby reached the big house, out of breath, the tears she'd hidden from Jesse wet on her cheeks. She paused at the porch, sitting down in the white wicker chair to wipe her face and pull herself together. It wouldn't do to let her family see how upset she was. There was no telling what her father would do with this piece of news. But her mother worried her more.

Joyce Martin was a paradox, in her daughter's view. Alternately loving and shrewish, she was a difficult woman to figure out. Abby knew she'd had back trouble for years and been taking medication for it, not to mention her more frequent migraines. Perhaps the pills were the cause of her inconsistent behavior. It was clear that she loved her children, though she particularly favored Lindsay, who resembled her the most. She rarely spoke of her life before marrying Vern. However, in a moment of weakness, Joyce had told Abby that she was illegitimate, that she'd not known her father, and the shame had affected her deeply. That was undoubtedly why she was overly protective of her daughters and very disappointed that neither was happily married.

No, her mother would figure things out quickly and that would be disastrous. Abby had gone to so much trouble to put her life back together after Jesse that she dare not risk another upheaval. Not only would she suffer, but Grace would, too. No matter the cost, she would have to protect her daughter.

Finally composed, she went inside.

It was only nine o'clock, but the downstairs was empty with nothing but a dim light on in the living room. Abby climbed the stairs and walked quietly down the hallway. She'd asked her mother to supervise Grace's bath and put her to bed. At Grace's room, she saw the door was ajar and went in.

A smile formed without her conscious knowledge as she gazed down at her sleeping daughter. Grace was on her tummy wearing her favorite Peter Pan pajamas, clutching the somewhat ratty stuffed dog she'd named Fred. Abby had rented the movie version of Peter Pan and Grace had loved watching it so much, Abby had finally bought it for her. The little girl viewed it almost daily, telling everyone she wanted to fly just like Peter Pan.

Leaning down, Abby brushed the golden hair from Grace's face and rearranged the sheet so it covered her. For a long while, she stood, just looking at her child. The best part of her, the best thing that had ever happened to her. How could she regret any part of that year that had changed her life when it had given her this wondrous little girl?

She kissed Grace's cheek, then quietly left the room.

Her parents' bedroom door at the far end of the hallway was closed, no light showing beneath. Dad always went to bed early because he was up by five o'clock. Mom also was an early riser, in the kitchen by seven o'clock, even though she often stayed up late reading or knitting, saying she couldn't sleep. Abby was grateful she didn't have to face them tonight.

She paused at Lindsay's room and knocked lightly. When she heard no response, she opened the door. The bedside lamp was on, but her sister's bed was empty. Lindsay had probably gone to that new club she'd mentioned at dinner. Abby decided she'd have to wait until tomorrow to ask her about the phone call from Jesse. Not that she didn't believe that part of his story. It would be just like Lindsay to throw cold water on any attempt a man might make to contact Abby. Things may have turned out very differently if she'd have taken down Jesse's number and told Abby to call him.

Sighing, she left her sister's room and went to her own. She undressed and put on her pale-green nightshirt, then lay back on her bed, knowing she was too churned up to sleep. More tears struggled to be freed from behind her eyes at the onslaught of the bittersweet memories being with Jesse again had evoked, but Abby ruthlessly blinked them away. She'd cried all she was going to over Jesse.

But once begun, she couldn't help remembering the shy, introverted girl she'd been six years ago, feeling very much in the shadow of her older, sophisticated and confident sister.

She'd been so young, not yet twenty, but already finished with her junior year at Arizona State, having skipped a grade in high school. She felt comfortable with books and learning, almost as much as she enjoyed being with the horses. Casey had taught her to ride at six and she'd turned out to be a natural, able to ride like the wind. She'd spent hours in the barn, grooming her favorite horses, giving them treats and talking softly to each one. She didn't mind that her interests were mostly solitary because she didn't feel as socially adept as Lindsay or even her mother. With books and horses, she felt the confidence that eluded her with people.

Until Jesse showed up the week she'd come home for summer break.

She'd noticed him in the barn that first time. Most of the men came in from a long day in the saddle on the range and handed their horses over to the two young grooms before heading straight for the mess hall. Not Jesse.

Standing by one of the far stalls, she watched him rub down his mount, talking to the stallion all the while. It was beastly hot so he'd taken off his shirt. Wearing jeans and scuffed boots, his damp chest gleaming from his exertion, he looked like the pictures of James Dean that Abby had seen, only with dark hair. There was a restless energy about him, a devil-may-care look in his impossibly blue eyes. Yet he was gentle with the horse, revealing a soft side.

Abby thought he was every girl's dream.

Suddenly the horse nearest her whinnied and Jesse glanced over. He spotted her and stopped working. He just stood there, staring, not smiling, sort of assessing.

Abby stared, too, and time seemed to stand still as she drank in the sight of him. He had a face carved by the sun, his chin square and strong. But her timid nature won the battle and she turned, leaving the barn, her cheeks burning.

Afterward, she couldn't get him out of her mind. Each time she was outside—and she made sure she had lots of reasons to be out—she'd surreptitiously search the area for a glimpse of him. She'd learned that his name was Jesse Hunter and he was new to the Martin ranch, but he'd had ranching experience elsewhere. At dinner one night, her mother said he'd arrived in a red convertible, as if that said it all. Then Joyce had proceeded to say that he had a cocky walk, and warned both her girls to stay away from him.

Abby had glanced at her sister and knew that Mom had made a tactical error. Lindsay was drawn to the forbidden.

She'd been so certain that Jesse would soon be wrapped in Lindsay's web that she'd literally given up before she'd begun to try to make him notice her. That evening, she'd saddled Freda, a gentle old mare way past her prime, although she still enjoyed a ride now and then. Abby had headed Freda to a big old cottonwood tree alongside the stream quite a ways past the ranch buildings. It was the spot she went to when she wanted, needed, to be alone.

Dismounting, she tied Freda to a solid limb, taking a moment to stroke between the mare's eyes and nuzzle her. Then she sat down in the grass, pulled a blade and stuck it in her mouth.

Why hadn't she been born more outgoing like Lindsay? Oh, she spoke easily and often to the ranch hands, but many she'd known from childhood. She wasn't afraid of men, it's just that if she was attracted to one, her mind emptied and she couldn't think of anything to say. But flirtatious thoughts and clever words rolled off Lindsay's tongue like water off a duck's back.

Maybe that's why Abby had such an active imagination, she thought, to the point where she often envisioned a dream lover who'd see only her, want only her, love only her. Lately her dream lover's features made a dead ringer for Jesse Hunter.

Rising, Abby held out her arms to the imaginary Jesse as she began to hum a romantic tune. Pretending he reached out to hold her close and swing her into a dance, she whirled about on the grass, smiling at the face she'd memorized from afar. Out here she could dream and no one would know about her feelings, her private fantasies. Around she twirled, turning and…and stopped.

Jesse was standing there, his arms stretching toward her in invitation. His eyes were shiny in the moonlight and there was a smile on his lips. She hadn't heard him approach, so wrapped up in her fantasy was she.

"May I have this dance?" he asked.

As if it were the most natural thing in the world to be dancing without music in the grass alongside the stream, she moved into his arms. He held her close, but not too close. She tried to hum the song, but her throat had gone dry. His eyes captured hers and held.

He twirled her around, keeping time with a melody in his head, and she followed, graceful as never before. Abby found herself smiling, then laughing as the dance ended.

"I'm Jesse," he said, still holding her.

"I'm Abby," she answered.

"I know." And he'd walked with her over to the tree and they'd sat down beneath it on the soft, fragrant grass.

That had been the beginning, Abby thought as she rose from her bed. What girl wouldn't have fallen in love with a man as romantic as that?

It was later that she'd learned that just because you fall in love with someone, even if you feel they care, too, it doesn't mean that happily-ever-after was a given.

At her bedroom window, she moved the sheers aside and looked out, thinking to see the moon. Instead, she saw Jesse leaning against the tall cottonwood in their front yard. He was staring right up at her as if he could see into her mind, her heart. She wondered what he thought he saw.

Closing the curtains, she sighed and turned off her bedside lamp.

It was noon before Lindsay came downstairs and wandered into the kitchen where Abby was making sandwiches for the kids in her schoolhouse. She poured herself a cup of coffee and yawned as she took a seat at the big oak table.

"Late night?" Abby asked her sister.

"Mm-hmm." Never too chipper when she first got up, Lindsay sipped the hot brew.

Abby placed the last of the sandwiches in her big picnic hamper, then turned to Lindsay. She would have to approach this diplomatically. It didn't take much to make her sister suspicious.

She sat down across from Lindsay and watched her light a cigarette with hands that were none too steady. "Lindsay, would you happen to remember a phone call you took for me quite a while back from Jesse Hunter?"

Lindsay blew smoke toward the ceiling and crossed her shapely legs. "You expect me to remember something that long ago? What made you think of him, anyway? This new guy with the same first name?"

"Probably. Did you ever talk to Jesse Hunter on the phone, maybe when I was away at college?"

Lindsay put on a thoughtful look as she drew deeply on her cigarette. "I believe he did call here, but it was shortly after we learned that you'd gotten married. So I told him and that was that." She tapped the ash off the end of her cigarette. "Why?"

"I just wondered." Getting to her feet, Abby moved to the fridge and pulled out a large milk carton.

"How about a letter addressed to me from California? Did you ever see that?"

"No. What's this all about?" Lindsay's interest was evident.

Time to back off. "Nothing, really." She couldn't very well fault Lindsay for telling Jesse the truth, as she knew it. As to the letter, giving the devil his due, maybe her sister honestly hadn't seen it—if there even had been a letter—or perhaps she didn't remember. Then again, Jesse had insisted his name was the only deception on his part.

"I don't understand why you want to know about some old phone call or letter from ages ago," Lindsay said. "This guy coming here and resembling Jesse Hunter's got you wired." Squinting through the smoke, something new occurred to her. "When you went out there to talk about Remus last night, did that guy make a pass?"

Good old Lindsay, Abby thought, grabbing a handful of

napkins before picking up the basket. So predictable. "No, he did not."

A shrewd look settled on Lindsay's features. "Maybe you wish he had."

"No, that's your department." With that, she left the kitchen, angry with herself for allowing Lindsay to rile her. She should have just let sleeping dogs lie. Now she'd planted a seed in her sister's fertile little mind. It was anyone's guess what Lindsay would do with it.

Remus was balking again, only more so. It was late morning and Jesse had been working with him for well over an hour. He'd tried shortening the rope, moving closer to the big stallion, but each time, he'd reared up angrily. It was time to try something else.

Leaving the pen, he spotted Casey watching. "I'm going to need your help," he told the manager.

Casey pushed off the barn wall where he'd been leaning and walked over. "What do you need?"

"I noticed this trench filled with water down by the east pasture at the end of that dirt roadway."

Nodding, Casey adjusted his hat. "Used to be a pond but it started drying up. Got three, maybe four feet of water, weeds on both sides."

"Perfect. I want to take Remus over and have him walk in it."

The older man frowned. "What for?"

"For one thing, it'll tire him. For another, I want him to know who's in charge, to make him acknowledge he needs to do as I direct him. It's all about control at this point."

Obviously skeptical, Casey looked up at him. "You've done this before and it worked?"

"Mostly. I can't say for sure. Will you help me get him over there?"

Looking like he'd rather do most anything else, Casey followed Jesse into the barn.

Word had spread and several men who'd managed to free themselves from their chores stood around watching as Jesse took hold of one lead rope on one side of the long, narrow pond while Casey held the other. Slowly, they led Remus into the water.

Nobody really noticed Abby, who'd heard about the experiment and had quietly walked over to stand alongside a paloverde tree.

Walking through the weeds, the two men guided the stallion through the water that came up to the top of his strong legs. At first, the skittish horse took high steps, but soon the somewhat muddy bottom slowed him down. Still, Jesse kept going, turning him at the far end and marching him back and forth again, with Casey doing the same on the opposite side.

More than a dozen turns later, Jesse, wearing high waders, went in, grabbing both lead ropes as Casey joined the others. Walking slowly alongside Remus, he walked him to the water's edge and stood there. He removed one rope, but held the other. Gauging the stallion's mood, he dared to reach up and stroke his long neck. Remus allowed the touch though he moved his big head up then down.

Jesse stepped closer to the edge, intending to lead the horse out, when the sound of a car approaching at a fast speed on the dirt road surprised everyone. Startled, Remus reared up, yanking the last rope from Jesse's hands as he pulled himself out of the water and took off into the east pasture. No one watching could miss the annoyance on Jesse's face as

Lindsay ground her red Corvette convertible to a halt and jumped out.

"What's going on?" she asked cheerily.

"You just messed up a real important exercise with Remus," Casey told her, his voice betraying his irritation with his boss's spoiled daughter. "That's what's going on."

Ignoring both of them, Jesse headed for the east pasture, his eyes on Remus who was still running, but slowing down.

Oblivious to the trouble she'd caused, Lindsay followed after Jesse as the men straggled back to work. "Hey, sugar, can I help?"

Not even stopping, Jesse said, "You've helped enough, thanks."

"Well, fine!" Lindsay whirled about and marched back to her car, suddenly noticing Abby by the tree. "What?" she asked her sister, who was eyeing her with displeasure.

"Your timing is impeccable, as always, Lindsay." Abby couldn't help wondering if the incident had hampered Remus even more.

"Why don't you go soak your head, dear sister?" Lindsay said with a saccharine smile. She got behind the wheel and backed up, then shifted and roared off, heading for the road, as if she couldn't wait to leave the ranch and everyone on it far behind.

Abby noticed Jesse strolling in the open pasture toward Remus. She wanted to see what he'd do, but she didn't want Jesse to know she was watching. But after all, Remus was *her* horse. So she followed behind carefully.

Jesse stopped walking after a while, gazing at Remus, who was now standing still, watching Jesse. He didn't want to crowd him, but rather to cause him to want to come back on his own. There was nowhere for him to escape since the pastureland was fenced in for miles. Jesse squatted on his haunches in the tall grass, visible only from the shoulders up, and waited.

Remus looked as if he didn't quite know what to make of this strange man. The horse studied him from a distance for long minutes, then slowly began walking toward Jesse. He took his time, sauntering along, occasionally sniffing the air, his big head bobbing up and down. The one lead rope was still hanging from his neck.

Calmly, Jesse remained as still as possible, his eyes on the stallion. Ever so slowly, almost reluctantly, Remus came toward him. When he was about a hundred yards away, Jesse rose. The big horse shuffled closer until he stood alongside the man. Reaching up, taking his time, Jesse stroked Remus's strong neck on his good side. When Remus turned his head, Jesse stroked down his nose, aware that a small measure of trust had been forged today. What he'd feared would turn disastrous when Lindsay had spooked the stallion, had turned into a good ending.

Taking hold of the remaining lead rope, Jesse led him back in the direction of the barn.

Minutes later, Abby followed. She was surprised and full of admiration for the way Jesse had handled Remus. If she could keep her personal feelings at bay, she was certain she'd have her horse back, able to trust again, once Jesse finished with him.

The problem was that once she'd discovered his real identity, she remembered far more than she wanted to about their time together, more than was good for her emotional health. And at night, she was plagued by dreams, scenarios that had her back in his strong arms. She would need to stay in the background, like today, and watch him from afar. He'd be gone soon and then maybe things would get back to the way they had been.

"Hi, Mr. Calder," Grace said, her big blue eyes looking up at Jesse as he sat on his front porch whittling. "Whatcha doin'?"

He smiled at her. "Trying to turn this piece of wood into a dog, one like him," he told her, pointing to where Jughead lay sleeping in a spot of late afternoon sunlight.

The little girl giggled. "You can't turn wood into dogs," she informed him.

"Not a real dog. A dog you can put on a shelf and admire." He scooted over and she climbed up and sat alongside him, watching as the knife he was using curled thin shavings off the block of wood. "Do you like dogs?"

"Mm-hmm. But Grandma won't let Mommy get me a puppy. She says dogs belong outside, not in the house."

"Well, at least you can play with Jughead and Spike, right?"

"Jughead's always down at the barn or out with the cows and Katie doesn't bring Spike over very often. Do you have a dog?" Her ponytail was tied with a piece of pink yarn to match her shirt worn with denim shorts and white sandals on her feet.

"Yes, I do. A Border collie named Roscoe."

"Do you miss him?"

"Sure do. That's why I keep Jughead around." Jesse set down his knife and the chunk of wood. Leaning back, he reached into his pocket and pulled out two packets of M&M'S. "Want some?"

Grace's eyes widened as she stared at the candy. "Mommy doesn't like me to eat too much candy. Spoils my dinner." She glanced over at the big house as if expecting her mother to materialize.

"It's hours yet till dinnertime and these are small." When she still hesitated, he brought out the big guns. "If Mommy gets mad, I'll talk to her, okay? Until then, it'll be our secret." He gave her a broad wink.

"Okay." Smiling, she took the packet, tore it open handily and popped a small candy into her mouth. "I like the red ones best."

He opened his own packet and studied the colors inside. "I think I like the green ones best. Did you know they have blue ones now?"

"I know. You shouldn't chew them, you know. You have to let them melt in your mouth."

"Is that right?"

Grace smiled solemnly. Getting comfortable, she scooched over and sat cross-legged facing him. "Are you done fixing Mommy's horse?"

"No, not yet. That takes time." Companionably chewing candy together, they sat quietly. Jesse thought that Grace was probably the most beautiful little girl he'd ever seen, not that he'd been with many small children. But then, look at the mother she had. Apparently she had no traces of her father, for her hair and features were like a miniature Abby. She'd probably gotten her blue eyes from Vern.

"Do you like to ride horses?" Grace asked.

"Sure do. Do you?"

She put on a sad face. "I can't, Grandma said. Not until I'm bigger. Grandpa wanted to teach me, but she wouldn't let him. I wish I could. Maybe one day Mommy will get me a pony."

"What does Mommy say about you riding?"

The banging of the screen door of the big house was followed by the sound of footsteps running down the stairs. Grace and Jesse looked over as Abby hurried toward them, a frown on her face.

She didn't say a word until she reached Jesse's porch. "So here's where you went. Grace, how many times have I told you that you can't just wander off without telling me?"

Grace didn't seem a bit afraid, but she did squish the bag of candy and hold it behind her. "I was just right here. Jesse's making a dog. Wanna see?"

Abby looked at Jesse as he reached behind his back and brought forth the chunk of wood that certainly didn't resemble anything yet.

Abby's brows rose. "That's a dog?"

"It's a work in progress," Jesse admitted.

"I'm sorry Grace is bothering you." She reached out a hand to her daughter. "Come on, Grace."

"She's not bothering me at all."

"We have to go."

Reluctantly, Grace took her mother's hand and slowly made her way down the steps. At the bottom, she turned back. "Thank you, Jesse." And she winked her eye comically, as he had done.

"Come back anytime," he told her, grinning.

Abby didn't like the sound of that. "Grace, you go on in. I'll be there in a few minutes." She watched her daughter hurry toward the big house, holding the candy she'd smelled on her.

Turning back to Jesse, she folded her arms over her chest, wondering how to put this. "Please don't encourage Grace to hang around over here. I need to keep her close to the big house. It's too easy to get hurt around a ranch."

Jesse picked up his knife and resumed whittling. "I was keeping watch on her, Abby. I wouldn't have let her get hurt."

"I'm sure you're right, but if she starts coming here, then next time she might wander farther, down toward the barn or the mess hall. She's only five. I don't like her to be out of my sight unless she's with a member of the family."

Which he certainly wasn't. "Okay. You're the boss." He thought she was being overly cautious, but then he'd never had children, so what did he know.

"Thank you." She started back, but his next comment stopped her in her tracks.

"Would you let me teach her to ride? There're a couple of really docile mares in the barn and…"

"Absolutely not!" She swung back to face him. "Listen, Jesse. I thought I made myself perfectly clear. You're here to work with Remus. Period. Nothing more."

She'd aroused his curiosity. "What are you afraid of? Surely you don't think I'd let any harm come to her, or any child?"

"She's *my* daughter. You'll just have to respect my wishes."

Why was she suddenly so adamant, almost belligerent? Studying her nervous gaze, Jesse thought he detected a hint of fear in her eyes. Was she afraid for Grace or afraid of him? And if so, why?

"Are we clear?"

"Crystal." He watched her turn again and this time run all the way to the big house, up the steps and inside.

Now, what was that all about? he wondered.

Chapter Four

Jesse had been at the Martin ranch for eight days and Remus was still giving him attitude. Occasionally, the stallion allowed him to come close, even to touch him. But then, the next minute he'd run off as if he regretted his weak moment.

The horse wasn't the only thing on his mind. Abby was front and center during most of his waking hours and she'd begun to invade his dreams. When he wasn't working with Remus, he could see Abby with her little charges from his cabin. She rarely even glanced over at him and she managed to avoid running into him. She also kept Grace all but glued to her side.

Too much time on his hands, Jesse thought. He couldn't work 24-7 with the damaged horse. So he'd wait to catch glimpses of Abby as she came and went, though she now spent less time outside with the children than before. Probably to evade him. There were times he spotted her standing off to the side, watching him work Remus, but the moment he appeared to head her way, she'd leave hurriedly. Still, the more she made herself unavailable, the more he wanted to be with her.

All too often, he recalled those delicious moments he'd spent with her all those years ago. He'd come here to face down that past and maybe he'd also been searching for his future. Because he was falling for Abby all over again.

And he kept remembering things, like the first time he'd kissed her.

After the impromptu dance on the riverbank, he and Abby had sat down in the fragrant summer grass under the old cottonwood. Jesse had wanted to know all about her, asking questions while his eyes took in the sight of her. Her long blond hair shifted lightly in the soft evening breeze. In her beautiful green eyes he could see interest mingled with an innate shyness. Not one to be easily awestruck, he'd felt jittery and tense in her presence, worried she'd run off.

They talked for a long while, about the ranch, the lovely night, even the weather and finally he got more personal.

"What are you studying?" he asked after she'd told him she'd just finished her junior year at the University of Arizona.

"I'm an education major. I'd like to teach, probably at grade-school level." Her slender hand caressed the high grass, her eyes downcast.

"Ah, you like children?"

"Very much. And you?"

Jesse wondered if he should tell her that he'd graduated from Stanford since he was supposed to be a simple ranch hand. He decided to finesse it. "Me? I love ranching. Everything about it. Horses, breeding them, working them." He gazed off toward the far west pasture. "I'm interested in raising cattle as well."

"I've seen you on horseback," she said, raising her eyes to his. "It's like you're one with the horse. That's pretty rare."

"Funny, I was going to say the same about you." Smiling at her, he took her slim hand in his large callused one. "I imagine you have lots of guys knocking on your door."

"Hundreds, actually." She laughed, then looked up at him. "None that mean anything."

Pleased, Jesse squeezed her hand. "Then maybe we could…"

"I don't think so." Reclaiming her hand, she got up. "My mother frowns on us—my sister and me—seeing any of the ranch hands privately." She checked her watch in the moonlight. "It's getting late…."

Jesse jumped up and moved close to her, placing his hand at her waist and urging her nearer. "Aren't you old enough to make your own decisions about the men you see?"

Her eyes revealed her conflicting emotions. He could see she was not used to going against her mother's wishes, yet the desire to be with him was very evident. Finally, she came to a decision.

"I go riding nearly every evening. Sometimes here and often to the east pasture along the river. There's a big weeping willow there that is so pretty. If you just happen to come along tomorrow night, well…"

"I'll be there." His hand at her back, he nudged her fractionally closer. Taking a big chance at possibly ruining things, he lowered his head and touched his mouth to hers.

She seemed surprised, barely responsive. Jesse knew she was nearly twenty. Surely she'd been kissed before. He ended the kiss and gazed into eyes filled with confusion. And something else.

Suddenly, rising on tiptoe, Abby went back for more, her arms encircling him. Jesse took over, deepening the kiss, crushing her against his hard body. His senses were flooded with the heat, the unexpectedly wild taste of her.

Then suddenly, as if her conscience had just kicked in, she pulled away and hurried to her mare, expertly climbing onto the horse's back.

Jesse stepped nearer, watching her take the reins in unsteady hands. "I'll see you tomorrow night."

"Yes." Turning the mare, she headed back toward the lights of the outbuildings.

He'd stood under the old cottonwood a long while, her taste on his lips, reliving that kiss.

That had been then and this was now, Jesse reminded himself. She'd said she forgave him, but it was crystal clear that she didn't trust him, not even to sit in plain view with her daughter. He wanted to ride with her along the riverbank again, to sit and talk with her the way they had before, to get to know this new Abby. And yes, he wanted to kiss her again, to see if what he'd been remembering was real or just a product of his overactive imagination. Instead he sat whittling all alone on his porch and tried to make a plan that would bring her to him.

He found his answer one afternoon as he left his cabin. A white pickup drove in through the arches and pulled up near Abby's school. Curious, Jesse stood watching as a tall man in a plaid shirt and work pants got out on the driver's side and walked around the truck. He opened the passenger door and helped a young boy of about ten wearing a leg brace step down. Abby came out to greet the man and boy. They talked for a few minutes, then the man drove off and Abby, her arm around the boy's thin shoulders, escorted him into the school-house.

Staring after them, Jesse felt an idea form. He hurried back inside his cabin and began looking through a stack of newspapers. He'd developed the habit of driving to Curly's almost daily for things he needed, a few toiletries, cold drinks and the daily paper flown in from Phoenix. He remembered reading an article just the other day.

In minutes, he found it. Skimming the reporter's story again, he thought this was something Abby might consider, especially since the program had begun at her old alma mater, the University of Arizona. It seemed some people there had tried a new method of working with children who suffered from a variety of problems, from injured limbs to autism, from mild retardation to parental neglect. The individuals in charge had begun teaching the kids to ride horses. They'd been amazed at the results, how well the kids had responded.

Ripping out the article, he folded it and put it in his pocket. He'd have to find the right moment to approach Abby. This could be his chance to work with her and the kids. Perhaps she'd regain her trust in him. It was worth a shot.

Whistling, Jesse left the cabin and headed for the horse barn.

It was at least an hour past dinnertime and the sun was low in the sky, the heat of the day somewhat less. Abby stood in the shadow of the barn watching Jesse with Remus, as she had been for about twenty minutes. She had to give the man credit. He was certainly not a slacker. This was his fourth session today with the big stallion and yet Jesse seemed as patient as he had early in the morning. She ought to know for she'd been quietly watching each time.

He'd managed to get Remus to willingly take the bit today, no small feat. It had taken him two hours, but man had won over horse.

Abby stepped into the doorway, sure Jesse was too busy concentrating to see her. He was doing the now familiar crowding, rattling Remus with the coiled rope, causing him to do some fancy footwork to evade the trainer. Even Casey was impressed with Jesse, stating that he didn't know many men who would step into a pen and challenge that much angry horseflesh.

Remus did look riled tonight. Abby thought he was getting tired of being confronted. Was Jesse trying to wear him down? She'd love to know, but she hadn't spoken to him since she'd warned him to stay away from Grace that evening at his porch. Her fears weren't only about Grace getting hurt. There was so much more at stake.

She watched the stallion back off, but Jesse whacked the coiled rope against his pant leg again, pressuring Remus. Suddenly the stallion had had enough. Snorting, Remus ran in a tight circle, then doubled back past Jesse, knocking him down. Startled, Abby gasped and moved out of the doorway to the fenced-in pen. Remus danced off to the far side.

The shoulder bump had hit Jesse pretty hard, but she'd expected him to get up quickly. He wasn't moving.

Acting instinctively, Abby opened the gate and stepped in, closing it behind her, her worried gaze going from the horse to the man. "Jesse!" she called out as she hurried to him.

Finally, he raised his head and shook it as if to clear his

vision. At his side, Abby helped him to stand, keeping an anxious eye on Remus. "Are you all right?" she asked.

"Yeah, fine." Jesse picked up his hat that had been knocked off. "Just blacked out for a minute."

"Here, let me help you." Abby had an arm around his waist as she led him to the gate, noticing that his limp was more obvious. Once outside the locked pen, she looked at his face. "You're bleeding. Let's go into the barn and I'll fix that cut."

He really was fine, Jesse acknowledged, but he let her assist him, enjoying her closeness. He'd been knocked down by horses more times than he could count and never been badly hurt, but Remus had caught him off guard.

Abby switched on the dim lights. A couple of the closest horses snuffled in their stalls. The smell of hay and animals and leather permeated the humid air.

In the far corner was a counter with a sink, a first-aid kit and a stool. She guided Jesse to sit down, then opened the kit and removed a thick gauze square. Dampening it with alcohol, she began to clean the cut on his forehead. "You take too many chances with that stallion."

"Not usually. He didn't mean to hurt me, just to get me to stop bothering him." He sucked in a breath at the sting, but she dug even deeper. "I didn't know you had a sadistic streak."

"You must have hit your head on a rock and there's dirt embedded in the cut. You need to get the stable boys to rake that pen again." She returned to her concerns over his work with the big stallion. "If you knew he wanted you to stop, why didn't you back off?" Rummaging around in the oversized kit, she found a tube of antibiotic ointment and proceeded to spread some on the cut.

"Because I can't teach him anything from a distance." It was a warm evening but her touch was cool. He inhaled and recognized the sweet, clean scent of her late afternoon shower, a fragrance he remembered so well. She wore a simple white blouse with a floral skirt that came to mid-calf and white sandals. Her toenails were painted a vivid pink. "You smell awfully good," he ventured. "Even in this barn. How do you manage that?"

"It's called bathing with soap and water." Determined not to let him get to her, she put an adhesive bandage over the cut and quickly put the kit away.

Jesse felt he had to get her attention before she hurried away. He took her hand. "Abby, thank you."

Frowning, she took back her hand. "It's not as if I saved your life. Don't make more of this than there is, Jesse." She started to leave, but he touched her arm.

"Wait. There's something I want to show you." He removed a folded newspaper from his pocket and held it out to her. "Read this."

Abby studied his eyes. Was this another ploy? Hesitantly, she took the paper and unfolded it before skimming the article. "I've heard of their work," she finally said.

"That little boy with the brace on his leg who arrived today. I'll bet he's shy and introverted around the other kids. Why don't we try this therapy on him, see if being around horses will help?"

Abby stared at the picture alongside the article where a young girl was on crutches in one shot and on horseback the next, smiling at the camera. She looked at Jesse. *"We?"* she asked pointedly.

"I could help with the kids," he told her, rising. "Do you have anyone else in your classes who has special needs?"

"Besides Sam, there's Charley. He's deaf." She had to admit that both boys were timid and seemed to feel hesitant and uncertain.

"Okay, that's two," Jesse went on. "We could try. I've checked out the mares. Dolly and Jasmine are both older and gentle. If the program doesn't work, we can always stop." He could see doubt in her eyes, but also interest.

Abby was beginning to warm to the idea, but she also had reservations. "I don't have a lot of time to devote to this. Susie, my teenage helper, can't be responsible for the other children for long periods of time."

"She wouldn't have to be. You could bring the kids over to me, stay until they got familiar with me and the horse, then go back to your kids." He paused as a new thought hit him. "Unless you don't trust me with the children."

Actually, she did trust him in this capacity. She knew he was capable, kind, patient—all the things necessary for working with special needs kids. What she didn't trust him with was her heart, which would be exposed to him more if they worked together. "I don't know." She turned from him, walking toward the door thoughtfully. "I'd have to present it to their parents and to the kids themselves."

Jesse followed her outside. "Sure. I'd be willing to bet they'd vote to give the plan a try."

She stopped to look up at him again, so aware of him that her skin tingled. Why did he have to be so damn good-looking? She'd never much cared for hairy men, but on Jesse, the short beard added to his appeal. As if he needed more.

The real question was, could she work with him and take a chance on all those old feelings surging back? "You'll be leaving soon and…"

"Not for weeks yet. I won't leave you hanging. By that time, the kids will be back in regular classes. Maybe we can find someone to train for an after-school program."

He seemed sincere, but she'd believed in him once before. Dare she gamble that he really was all he claimed to be? "Let me think about it, okay? I'll let you know tomorrow."

"Fair enough." She held out the article, but he shook his head. "Keep it. Read it again, the part about their results."

"All right, I will. Thanks." Abby turned and walked home slowly as Jesse stood watching her. He hoped she'd try this program because if she didn't, he was fresh out of ideas on how to legitimately spend time with her.

By late afternoon of the next day, Jesse hadn't heard from Abby. He was plain too hot and tired to confront her. Maybe later.

He'd worked with Remus twice and made some headway, but not much. The stallion was more resistant than most horses he'd worked with, probably due to the fire but also his previous abuse and neglect that made him distrust humans. Jesse couldn't blame him, but he also wasn't prepared to give up.

He'd talked with Vern, explained the situation and the rancher had stressed that he could wait it out if Jesse could. Then he'd used his cell phone to call home and talk with Jake. Everything seemed to be going well there. His father was feeling fine and, although his brother would be happy if he returned, Jake urged him to stay until he'd accomplished what he'd set out to do. His brother also warned him to guard his heart.

Jesse wondered if perhaps the warning had come too late. Feeling restless, Jesse had ridden out with Casey and helped repair fencing in the west pasture, an ongoing thing in a ranch as large as the Martins'. On his way back, around four o'clock, he decided to take a swim in the river that snaked through the property. With Jughead running alongside in that clumsy, comical way he had, Jesse headed out, keeping Domino to a trot so the silly dog could easily keep up.

Reaching the narrow ribbon of river by the weeping willow that he remembered with fondness, Jesse dismounted and tied Domino to a tree limb. He sat down to remove his boots as Jughead came bounding over, nearly knocking him flat in his eagerness.

"Don't you ever run out of energy?" he asked the dog. He'd barely gotten his boots off when Jughead forgot he couldn't swim and went splashing into the river. "Hey, wait! You crazy dog. What are you doing?"

Quickly, Jesse tugged off his jeans and shirt, tossing them aside as he rushed to the water's edge. Shading his eyes against the sun, he finally spotted the pooch midway across, disappearing under, then rising up, floundering. "Stupid dog," he muttered as he rushed into the cold river.

Clearly frightened and well over his head, Jughead struggled against a mild current, gasping and coughing as he tried desperately to keep his head up, but sinking repeatedly. Jesse reached him and grabbed him from behind, one arm around his solid body. But the dog was too scared to just relax and let Jesse take him ashore, fighting his rescuer, scratching everywhere his paws landed.

"All right, all right. Stop it!" Jesse shouted, trying to side paddle back to shore with the squirming animal in his grasp. "I've got you." Finally realizing that Jughead wasn't listening, he swam faster until his feet finally touched bottom.

Walking gingerly over stones, he was in water waist-high before the dog went limp.

"Great," Jesse said. "Now you pass out on me." Carrying his heavy burden to shore, breathing hard from his struggles, he placed the dog on the grassy bank. Jughead lay perfectly still.

Jesse ran his hands over the dog's stomach, moving strong fingers up toward his neck, trying to get him to release any water he'd swallowed. "Listen, boy. If you think I'm doing mouth-to-mouth on you, you better get ready to meet your maker."

Standing alongside the tree back a ways from the river's edge, Abby tried not to smile. She'd arrived in the middle of Jesse's rescue of Jughead and hadn't been able to resist stopping to watch. He was on his knees, the dog on his side, literally trying to push river water from Jughead, muttering the whole way.

"You're the only dog in the universe who can't swim by nature," he told the inert animal. "Who'd believe this? And then you jump in over your head. You got a death wish, bud?" He squeezed, pushed, tilted the dog's head.

After several long seconds, Jughead started coughing, then got to his feet sort of wobbly before coughing up a fair amount of water.

"Well, it's about time," Jesse said.

After he gave two hard shakes, spattering water over his rescuer, Jughead seemed fine, hurling himself at Jesse, licking his chest, trying to reach his face.

"Yeah, yeah." Noticing that the dog was shivering despite the sun, Jesse reached for the shirt he'd tossed aside and began rubbing Jughead's wet fur. Which wasn't easy with the grateful pooch continuing his licking and shaking. "Okay, okay."

Finally, holding the still-quivering dog wrapped in his shirt in his arms, Jesse sat back and sighed. "You sure managed to get us both cooled off, didn't you, boy?"

Noticing a shadow moving toward him, Jesse turned and saw Abby walking over, a smile on her face.

"So you not only train horses, but you give swimming lessons to dogs, eh?" she asked, still amused at his conversation with Jughead.

"I doubt anyone can teach this dog anything," Jesse answered as Jughead squirmed out of his grasp and went to meet Abby.

"I didn't mean to interrupt, but I had to see if you were going to do CPR on him." Squatting, she rubbed the dog's wet head. "That I'd have paid to watch."

"Yeah, well, he's just lucky he came around." He hadn't seen a genuine smile like she was wearing now since…since before he'd left six years ago.

He nodded toward her gelding tethered near his horse. "You taking a break or were you looking for me?"

Abby was glad she had sunglasses on so he couldn't see her eyes as they roamed over the tan length of him. He was wearing only gray-knit briefs and she couldn't help noticing a long scar on his left leg, healed a while ago but still visible. The cause of his occasional limp and a permanent reminder of his accident, she was certain. She felt a softening inside, one she'd struggled against.

If she'd really forgiven him, she should let the animosity go. It was time. Only she couldn't afford to get too close to Jesse a second time. Because then all of her secrets, the ones she'd guarded so carefully all these years, would come tumbling out. And she wasn't the only one who'd be hurt.

"Actually, I went for a ride after the children left. I can

think my way through problems sometimes when I ride." She sat down as Jughead insisted on crawling into her lap.

He nodded, running a hand over his beard to get rid of excess water. "I know what you mean."

"But I did want to talk with you. I spoke this morning to Sam's father and to Charley's mother about the program you suggested. They're both interested, but they want to meet you and maybe watch what you do with their children a time or two."

Jesse didn't let her see how pleased he was. "That's fine."

"All right, then. Tomorrow I'll talk with Susie and make sure she's okay with extending story time so I can go with the boys, at least the first few times."

"Great." This would give him an opportunity to interact with Abby, to see her work with the children, to ascertain whether these new feelings for her were real or just some leftover romantic memory. *Memories define who we are,* his father always said. Jesse wasn't sure he agreed.

Abby gently shoved the dog from her lap and stood. "There's also this little girl named Maddy. Eight years old. She only comes to class three days a week. She lost an eye to cancer and has to wear an eye patch. She's too young to be fitted with a replacement yet. She's been coming since she was five and used to be so outgoing. Since her surgery, she rarely speaks and seems so sad. I want to see how the boys make out and then possibly add her."

"I'm sure we can accommodate her as well." Jesse got to his feet, aware he was wearing only his underwear. It didn't bother him, but he wondered if it would rattle Abby.

She felt her color rise and kept her gaze riveted on his face. "You sound very confident that this program will work."

"I am. We both have experience with horses and you know children. I think we can make it work. Together." He reached to pick up his jeans.

Abby couldn't resist allowing her eyes to skim over him. How well she remembered those great buns. And that wasn't all.

Hastily, before he could notice her flushed face, she untied her horse and climbed up.

"Are we starting tomorrow?" he called after her.

"Yes," she yelled over her shoulder as she nudged the mare into a gallop.

Grinning from ear to ear, Jesse pulled on his shirt. *I saw that, lady,* he thought. *Deny it all you want, but you're interested, too.*

He couldn't sleep. Tired of fighting the covers, Jesse got up and pulled on his jeans. The bedside clock read nearly midnight and he'd been tossing and turning for over an hour. He'd been getting up at five o'clock along with the rest of the men since breakfast in the mess hall was served at five-fifteen. Besides, that had been his routine back in California. There, he'd rarely had trouble falling asleep.

But then, Abby Martin hadn't been under his nose.

Grabbing a root beer from his fridge, Jesse went out on his porch and sat down on the top step, leaning back against the post. He gazed up at a cloudless night sky filled with winking stars. Crickets serenaded and the occasional whinny of a restless horse could be heard. The fragrant lilac bushes in bloom nearby and the honeysuckle along the driveway couldn't quite overcome the smell of cattle and horses that permeated the area. Still, it wasn't unpleasant.

Tilting his head back, Jesse drank deeply. At times like

this, he wished he still smoked. He'd stopped years ago
when his father had developed heart trouble.

He glanced over at the big house and saw only a dim light
glowing from the downstairs living room window. Undoubtedly everyone there was asleep. Most ranch people worked
hard from sunup to sundown and retired early.

Jesse yawned expansively. He could go back inside and
read, but he just wasn't in the mood. He could go out back
and work on his newest project. After dinner and another un-
fruitful workout with Remus, he'd poked around the barn and
found some leftover pieces of lumber. They'd given him an
idea so he'd asked Casey if he could have them. The old man
had been obviously curious, but he hadn't asked, just told
Jesse he could have all of them plus the use of the tools in
the barn.

So he'd taken what he wanted and set to work on the cement slab in back of his cabin. He would make a surprise
for Grace in the hope that he could soften her mother's heart
toward him, and maybe allow him to sit and talk with the cute
little girl now and then.

Jesse took another long swallow and decided he didn't
feel like working with the wood anymore tonight, either.
He felt as restless as Remus had been today. Was it the full
moon? he wondered, looking around the sky. There it was,
but only half-full.

He probably wouldn't have noticed the light go on in the
upstairs room of the big house that he knew belonged to
Abby if he hadn't been looking up. Was there a problem or
did Grace wake up and need comforting? he wondered. He
sat staring at her window, thinking that maybe Abby couldn't
sleep either and had turned the light on to read. He'd just
about decided that was it when he saw the front door of the

big house open and Abby come rushing out. She was dressed in jeans and a white shirt, her shoulder bag over her arm.

Instinctively, he stood, wondering if there was an emergency. Glancing neither to the right or left, Abby hurried to the Martins' sleek Lincoln Town Car parked on the asphalt apron, the car that hadn't moved since Jesse had arrived. He heard Abby try to start the car, but the motor wouldn't turn over.

Thinking to go help her, Jesse walked down his steps in time to see Abby leave the Lincoln and march over to the black pickup parked alongside the family car. In the still night air, he heard her muttering to herself, sounding greatly annoyed. She opened the truck door and looked inside. This time he heard her clearly.

"Oh, no! Damn!"

Though barefoot, Jesse walked over and found her with one arm braced on the door, her eyes closed in frustration.

"Can I help?" he asked.

Startled, she jumped. "Oh! You scared me."

"Sorry. Is there a problem?"

Abby made an exasperated sound. "Yes. The Lincoln won't start, probably because it hasn't been driven in weeks and I forgot that this truck isn't automatic. I've never driven a stick shift and I…" She glanced up at her parents' bedroom window and shook her head.

"You have to go somewhere?" he asked, though that was obvious.

"You could say that." She debated how much to tell him, then decided to confide in him. The Jesse she remembered had been very closemouthed and besides, she needed his help. "A familiar problem. The bartender at the Thirsty Camel just called. Lindsay's there, drunk and disorderly. I have to go get her before she gets in real trouble." She met his eyes and saw no censure there. "Do you know how to drive a stick shift?"

"Yes, but I'd rather we took my Bronco." He touched her elbow, guiding her across the wide driveway to where he kept his vehicle. "I'll just run in and get my keys."

Abby brushed back her hair. "I hate to involve you, but I don't want my parents to know about this."

"No problem." Jesse bounded up the steps and disappeared inside.

Waiting alongside the Bronco, Abby searched her pockets for a band to tie back her hair. She found a gold clip and just finished anchoring it in place at her nape when Jesse reappeared wearing a denim shirt with his jeans and sneakers.

He unlocked the doors and helped her up before getting behind the wheel.

"I want you to know I really appreciate this," Abby told him.

"Where are we going?"

"Take Highway 61 north about fifteen miles. The club's on the right-hand side, set back a ways."

Jesse eased the Bronco through the arches and turned right toward the highway. "I take it you've done this before."

"Twice before." Abby stared out the windshield at the dark night. "Lindsay's not a bad person." She felt compelled to explain her sister's behavior. "She's had a really bad year."

Turning onto the highway, Jesse glanced at Abby and noticed her worried frown. "Casey mentioned a wedding that didn't take place."

She wasn't surprised that Casey had mentioned her sister's problems to Jesse. She was sure the older man, who loved both of them, did it to explain Lindsay's often disturbing behavior. "Lindsay's had a rough time with men. Three or four years ago, she fell for this cowboy from the Walker ranch just west of ours. The Walkers have an arena for show horses and once a year, they throw a big party. Lots of food, music, dancing, an all-day affair. That's where Lindsay met this man. Kobi Randall was his name."

In the intimacy of the dim interior, not another vehicle on the road, Abby went on, needing him to understand what Lindsay had gone through so perhaps he'd understand what led her to drink too much. "He was handsome and charming. Dad didn't like him and Mom warned her repeatedly that he was a gold digger, more interested in her future inheritance of the ranch than in her. Naturally, Lindsay rebelled and got engaged. Finally Dad insisted that she offer Kobi a prenuptial agreement, to test him. Lindsay was certain he wanted her and not her money. But she was wrong. As soon as he saw the agreement, Kobi took off."

"That must have hurt."

"I'm sure it did. But not as much as her breakup with Adam Maxwell last December."

Jesse glanced over at her. "You're telling me he was a gold digger, too?"

"No. Lindsay went on vacation with a friend to San Francisco and met him there. She came home all starry-eyed. This time, I think she really loved the guy. Mom and Dad invited him to spend a couple of weeks at the ranch, hoping things would get serious. And they did. Mom planned this big wedding right before Christmas. But the more time Adam spent here, the more the two of them fought. I don't know exactly what happened, but a week before the wedding, Adam went home and Lindsay fell apart. She told me one tearful night that Adam said they could live on the ranch, but not in San

Francisco because she'd never fit into his parents' and friends' social circle."

Jesse groaned. "That must have shattered her."

"It did. She didn't leave the house for weeks, stayed in her room, hardly ate. Dad was furious. Mom and I had to call all the guests, cancel all the arrangements. It was a nightmare."

"I can imagine."

"I can't blame her for losing faith in men. It's easy to do once your trust is broken."

There was a message for him in this conversation, Jesse realized. But he decided to ignore it. "So when did she begin to drink?"

Abby sighed. "A couple of months ago, she began going out to these bars and clubs. There aren't that many around here, but she finds them. The first time I had to go get her, when I sobered her up, I asked her what she was doing to herself and why. She told me she's decided that men are no damn good and she's just going to have fun and forget about forever after. She stopped seeing most of her women friends, the ones who were married. I think she's jealous."

"If she keeps getting drunk and disorderly, that doesn't sound like she's having all that much fun."

"I agree, but I haven't been able to get through to her." Abby spotted the sign. "There it is, up ahead."

Jesse left the highway and headed for the Thirsty Camel, which was doing a thriving business on a weeknight. The parking lot was crowded but he managed to find a spot in the second row.

Abby turned to him. "Let me warn you. She's liable to be belligerent or boisterous or, and this is the worst, in the middle of a crying jag. Are you up for this or do you want to wait here?"

"I'm sure I've seen worse, Abby. I'm going with you."
Suddenly, she was glad he was there.

Lindsay was none of the things Abby had warned him she
might be. Instead, she'd gotten sick, then quietly passed out.
Jesse carried her out to her car parked near the entrance
while Abby settled up with the bartender.

Now, following Abby driving Lindsay's convertible with
Lindsay passed out in the passenger seat, Jesse thought about
their previous conversation. Her sister was definitely troubled, and with good reason. Maybe she needed professional
help, though he wasn't sure if that suggestion would be welcome, especially with her parents who seemingly didn't
know how far gone Lindsay was.

Jesse tried to put himself in her place, the two broken en-
gagements, the embarrassment, her parents upset. His guess
would be that by now Lindsay had a very bad self-image and
was probably acting up because she wanted to escape from
a reality she couldn't face. He was no psychiatrist but it
seemed that Lindsay no longer cared what people thought.
Or maybe she cared too much.

Usually this sort of behavior was a cry for help, Jesse
thought.

Pulling into his usual parking space, he shut off the
Bronco and walked over to where Abby had parked her sister's car. Lindsay had her head back and her eyes closed. He
looked at Abby as she came around to the passenger side.
"Do you want me to carry her up to her room?"

Abby sent a nervous glance up to her parents' bedroom
window and saw that it was quite dark. The other times she'd
been called out in the middle of the night to get Lindsay,

she'd at least been awake and mumbling. This time, she was out like a light.

"I'd appreciate it. I don't think I can manage her."

Jesse opened the car door and scooped Lindsay into his arms. She reeked of alcohol and heavy perfume. She moaned once, then was quiet.

He followed Abby through the door and up the stairs. He noticed that she was trying to be quiet so as not to wake anyone. As soon as she opened the bedroom door, he carried Lindsay to the bed and lay her down.

Again, she moaned and this time opened her eyes. It took her a moment to focus as she gave Jesse a boozy smile. "I knew I'd get you in my bed." Jesse stood back as Abby removed her shoes and settled a light blanket over her sister.

Back downstairs, Abby walked out onto the porch with him. "I can't thank you enough for helping me tonight."

He decided to say what he'd been thinking. "Abby, do you think some sort of counseling therapy would help Lindsay? She can't go on like this."

Abby hugged herself as a cool night breeze rearranged her hair. "I think you're right. I'll talk to her." A glance at her watch told her it was nearly two in the morning. "Listen, I know you usually are up at five. Why don't you sleep in tomorrow and come here, have breakfast with me, say around eight o'clock?" The moment the words were out of her mouth, she worried that he might take the invitation as more than it was. To her, it was just her way of thanking him.

Moonlight played across her lovely features, making Jesse wish he could take her in his arms and offer her comfort when she was so obviously worried. But her somewhat defensive stance didn't invite his touch. "Thanks, but I'll be fine. I've been working with Remus most mornings by seven o'clock and I don't want to change that."

"All right, if you're sure." He'd let her off the hook and she wasn't sure if she was glad or disappointed. This ambivalence was making her crazy.

There was a war going on in that beautiful head of hers, Jesse decided, studying her eyes. Anyone's guess as to which side would win.

"What do you think Lindsay wants?"

She didn't hesitate. "What we all want. Someone to love who loves her just as much. A home of her own, children, a family."

Jesse had no quarrel with that. He dared to reach up and trail the backs of his fingers along her silken cheek. "Get some sleep. Your little charges will be here before you know it."

She nodded, then stood watching him walk to his cabin, the limp only slight but still noticeable. Reaching up, she stroked her cheek where the warmth of his touch remained.

It was happening, despite her resolve. She was falling for Jesse Calder all over again.

Chapter Five

Jesse handed Sam the carrot. "Horses love carrots," he told the ten-year-old. "When someone gives them something they like, they become friends. So, you want to offer that to Dolly?"

Still hesitant, the boy looked up at the big horse standing inside the round pen. Slowly, he raised the carrot toward the mare. He watched as she bobbed her big head and reached over the fence. Suddenly she opened her mouth and snatched the carrot, surprising Sam so much that if Jesse hadn't been standing behind him, he might have fallen backward. Then he giggled.

"See?" Jesse asked, smiling as they watched Dolly chew her treat. "Now she likes you. You're her friend."

Jesse turned to Charley, the six-year-old deaf boy, standing between his father and Abby. He'd been told that the youngster could read lips if a person talked slowly, something Charley had learned at the school for deaf children that he'd attended since he was four.

Leaning down, Jesse touched the boy's shoulder. "Do you want to give a carrot treat to Jasmine?" he asked, indicating the older gray mare waiting patiently alongside Dolly.

Charley shook his head vigorously. "He's got awfully big teeth."

"*She,* honey," Abby corrected, making sure the boy could see her face. "She does have big teeth, but she wouldn't bite you in a million years. How about if I stand with you and we both offer her a carrot?"

Somewhat reluctantly, Charley nodded.

"I'll give her a carrot, Mommy," came a voice from behind them. "I'm not afraid."

Abby turned to see her daughter standing behind them. "Maybe later, Grace. Please go back to the schoolhouse. Susie's about to start story time."

Grace's little face screwed up as if she might cry. But she didn't, instead she turned and ran back across the driveway.

Jesse watched as Abby got Charley to give the horse the carrot, but his mind was on Grace. *What a little cutie!* And spunky. He'd have to try harder to get Abby to let him teach her to ride. She was as tall as Charley even though she was a year younger. He was almost finished with the surprise he was making for her.

Charley ran back to his father, proud of his bravery. "I did it!" he yelled. Because of his deafness, Charley spoke loudly, his words not always clear. Jesse wondered if his father had checked into a cochlear implant for his son.

"What's next, Abby?" Sam's mother wanted to know.

Jesse answered for her. "Next we'd like to put each child on a horse, Abby behind one and I'll be with the other. We'll trot around the pen slowly, getting them used to the feel of being on horseback."

"Is that safe?" the mother asked with a worried frown.

"Perfectly safe," Abby answered. "We'll have our arms around each one and, as you can see, these two mares are quite docile."

"Then you'll let them ride alone next?" Charley's father asked.

"Not until we're absolutely certain they're comfortable in the saddle and unafraid," Abby answered. "And, of course, we'll lead the horses around at first." She and Jesse had worked out the routine before the parents had arrived with their children. Jesse was so sure of himself, so strong and confident that he'd put her at ease. She could see the two parents relaxing as well.

Abby took a minute to check on the other children to assure herself that Susie was handling things well with four little ones napping on their mats and the others gathered around for story time. She hurried back, hoping these riding sessions would help as Jesse seemed to think they would. She'd checked out the program at the U. of A. and on the Internet, and the results had been mostly positive. In theory and in experiments. Now if only they'd work out in practical application.

They spent the next hour initiating the two children to riding in a saddle surrounded by an adult. There hadn't been any bad moments, just a few nervous ones. When they handed the boys over to their parents after the session, the adults seemed pleased at their progress and agreed to more lessons, deciding on twice a week. As they drove off, Abby let out a sigh of relief.

"That went off better than I'd dared to hope," she commented as they led the two mares back into the barn.

"Oh, ye of little faith," Jesse teased her.

"Did you notice that Charley, who's four years younger than Sam, lost his fear of being up so high first?"

"Yeah. I think that Charley's father is open to new experiences for his son whereas Sam's mother has kept him too sheltered, made him afraid of trying new things." Jesse opened Dolly's stall, let her in and closed the door before offering her a couple of sugar lumps.

"I suppose you're right," Abby reluctantly admitted as she followed suit with Jasmine.

Leaving the barn together, Jesse decided to drive his point home. "I've read where they've done studies that prove that kids can learn things much earlier than was originally thought, with the proper adult supervision. And with each accomplishment comes a confidence and a self-esteem that they can't get any other way."

Did he think she was obtuse? "You're talking about my daughter and the fact that I haven't let her learn to ride, right?"

He stopped, turning to face her. "Guilty as charged. You saw her come over today. She *wants* to learn. Whenever you deny a child the opportunity to learn, you delay their progress."

"And just what makes you such a child expert?"

He shrugged. "Never said I was. But there's my nephew and we have seven families living on the Triple C ranch in housing we provide for long-time employees, like you have here. My brother and I have taught more than a dozen kids to ride and later when they were older, to rope, to bronco bust, all sorts of things. Size and age isn't as important as the desire to learn. We've already had Jack on horseback, with his father, of course, and he's only two. Naturally, you have to have a good instructor."

"I suppose that means you," she said, with a smile.

"Yes," he said modestly. Jesse laughed. "And you. I've seen you ride, before and now. You're really something."

Abby didn't know how to handle compliments from this man. So she looked across toward her schoolhouse, getting ready to bolt. "I think I'd better go." Her gaze swung back to him. "Thanks for your help. I'm going to have to get Dad to double your salary. I think you're doing far more than just helping Remus. Casey tells me you often ride out and help the men round up, mend fences, whatever needs doing."

"They're shorthanded and I get bored just sitting around. I'm used to being active. I volunteered so no pay increase is warranted." From his observation so far, the Martin ranch was barely getting by.

"I just wanted you to know, your work is appreciated."

His eyes grew serious. "I like working with you, Abby. I think we make a good team."

She saw the hope in his face and didn't know how to respond. "I really do have to get back to the kids."

"One more question. How's Lindsay this morning?"

Abby sighed. "I don't know. She wasn't up yet when I left the house. I'll check on her at lunchtime." She started back, calling over her shoulder, "I'll see you later."

Jesse watched her hurry to the schoolhouse, wondering if he could ever break down the walls Abby had built around herself. In her own way, she was as troubled as Lindsay. Both were afraid to trust again.

And he wasn't sure he knew how to rebuild that trust.

Jesse wiped his damp brow as he walked out of the round pen. Remus had been especially frisky today, probably because he'd brought in a saddle. He hadn't tried putting it on the stallion, but Remus had guessed he might so he did everything he could to evade Jesse, short of jumping the fence. After an hour, Jesse decided to end the session since they were getting nowhere.

He left the saddle in the pen, hoping Remus would check it out when he was alone. If the bullheaded stallion kept this up, he'd have to resort to more drastic measures to gain his cooperation. Turning from latching the gate, he saw that Lindsay was by the barn door, and he wondered how long she'd been watching.

"You're very good with that stubborn horse," she said as he walked over, coiling the cotton line.

"If I'm so good, why won't he let me saddle him?" Squinting in the harsh afternoon sun, he noticed that her eyes were a little bloodshot and her skin had an unhealthy pallor. Did she realize that if she kept up her heavy drinking, her body would soon pay the price?

"Oh, he's just toying with you. I have no doubt you'll bring him around."

"Thanks for the vote of confidence." Lindsay wore a loose-fitting T-shirt over tan slacks, a subdued outfit for her. But she'd still doused herself in the same heavy perfume.

"You don't need my vote. Around here, everyone thinks you walk on water. Dad, Casey, the men. And Abby. She watches you all the time."

"Well, Remus is her horse, so naturally she's interested in his progress."

"You think it's the horse she's interested in?" She removed a rumpled pack of cigarettes from her pocket, but didn't light one, remembering her father's repeated warnings not to smoke around the barn.

"What else?" Jesse decided to play innocent, wondering if this shrewd woman knew about his history with Abby.

Lindsay chuckled. "They must not have hung any mirrors in that cabin of yours."

"That's certainly flattering, but Abby's got too much on her plate with her daughter and her schoolkids to bother with me." He could see she remained unconvinced. Time for a change of subject. "How do you feel this morning?"

"Fine. I am sorry that when I finally got you in my bedroom, I fell asleep before we could have some serious fun. I must have been really tired."

Most women would feel a bit embarrassed about last night, but Lindsay was in denial, Jesse decided. Though he knew it wasn't his place, he couldn't pass up the opportunity to try to convince her to face the truth. "You weren't tired, Lindsay. You passed out because you were drunk."

Color moved into her face as she removed a cigarette from the pack and looked at it longingly. "Is that what my saintly sister told you?"

"No one had to tell me. I saw for myself." He took a step closer. "That wasn't the first time, either, was it? Why do you drink so much, Lindsay?"

She made a sound deep in her throat. "You'd drink, too, if you were stuck in this hellhole day after sweltering day. My father loves it here and so does Abby. My mother hates it, too, so we're both stuck. I'm not meant for the ranching life. I hate the horses, the stupid cattle, the grimy cowboys, the smell that gets into everything, even your hair."

"Then why don't you move? Your mother probably doesn't want to abandon her family, but you're old enough to leave the nest. It beats drinking yourself into a stupor to escape." Her eyes were shuttered and he wondered if he was getting through to her.

"Ha! And go where? I loved San Francisco, but…that didn't work out." She rolled the cigarette between her fingers.

"There're a lot of other cities. Find a spot you like, get an apartment, a job. Meet people. What's so hard about that?" He saw that she was actually mulling his suggestion over. "What kind of work are you trained to do, or would like to do?"

Another throaty chuckle. "That's just it. I have a liberal arts degree, which trains you for nothing practical. Besides, I've never had a job. I don't think I'd do well with nine-to-five, people telling me what to do." She put on a seductive smile. "I'm having too much fun right here, meeting people." Reaching up, she trailed a hand along his bearded jaw.

"I don't think you're having fun at all." Jesse removed her hand. "Look at Abby. She didn't finish college, but she knew she liked kids. So she started a little business and she's happy with it."

"Yes, perfect little Abby with the perfect daughter found the perfect job. She's a marvel, that girl."

He was getting annoyed. "You could discover what it is that you like to do and that you're good at doing, and go for it. Like she did. At the very least, you might consider getting counseling. It could help you deal with things without depending on alcohol."

"Sugar," she drawled, moving nearer until she was close up against him, "I can deal with things just fine." She ran a red-tipped nail up his chest. "As for what I'm good at, I'm really good at making a man happy. Don't you want me to show you?"

Moving away from her, Jesse shook his head. She wasn't interested in changing, so he was wasting his time. "Have it your way, Lindsay." He circumvented her and went into the barn.

"Sure, walk away," she said, her mood shifting to anger. "Bet you wouldn't walk away from Abby." With that, she marched off.

So much for trying to help, Jesse thought as he put the cotton line away. Remus was balky and Lindsay was impossible. Maybe he should have stayed in bed today. He certainly should have followed his first instinct and steered clear of Lindsay Martin. She was trouble waiting to happen.

Abby was in the kitchen putting away the groceries her mother had bought when Lindsay stormed in and went straight for the refrigerator. She quickly poured herself a glass of iced tea and drank half of it before pulling out a kitchen chair and dropping into it. With unsteady hands, she lit a cigarette and blew smoke toward the ceiling in an angry stream.

She turned her wrath on her sister. "Why are you staring at me?"

Abby shoved a cereal box into the cupboard. "Just wondering what's got you so steamed." She'd seen Lindsay talking with Jesse by the barn when she'd helped unload the groceries and wondered if her sister had sought him out to thank him for last night.

Lindsay pulled more smoke into her lungs. "Where's Mom?"

"Upstairs lying down. She has a migraine."

"I don't know what you see in that bearded jerk," she spat out, returning to the original subject.

Apparently their talk hadn't gone well, Abby surmised. But she wasn't going to discuss her feelings with Lindsay, especially in her current mood. "What I see is a man who hopefully can help Remus, and that's all."

"Oh, cut it out, Abby. When you watch him, you practically drool. I have eyes, you know." Another deep drag on the cigarette.

"That's ridiculous. I don't drool over anyone." Abby put the fresh vegetables in the refrigerator bin, then shut the door.

"Yeah, you do. There must be something about the name Jesse that turns you to mush. I saw you sneak off to meet that other Jesse way back when. You're probably skulking around with this one, too." As Abby stared at her openmouthed, Lindsay crushed out her cigarette in the ashtray with two vicious strokes. "You must think I just fell off the turnip truck, sister dear."

With that, she left the kitchen and went upstairs.

Abby stood staring after her. Lindsay had seen her with Jesse six years ago? Yet in all this time, she hadn't said anything? Hard to believe. Maybe she was guessing, fishing for answers. What had happened between Lindsay and Jesse that riled her so?

After she put away the grocery bags, Abby went upstairs to check on her daughter, who still took naps because she was always up so early. Grace was sprawled out on her bed hugging the ratty stuffed dog named Fred.

Closing her child's door, Abby went to her room and lay down on her bed. She'd thought about those times she'd snuck out of the house to meet up with Jesse six years ago over and over. She'd been very cautious, very careful, yet she'd never once noticed Lindsay lurking nearby. They'd never been close as sisters only two years apart usually are. They had very different personalities. Still, she couldn't imagine Lindsay having something on her and not spilling the beans.

Abby slipped off her shoes and gazed out her window through the gauzy drapes at the blue, blue sky. But she wasn't really looking at the outdoor scene. In her mind, she was riding alongside Jesse on one particular moonlit night as they urged their mounts to hurry, to rush to their meeting spot by the old cottonwood so they could hold each other. Jesse had spread an old blanket from the barn on the grass and invited her to join him. He'd never had to ask twice. Abby closed her eyes and saw him as clearly as if he were in the room with her.

"You're so beautiful," he whispered, removing her gold clip and thrusting his hands through her thick hair. "My blue-eyed golden girl." And then he kissed her.

Abby had been kissed before, mostly college friends she'd dated occasionally. She was too shy to have experienced much, and she really hadn't wanted to know more. Until Jesse.

To her, Jesse was worldly, twenty-five years old, mature. He was a man compared to the boys she'd known before. He'd undoubtedly known many women. Abby felt inadequate.

"I'm not beautiful," she told him honestly. "My skin burns instead of tanning the way Lindsay's does. She's tall, probably could be a model, and I'm short. I can't believe you're attracted to me." She'd been worrying about her shortcomings ever since meeting him.

To her surprise, Jesse laughed. "And I can't believe you don't see what I see. Your skin is lovely and so soft. You're not short, just the right size." He trailed his hands through her hair again. "I love your hair." He buried his nose in it. "It always smells so good." Easing back, he looked into her eyes. "Your eyes are the best part, so big and blue a guy could drown in them." Then he turned serious. "Don't ever compare yourself to Lindsay, or anyone else. I'm attracted to you just the way you are."

Her heart beat so fast she was certain he could hear it. "You really mean it?"

"Yes. I've never felt this way about anyone but you, Abby." He touched his lips to hers.

Passion flared just that quickly, that fiercely. He kissed her mouth, a long lingering brush of lips, then sent his tongue in to duel intimately with hers. Abby had never known such sensations, such craving for she knew not what. Her restless body shifted, wanting to be one with him.

She heard soft sighs, gentle murmuring and deep throaty moans and wasn't sure if they came from her or Jesse. His busy hands stroked everywhere, her cheeks and hair and shoulders. The need to be closer and closer still was huge, a new feeling that engulfed her.

Breathing hard, Abby felt him pull back to study her intently. He seemed to be a man at a crossroads, coming to some serious conclusions as he searched her eyes.

"I want things to be right between us. I don't want to mess up and lose you."

"You could never lose me, never."

He trailed his fingers along her cheek, cupping her chin. "I don't know what I'd do if I couldn't have you in my life."

"You have me. You've had me since that first day." Emboldened by his words, her hands moved to the buttons of his shirt, slowly freeing them, needing to touch his broad chest.

After pushing the shirt from his shoulders, he let her explore, touching where she would, her fingers tangling in the dark curly hair. But when he took hold of the hem of her shirt to remove it, she put her hands on his and stopped him.

"What if someone comes along?"

"No one rides out this way, especially not at night."

Still, he waited, allowing her to make the decision. Abby acknowledged that her need for him, to discover more of him, was stronger than her fear of discovery. She removed her hands and let him tug off her shirt and then her bra.

Her face grew warm as his eyes caressed her naked breasts in the moonlight. She sucked in a breath as he raised a hand to cup her breast, then closed her eyes as a myriad of new feelings spread through her. Awash in awakened desire, she swayed toward him.

"I want you to be sure, Abby. No regrets."

With both hands pressed to his chest, she could feel his heart beating, strong and sure. "Yes, I'm sure. This feels right."

Jesse slipped his arms around her, edging her up close against his chest, his hands caressing her back. Locked in his arms, her sensitive breasts gently rubbing against the soft hair of his chest, again Abby closed her eyes, holding in the delicious feeling.

He lowered her to the blanket, then followed her down. With unsteady hands, he removed his boots and hers, then quickly rid them both of the rest of their clothes. A warm night breeze caressed Abby's skin as she welcomed him back to kiss her again. And again.

She felt his lips skim down the line of her throat and lower to claim the breasts his hands had lovingly prepared. She couldn't lie still as he tasted and teased, his clever fingers touching everywhere, setting her on fire.

Abby was whirling away on a sea of sensation. For years

she'd nurtured needs deep inside, storing them away secretly, and Jesse was answering each one in turn. From a distance, she heard a coyote call to his mate, heard the soft whisper of the leaves overhead, heard her own shallow breathing. Her limp arms fell away and she gave herself up to each wondrous new pleasure, helpless to do anything but allow him to do what he would.

His breath choppy, Jesse paused to look at her flushed face. "You can't know how many hours I've lain awake dreaming of seeing you like this. You're even more beautiful than my dreams."

Abby could think of no words to answer him, could only look at him with her heart in her eyes as she caressed the hard line of his jaw. Gently, she traced the slight indentation in his chin, running a finger over his full lips. She could hardly believe that he was here, hers to touch freely, hers to love at last.

He lowered to her, his mouth distracting her with deep, openmouthed kisses while his fingers explored and found her. Startled, Abby arched and froze.

"It's all right," Jesse murmured. "Trust me."

He waited until he felt her relax, then resumed his explorations, his touch becoming more intimate, more exhilarating. Moments later, so aroused was she that in two tender strokes, he had her soaring as her hands gripped his back. The rippling pleasure had Abby sighing, had her moaning his name as her breath shuddered from her.

Jesse waited as long as he could for her to come down. Finally, close to the end of his endurance, his legs trembling, he raised himself above her. "This may hurt a little," he cautioned.

"It's all right," Abby whispered. She was floating in such

euphoria that she couldn't believe anything could hurt her now.

It did hurt, for a brief moment. Then his hands lifted her hips and he joined with her more fully. The movements were slow and steady, then suddenly faster, longer and then unbridled in their intensity.

Abby's hands clutched at his biceps as she hung on. Then there was only a mindless pleasure that rocketed through her and went on and on. She let the sensation take over, let herself go.

She'd heard her friends talk and she'd dreamed, but she hadn't believed it could be so breathtaking, so wondrous. Until now.

And when long minutes later, she opened her eyes, Jesse was smiling down at her. She didn't say the words aloud, only to herself. *I love you, Jesse.*

Stretched out on her bed, still adrift in her memories, Abby sighed. No, she'd never once said the words aloud to Jesse. But she'd felt them even before they'd made love.

After that first time, Jesse had suddenly grown angry— with himself. Over and over, he berated himself for not being prepared, for not using a condom. She'd sat listening to his tirade, thinking she should feel bad, too. But truth be known, she hadn't given protection a thought once Jesse kissed her.

When she'd told him that, he'd merely said that it should be up to the man to protect the woman. Finally she'd said that it would probably be all right, considering where she was in her cycle. He wanted to believe her and he'd fervently promised that next time, he'd be prepared.

All Abby had focused on were the words *next time.* There would be a next time because Jesse wanted her. Her heart had been so full of love for him, but she'd had enough sense not to say it out loud. Not until he said he loved her, that is. They'd gotten together nearly every night for four weeks after that first time, and Jesse always had a condom. Then abruptly he'd had to leave.

But that hadn't stopped her from weaving dreams built around their future together. Big fantasy dreams. Like her parents would get to know Jesse and love him as much as she did. That he'd return, they'd marry and Jesse would run the ranch with Dad. That they'd all live happily ever after.

How young and naive she'd been, Abby thought as she left her bed to gaze out the window. Happily-ever-after was a myth, a Hallmark card, a fairy tale. He'd left before they'd gotten to the point of a love so deep it was followed by commitment. No matter that he had a really good reason for going—his father's heart attack—and a serious reason for not calling to explain—his accident. Then there was the fact that Lindsay hadn't told her that Jesse had been looking for her. And let's not forget the deception of his name which kept her from being able to locate him.

All those things conspired against their blossoming love. Who knows if it would have turned out to be the real thing. Now, seeing Jesse again, watching him, Abby knew that despite her words to the contrary, she was drawn to him. Again.

What was wrong with her that she couldn't learn from her past mistakes?

Because when she'd told Jesse the first night they'd made love that things would probably be all right, that her cycle wasn't in the danger zone, she'd been wrong. It turned out that things weren't all right. But by the time she learned she was pregnant, Jesse had left, promising to come back and explain everything. And he had. Six years later.

Wearily, Abby sat down in the bentwood rocker that had been her grandmother's. She'd been so scared after she'd taken that drugstore pregnancy test. She hadn't dared tell her mother or father. No one knew until the day Casey found her crying in the hayloft.

Casey had always been like a kindly uncle to both her and Lindsay. He'd guessed what her problem was because he'd seen her and Jesse ride off to be together several times. Like the loyal man he was, he hadn't told anyone. She trusted him not to tell her secret this time, either.

So together, they concocted the story of a quickie elopement after she returned to college and then the accidental drowning. Abby knew she couldn't allow her mother to know the truth because Joyce was the result of a one-night stand, raised alone by her single mother, and the stigma bothered her enormously. Casey had helped Abby put it together and had even come up with a picture of a nephew of his who was about the right age and had died a while back. She'd been scared to death, but her family accepted her story more readily than she'd dared hope.

Things went along smoothly—until Jesse had come back and filled her with confusion again. And given her a new worry.

She knew Jesse would be leaving soon, right after Remus was as good as he could get him to be. She also knew that Jesse and his twin brother were heirs to the Triple C ranch in California, one of the largest and best of its kind. Jesse might well want to take his daughter there if he learned that Grace was his. A judge might just rule in his favor, if it came to that. His father and brother both had managed to get custody of their children. The very thought of losing Grace to shared custody made Abby break out in a cold sweat.

No, she couldn't let that happen. She would work with Jesse while he was here, with Remus and the children's riding lessons. But that would be all.

She hated keeping up the lie, but she couldn't take the chance, not when her daughter's future was at stake.

Chapter Six

Abby liked the early morning hours before anyone in the household was awake, except for her father, who was already out on the range. She enjoyed taking her first cup of coffee on the porch, sitting in one of the rocking chairs and listening to the birds chasing one another in the branches of the big cottonwood. Strolling to the far end of the wraparound porch, she sipped the hot brew as she gazed about.

There'd been some light rain during the night and it seemed as if everything had been washed clean—the trees, the grass, the flowers her mother kept in bloom all year round. She took a deep breath and thought even the air smelled fresher. The familiar sounds of the ranch—the occasional horse whinny, distant cowbells and the pounding of horses' hooves as the men left the barn—soothed rather than annoyed her today.

Coffee mug in hand, she walked back and stopped short. Jesse was up in the big tree tying some sort of rope to the largest branch. Curious, she wandered over.

"You're up early," she said, gazing up.

"I wanted to get these in place before the kids came." Finishing with the last knot, he gingerly climbed down and dusted off his hands.

Abby checked out the two sections of rope now hanging from the limb as Jesse tested the strength of each. "What are they for?"

"You'll see." He walked to the base of the tree and picked up two boards, one painted bright red and the other blue. He fastened a loop of rope at each end of the red board and tied it firmly in place, then did the same with the blue. Yanking hard, he positioned each, then sat down on one and began swinging. "I figure if it holds my weight, it'll hold any of the kids."

"You made swings for my kids?" She was surprised and pleased. It would give the children one more thing to do when they were outside. "That was awfully nice of you."

He moved to test the other swing. "Grace told me the other day that she'd like a swing." Noticing the sudden narrowing of her eyes, he shook his head. "Don't worry. She was taking a walk with Vern and I went along."

"I wasn't worried." But she knew her face had given her away.

"Uh-huh." His half smile told her he didn't believe her, as he pushed off with his feet so the swing would go higher.

Abby didn't much care if he believed her or not. She had every right to protect her daughter. Draining the last of her coffee, she set down the mug and sat on the other swing, holding on to the sturdy ropes. "A little close to the ground," she commented, shoving the swing into motion.

"Well, yeah, for the kids." Holding his legs straight out, he swung all the way forward.

"Funny you should think of swings. Dad put up a couple for Lindsay and me when we were little. I used to love swinging, the higher the better. Lindsay wasn't too keen on it." Holding on to the heavy rope, she looked through the leafy branches at the blue sky. "I wonder whatever happened to those old swings. I remember Dad used chains instead of rope."

"Chains get rusty." Stopping the motion, he got off just as the screen door banged shut and Grace came running over.

"Swings! Wow! Who put these up?" Quickly, she climbed on the empty swing and put it in motion, her little legs pumping away.

"Jesse put them up. For all the kids to use." She didn't want Grace to think he'd done it especially for her.

"You did?" Grace jumped off and gave him a big hug. "Thank you, Jesse." Just as quickly, she got back on.

"You're welcome," he said, smiling.

So much for trying to keep Grace from getting too close to Jesse, Abby thought. Getting off, she picked up her mug. "Time for breakfast, Gracie. You can swing later."

But her daughter was flying high now, in seventh heaven.

"Did you hear me?" Abby asked in her no-nonsense voice.

"Okay." Reluctantly, the child slowed, then got off. She started to follow her mother inside, but stopped to beam a smile at Jesse. "I really love the swings." Turning, she noticed Abby's frown and ran after her.

Jesse frowned, too. Abby was a puzzle, he decided. She'd seemed pleased that he'd put up the swings, but as soon as Grace had come out, her defenses went up. Why? he wondered. And what would she do when he presented Grace with the surprise he was building?

Strolling back to his cabin, Jesse decided that because she was raising her daughter without a father, Abby wanted to keep it that way. The fact was it was nearly impossible to shield Grace from half of the human race. But Abby would have to learn that on her own.

"I'm really not a teacher," Jesse told Vern as he propped one booted foot on the bottom rung of the round pen. "I work with horses the way my father taught me, but I've never given others instructions."

The rancher nodded. "I guessed that was the case. And I know this wasn't what we hired you to do. But Abby mentioned that you might be willing to try to break our new two-year-old Thoroughbred. I acquired her last month and I think she has the makings of a gentle horse, but she's high-spirited and never been ridden. All I'm asking is that you allow a couple of my men to watch and maybe to explain what you're doing and why. So they'd be able to follow your ways after you're gone."

Jesse removed his hat and wiped his brow, damp from his afternoon workout with Remus, who'd been taken back to his stall. He studied the chestnut filly who was prancing about the pen, noticing that she was understandably a bit nervous, but she looked intelligent.

"First, I have to tell you that I don't *break* horses. That's a term I never use. I communicate with them, discover their character, get them to trust me so they *want* to do what I ask of them."

Casey, standing alongside the owner, looked even more skeptical than Vern. But he kept silent.

Vern, having noticed that Jesse was fond of Grace, decided to bring out the big guns. "Her name's Red. I want to groom her for my granddaughter. So far, I haven't convinced my wife or Abby to let Grace learn to ride. But if we can show them a well-trained, gentle horse, I believe they'll give in. Both of my daughters were riding by the time they started school and Grace is five."

Jesse considered the request. Each horse was different, but he wasn't worried. He felt reasonably certain he could gentle the filly, but he disliked putting his methods on display. But perhaps when Abby saw the results, she'd let him teach Grace to ride.

"All right," he told Vern. "Round up the men you want to learn and warn them, please, that they have to be quiet so as not to distract the horse."

Vern smiled and clapped Jesse on the back. "I'll have everyone here in half an hour. Casey'll get you anything you need." He hurried off.

"Son, I hope you know what you're doing," Casey said. "That's one very frisky filly."

"I hope so, too, Casey," Jesse said. He would hate to fail and have word spread throughout the ranch, including to Abby.

At four o'clock, Jesse made his way to the round pen. There were five men standing back a ways, presumably the ones Vern wanted to learn Jesse's methods. Four he didn't know, but the fifth was a rough-and-tumble guy who went by the name of Tex. He'd been at the Martin ranch six years ago and had been just as cocky then.

Curly had heard the news and was leaning against the barn alongside Vern and Casey. But the surprise was that Abby was positioned near the gate, an encouraging smile on her face. He walked over to her.

"You waiting to see me fall on my face?" he asked softly.

"Not hardly. I know you can do this."

"How about a friendly wager? If I'm able to turn this filly into a docile animal, you'll let me teach Grace to ride."

A frown came and went on her face. "And if you can't?"

"Then I won't badger you about her riding lessons."

Abby looked reluctant, but she didn't want to hold things up. "Fair enough." She'd seen Jesse with the handicapped children, noticed how sensitive and patient he was. Maybe he should teach Grace, with Abby right there, of course.

Jesse removed his hat. "Will you hold my hat, Abigail?" he asked softly.

Abigail. She remembered the night up in the hayloft, talking after they'd made love, and he'd coaxed and charmed her until she'd told him her full name, Abigail Amelia Martin. After that, when he wanted her to smile, he'd called her Abigail.

Her eyes soft with memories, she took the hat he held out, and he gave her that heart-stopping smile.

Jesse picked up the light cotton line he'd left on the fence, coiled it and draped it over one shoulder before entering the pen. He kept his eye on the horse, but spoke to the men.

"Just so you know, I have to give credit for this method called *joining up* first begun by a man most of you have probably heard of, Monty Roberts. He spent many years, from boyhood on, observing and learning the ways of horses, then taught others, including my father. Watch closely and then I'll explain the sequence so you can understand what I'm doing and why."

Jesse settled his eyes on the filly's eyes as she ran around the perimeter, frisky and high-stepping. Suddenly he shifted his gaze to her shoulder and the horse slowed noticeably. "I can control her speed by where I look at her with my body squared to hers. Eye to eye and she hurries away from me, but if I look away, say at her shoulder, she slows down, the challenge perceived to be less."

He demonstrated the control over the horse's speed again. "Next, I want her inside ear to lock on me, so she'll listen to me. Once she does that, she's showing me a mark of respect."

They all saw the filly's ear turn in Jesse's direction no matter where she was in the pen. He pitched the coiled line just ahead of her and they watched as the filly turned sharply in the opposite direction. Although she was now going counterclockwise, her ear was still aimed in his direction as she settled into a steady trot.

"These steps are all important in gaining the horse's respect and her trust," he further explained. "Next you're going to see her licking, her tongue coming through her teeth, then she'll pull it back and start a chewing action."

With his peripheral vision, Jesse saw a couple of the men ease closer to the fence. Calmly, he waited and, sure enough, Red began to lick and chew just as he'd said she would. "She's letting me know that it's all right, that she's with me."

"The last thing I'm looking for is for her to drop her head, to come toward me with her nose a couple of inches from the ground." Standing still, Jesse waited and within a few minutes, the filly trotted toward him, blowing at the dirt in front of her feet, her ear still turned to him.

"That was the final step where she indicated that she trusts me. Now just watch." Jesse stood still, his body at an angle to the horse, avoiding any eye contact with her. Red stopped, head cocked as if trying to figure out this man. Finally, she took a tentative step toward Jesse, who was still not looking at her. In moments she was standing next to him, her nose at his shoulder. He walked slowly in a circle to the right, then to the left and both times, she followed him. "Now the join up is completed.

"One more thing. I'd like to confirm for you that she trusts me completely. You see, horses are flight animals. When they sense danger, they run away. But man is just the opposite, a fight animal. Her trust is complete if she allows me to touch her vulnerable spots."

Jesse demonstrated these spots where predators, man or beast, might attack a horse. He ran his hand over her withers and her neck, across her flanks and under her belly, then picked up each foot for just a few moments. "She trusts me from top to toe since as a flight animal, she allowed me to touch her vulnerable spots as well as her means of escape, her feet."

Feeling comfortable with the filly now and certain she was with him, he stroked down her nose and she actually nuzzled him. As he walked to the gate, she followed, not wanting their session to end. Jesse stepped out, latching the gate.

"Damn, if I hadn't seen that with my own eyes, I wouldn't have believed it possible," Vern said.

"Maybe," Tex allowed, "but the real test is getting on her back and riding her."

"I'll show you that tomorrow," Jesse told him. "You never want to rush these things. She's come a long way. Let's let her rest now."

The men straggled away, talking among themselves as Casey joined Vern alongside Jesse. "Son, I got to hand it to you," the ranch manager told him. "You do know how to handle horses."

"I owe it all to my dad and Mr. Roberts."

"You going to saddle her tomorrow?" Vern wanted to know.

"Sure, if you want me to."

"You bet I do." He reached to shake Jesse's hand. "Thanks." Vern walked off with Casey, both of them shaking their heads as if having trouble believing what they'd just seen.

Winding the cotton line into a tight circle, Jesse walked to where Abby was sitting on the fence, holding his hat. He stopped in front of her expectantly.

"You done good, cowboy," she said in an exaggerated drawl. "And you make it look so easy." He'd looked more than good out there, a man in control of himself and the horse. That self-assurance more than anything conveyed itself to the mare.

If only she could trust him as easily as Red had.

"It is easy once you learn. I think horses want to communicate with humans, want to please. We just had to figure out their language." He dropped the coiled line on the closest fence post. "So, do I win the bet?"

"Not yet. Maybe after you ride her. *If* she lets you ride her."

"Oh, ye of little faith. She'll let me. You wait and see." He helped her down off the fence, then kept his hands at her waist. Searching her gorgeous eyes, he saw only a hint of wariness. That was progress.

Abby's heart beat erratically at his closeness. Would it always be like this with Jesse? Would she always long for him as strongly as before? She could give herself all kinds of warnings, but when he touched her, even briefly, her reaction both thrilled and frightened her. Her eyes shifted to his mouth, that strong, full mouth that had wreaked such havoc with her senses.

Jesse saw her gaze slip and his followed, noticing that her lips looked soft and inviting. But he dared not give in, not here where anyone could come by. Nor would she probably allow him to kiss her. Even though she looked as if she wanted him just as badly. Maybe he should…

The sound of two men talking as they rounded the corner had Abby stepping back guiltily. "I'd better go check on Grace," she said, walking backward away from him. "See you later."

Jesse cursed the interruption, though he knew it was probably for the best. What kind of a masochist was he, wanting to jump back into that blazing fire again? he wondered.

Feeling restless, Jesse wandered the compound at dusk. He felt fidgety, jittery, which wasn't like him. Maybe he was just plain homesick.

If he were back at the Triple C right now, he'd probably be with Jake, checking on the new foals maybe, or riding out to pasture to see how the cattle were settling for the night. Or perhaps he'd be in the house, playing a game of chess with Dad after one of Angel's great dinners. Their cook-housekeeper-maid and past nanny disliked her real name, Angelita. So when he and his brother had been youngsters and Cam hired her to help raise them, they'd settled on calling her Angel and it had stuck.

Angel was a wonderful cook and Jesse missed her meals. He missed sitting around the big oak table with Dad and Jake, rehashing the day's events. He knew that since his accident, since nearly losing his life, he was more introspective and certainly more aware of how much his family and home meant to him. He was getting anxious to get back there, but he'd made a commitment and he would see it through.

Strolling past the horse barn, he looked up at the slowly

sinking sun. Casey had told him that Remus was off his feed, that Vern had called the vet to come take a look at him tomorrow. Another delay.

He walked on, kicking at a stone in his path. Then there was the problem of Abby. She was every bit as attractive as she'd been six years ago, if not more. She was more womanly, still slender but more curvaceous, probably since giving birth to Grace.

She was still wary of him, but warming. The question was, where did he want to take this? She was bright with a good sense of humor, honest, a hard worker and a good mother. He admired her, cared about her, wanted her. But could she ever learn to trust him fully again? Did she care deeply for him, the way he'd want a woman who would be his wife to feel? Did he love her?

So many questions and so few answers. As Jesse mulled over his thoughts, he heard a horse trotting along the walkway dividing the two barns. He stopped to check out the rider. In moments, Abby appeared riding Jezebel, a frisky Thoroughbred. Looking neither to the left or right, she cleared the buildings and urged the mare into a gallop. Certain she didn't see him, he watched her turn the horse in the direction of the weeping willow alongside the stream.

Without hesitation, Jesse hurried back to the barn, saddled Domino and followed her. In no time, he spotted the mare tied to a limb of the willow and slowed Domino to a canter. Abby was wading in the stream, bending to pick up stones and throwing them downstream. She'd taken off her boots and rolled up her white pants.

Quietly, not wanting to startle her or Jezebel, he moved closer and tethered his horse to a small tree downwind from the mare. Walking along the water's edge, he saw that she was so wrapped up in her thoughts that she didn't notice his approach.

Finally he stopped and, hooking his thumbs in his back pockets, stood watching her.

"Yes," Abby said, her voice barely audible as she sent another stone flying. Moments later, she pitched another and called out, "No."

What was she doing? Jesse wondered, listening carefully.

"Last one," she said, then threw the stone. "Yes," she said. She watched it land, then shook her head. "If only it were that easy," she muttered as she turned to go back to shore. Her eyes landed on Jesse standing by the willow tree, his expression inquisitive.

Clearing her throat to cover her embarrassment, she waded out. "Sneaking up on me, are you?"

"I didn't mean to startle you." He indicated the stream. "What were you doing out there, with yes and then no?"

"It was nothing." Abby sat down on the thick grass. How could she explain her private version of *he loves me, he loves me not* to the man in question? "What are you doing out here?"

Dropping down to sit beside her, he decided honesty was the best policy. "I followed you."

"I see." Only she didn't see. "Why?"

Jesse crossed his feet and leaned back, supporting himself on his elbows, trying to choose the right words. He took a deep breath, noting how much fresher the air was this far from the barns. "Because there was a time when you and I could talk for hours, remember?"

So he wanted to drag her down memory lane. "Yes, but that was a long time ago, Jesse. We can't live in the past."

"I'm not trying to. I want to get to know this new Abby, the grown-up version."

Sitting cross-legged, she kept her eyes downcast as she pulled up a piece of grass. "For what purpose? You're only here for a short while, then you're going back to California. We live very different lives."

"Not so different. We both live on a ranch. We love the ranching life. We've both been to college." He sat up to face her. "Did you ever finish out your last year?"

Somehow Abby knew he'd turn the focus of the conversation on her. "No." Like the courtroom dramas she enjoyed on television, she would only answer the question and offer nothing more. And she'd turn the tables on him. "What about you? Did you ever do anything with your degree?"

"Sure. I studied animal husbandry, accounting, business courses—all things I use at the Triple C." But he wanted to know more about her. Much more. "So you quit college when you got married. Did you meet your husband at school?"

He was moving her onto shaky ground. "Not exactly. Why is it you've never married? You're what, thirty-one? And your twin's not married, either? Aren't there any eligible females in California?"

"Sure. Jake was married. He has a two-year-old son."

"Oh, that's right. And Jake has custody."

"Yes." Jesse wanted to pull the conversation back to them. "As for me, there aren't any females in California like you. You were the girl I measured every other woman against. And they all came up short."

A look of astonishment had her eyes widening. "I find that hard to believe."

"And I find it hard to believe that you got married only weeks after you and I had made love."

Abby tossed aside the grass she'd been mutilating, annoyed to see that her hands were unsteady. "We made love,

Jesse, but we never spoke of love. And, in case you've forgotten, you left and I didn't hear from you until recently when you magically reappeared."

"I know that. I also know you, or thought I did. We might not have said the words, but you knew I cared about you. Who was this guy who apparently swept you off your feet so quickly? He must have been *some* charmer." Jesse knew he was beginning to sound bitter and reminded himself to lighten up.

"I don't want to talk about him. I don't have to explain myself to you. You and I had a fling, it's over and that's that." Swallowing around a dry throat, she reached for her boots and tugged them on.

He didn't know which was worse, the anger or the hurt. "A fling? You call what we had a fling?"

Abby scrambled up, realizing she had to leave before she said some things she'd surely regret. "I've got to go."

Unwilling to let her leave with things so unsettled between them, Jesse stepped close, blocking her path to Jezebel. "Wait. I…"

Suddenly, their eyes locked together as awareness surged through Abby's system, at once familiar and unwelcome.

Jesse took hold of her arms, watching those gorgeous eyes turn a deeper blue.

"Jesse, don't. I…"

But his hand reached up to tuck a lock of her lovely blond hair behind her ear. "Don't what? Don't look at you, don't touch you, don't want you? If only I could stop." There might be hell to pay, she might slap him and walk away, but the reward was worth the risk. He lowered his head and took her mouth.

He'd caught her off guard. Of all the things Abby hadn't expected tonight, kissing Jesse was at the top of her list. But she was in his arms, her mouth locked to his, before she could dodge him. And in another heartbeat, she didn't want to.

There it was, the heat, the incredible heat he alone released in her. Like a match set to very dry tinder, he had but to touch his lips to hers and she was hot and needy and filled with renewed longing. She'd dreamed of this, consciously and unconsciously, month after solitary month and finally year after year. And now it was here and six lonely years fell away.

Fire. There was such fire in her, Jesse thought. Her response was instantaneous, like a fallow field springing to life overnight, like a dead man suddenly awakening. Yet he could sense her inner struggle as her hands moved restlessly up and down his arms, finally bunching in the denim of his shirt as she tightened her hold, shifting closer.

Her mouth was the stuff dreams were made of. Her lips greedy on his, her tongue slipped inside without hesitation. Then he felt her hands inch up his back and curl around his shoulders as she pressed her slender frame against him. And he was once more lost in the wonder of her.

Familiar. How could that be after such a length of time? Abby asked herself. Yet he felt and tasted familiar. Still, there were subtle changes. His hold on her was more self-assured, for the cocky young cowboy had been replaced by a mature, confident man. He'd always been clever, his hands roaming her body with a thoroughness that had stolen her breath away. Now, there was no vacillating, but rather a certainty to his touch that was even more thrilling.

She had no willpower when Jesse touched her, never had. She was like a puppet who danced willingly to his tune, like a piece of clay he molded to his liking. Never had anyone ruled her so completely or stolen her breath along with her firm resolve.

Shaken to her core, Abby stepped closer to the flame and let the fire take her.

Jesse had wondered how she'd react if he kissed her, if she'd struggle out of his grasp and curse him for daring to touch her. From the moment he'd seen her again that first day riding Jezebel, then later gazing up at her window, he'd wondered if she'd taste the same, respond the same as she had all those years ago. His heart leaped to realize that she'd opened to him as if they'd been apart six days rather than six years.

A homecoming. It was like a homecoming, the feel of her in his arms once more, her generous mouth moving under his, the soft sounds she made that he remembered from long ago. Pressing her closer, Jesse thrust his hands into her hair and deepened the kiss.

Later, Abby was to wonder what would have happened if the sound of horses' hooves in the near distance hadn't startled them apart. She opened her eyes and saw the jolt of irritation in his at the interruption. Breathing hard, she stepped back into the deeper shadows of the big tree.

Jesse ducked under a low hanging branch and peered toward the two riders, but he couldn't tell who they were in the darkening twilight at this distance. In minutes, they were out of earshot, heading toward the barn.

Annoyed with himself, Jesse frowned. "I don't know why we hid since we weren't doing anything wrong. We're both free."

"Yes, but you know how gossip spreads on a ranch." She was vexed to realize that her voice wasn't quite steady. "I've got to get back."

"Wait. Don't go yet. It's early." He wanted to explore what they'd just discovered.

"I can't. I promised Grace a bedtime story." It was as good an excuse as any, especially since it was true.

Jesse walked with her to where Jezebel waited, but she jumped up before he could lend her a hand. *Always was independent,* he thought.

Reins in her hands, Abby tried to think of something fitting to say, but her mind was a blank. Finally she looked down at him. "I don't want you to…"

"If you tell me not to make too much of this, I'm going to grab you off that horse and prove you wrong." Now that he'd kissed her and she'd kissed him back, he knew. There was no denying the obvious.

Abby nodded. "All right, then. Good night." Turning Jezebel, she headed back, her mind and heart in turmoil.

Jesse decided to wait a bit before following her since she was so all-fired nervous about ranch gossip. Her fears were probably based on her mother's constant warnings about mingling with the cowboys. Well, he was a damn sight more than a cowboy.

Some minutes later, he swung up on Domino and eased him into a mild trot as he wondered just what difference that kiss made in his relationship with Abby. He had to convince her to let him tell her parents the whole truth so they could see each other out in the open. They needed to get to know one another better, to talk. Yes, he was interested, very much so. But time would tell if this would develop into a forever love.

With that thought, he urged the stallion to gallop home.

The bunkhouses were dark and even the horses were quiet by the time he settled Domino in his stall. His mind going over possibilities, Jesse walked to his cabin and went inside.

He'd left a light on, as was his habit. His back was giving him a little grief so he went into the kitchen and poured himself two fingers of Scotch, neat. Drinking it down, he made a face. Still tasted better than any pill he'd ever had.

He turned off the table lamp and, yawning, went into the only bedroom, removing his shirt as he walked. He doubted he'd get much sleep with Abby foremost on his mind. Though he'd taken a shower earlier, maybe another would help him relax.

Going by feel in the dark room, he found the doorway to the connecting bath and snapped on the overhead. He heard a sound and swiveled about.

To his great surprise, there on his bed, clearly visible in the splash of light from the bathroom, wearing something black and slinky, was Lindsay Martin, a seductive smile on her face.

Chapter Seven

"What are you doing here, Lindsay?" Jesse asked, raising his arm and bracing his hand on the doorjamb.

"Why, sugar, I've come to see you. Neighborly-like," she drawled. Lying on her side facing him, she ran a manicured hand lazily along her thigh.

"You can drop the southern accent. You're no more from the South than I am." He saw her eyes narrow slightly as she revised her game plan. "Listen, I'm tired and my back hurts like the devil. Whatever it is you have in mind, I'm not up to it."

Slithering to the edge of the bed, she sat up. "I don't want to do anything that'll tire you, sweetie. Come over here and I'll show you. You just lie back and I'll do all the work."

Jesse wondered how a woman as beautiful as Lindsay—and he had to admit she was stunning—could allow herself to get so pathetic. "Sorry, but I'm not interested, Lindsay. I just want a hot shower and eight hours of sleep." Unbuttoning his shirt, he decided that was plain enough.

Deliberately misunderstanding, Lindsay got up and walked over to him. "Water conservation is important, you know. Why don't we take that shower together?" She reached over and put her hand on his chest, her fingers twining in the hair.

Up close, he could smell her heavy cloying cologne that didn't quite cover the alcohol on her breath. He couldn't help noticing that she wore nothing beneath the black teddy that showed off her generous curves. Calmly, Jesse took hold of her wrist and removed her hand. "Lindsay, go home. You're embarrassing yourself."

Momentarily taken aback, she rebounded quickly, unused to men turning her away. "You got a girl back in California, sweetie? But she's there and I'm right here."

Jesse drew in a frustrated breath. "You need to understand that I'm simply not interested in going to bed with you, Lindsay. You don't have to do this, spend your evening drinking, then trying to seduce a man. You're a lovely woman. Stop hitting the bottle, straighten out your life and you'll find you'll attract men without having to resort to…to this." He dropped her hand and stepped back.

Lindsay's face reflected a flash of sudden anger at being rejected, then lectured. "Just who do you think you are, Mr. High-and-Mighty Jesse Calder? I was doing you a favor, but it looks like you're not man enough to accept." She grabbed her dress from the chair where she'd left it and hurriedly pulled it on over her head.

Jesse tried again to explain. "Calm down. I'm merely saying you have a lot to offer someone. Don't cheapen yourself. Get to know someone and—"

"Did I ask you for advice? Did I?" Shimmying her dress down her body, she looked daggers at him. "I'll bet you wouldn't be turning down Little Miss Perfect! Oh, no! If Abby came over and threw herself at you, you'd agree in a heartbeat." Slipping her feet in her sandals, she continued to glare at him. "Only she's *not* as perfect as she seems."

Jesse took hold of her arms and shook her slightly. "Stop it, Lindsay. Stop bad-mouthing and stop your self-destructive behavior. Just because your wedding was called off is no reason to drink too much and become wild. There're plenty of guys who are honest and want what you want."

Color tinted her cheeks. "Oh, so you know about that, too? What is it, on some billboard on the highway? Lindsay Martin, not marriage material. Nice guys need not apply." With a sob, she wrenched out of his hold. "I'll have you know *I* called off the wedding!" Turning, she rushed to the door and outside.

Walking after her, Jesse saw her stumble her way to the big house and go inside. Wearily, he closed his door.

That certainly went well, he chided himself. But to be honest, he wasn't sure how else he might have handled the situation. Lindsay was a walking time bomb waiting to go off. He didn't know when or how, but she was bound to explode sooner or later. He just hoped he wasn't around to see it.

She had said one thing that was certainly true. If Abby came through his door, he'd take her in his arms in a heartbeat. How had Lindsay known that? While it was true that he and Abby had spent time together, it was usually while working with Remus or with the handicapped children. There'd scarcely been a look or a touch that could have been misinterpreted.

Then again, in her present state of mind, perhaps Lindsay had said that to rile him, Jesse decided as he went in to shower.

Abby climbed off the large rock she'd been sitting on near the entrance to the west pasture. After leaving Jesse and tending to Jezebel, she'd gone for a walk to think, to clear her mind. Through the years, she'd often sought out this quiet place to sit and muddle through her problems. Sometimes it worked. Sometimes it didn't.

This was one of the times it didn't.

Strolling back, she realized she was no closer to an answer than she had been earlier. What to do about Jesse? There was no denying the impact of that powerful kiss they'd shared. It had been just like before, six years ago. The world went away when Jesse Calder kissed her, or even just touched her. It was as simple as that. And as complicated.

Rubbing her arms, Abby was chagrined to admit to herself that she'd been moments away from dropping to the fragrant grass and having a bout of mindless sex with him. She couldn't let that happen, not again. Look what had happened the last time she'd given in to her desire for that man. Mindless was a good word to describe her when Jesse was around.

You are the woman I compared all others to, he'd said. It had been the same for her. She'd come to believe that for some women, there was only one man who would do. And for her, it was Jesse. She hadn't made love with anyone before him, nor after. Hadn't even wanted to, not even slightly.

She'd been so certain she'd never see him again that she'd resigned herself to a life without a man in it, without a father for Grace. But that had been before Jesse had come back. Before he'd kissed her again and had her treacherous heart beginning to hope.

It wouldn't work, even if they ironed out their personal problems. His place was with his father, brother and nephew in California and hers was here. One day, with her father's health not the best and since Lindsay had no interest, she'd probably wind up running the Martin ranch. Why not? Lots of women were ranchers. Two or three miles up the road, there was Birdie McBride, widowed at thirty, who'd run her ranch for ten years now. Granted she had a ranch manager and a dozen or so cowboys, but she was in charge.

Then there was Grace to consider. If she told Jesse now that he was her daughter's father, her parents would learn that Grace was illegitimate, a fact that might change how Joyce viewed both Abby and Grace. And then, after confessing all, if Jesse left, all the upheaval would be for nothing. Plus if her father learned that Casey had helped her deceive them, he might be angry with the ranch manager. Too much at stake, Abby decided.

She'd wait him out, knowing he'd leave once Remus was mended. Maybe she was wrong to be afraid, but she really didn't know this new Jesse that well. If only she could stop wanting him, loving him. Still, she would give all that up to keep Grace.

Abby was almost at the barn when she saw someone ease out of the shadows and recognized Casey. The man never seemed to sleep, always checking on something. If she had to run the ranch one day, she hoped he'd still be around.

"Hello, there," she said as she came up alongside him. In the dim glow of the night lights, she saw his worried look and wondered what was wrong.

"Have you completely lost your mind?" Casey asked quietly. When Abby looked confused, he went on. "I saw you come back from your ride and not ten minutes later, Jesse came trotting in from the same direction. Don't take no genius to put two and two together."

Abby knew her face betrayed her. Besides, Casey was the one person she could never lie to, not after all he'd done for her. "He came by when I was out by the willow. We sat and talked."

"Uh-huh. You think I can't tell when a woman's been kissed good and proper?"

Pressing her lips together, Abby brushed back her disheveled hair. "Okay. One kiss. That was all."

Casey shook his head and ran a hand over his stubbly chin. "Girl, you're touched in the head, like my daddy used to say. You got burned real good, and you go back asking for more."

"You guessed his real identity?"

"Hell, yes. First day I saw him. I been worrying about you ever since."

She touched his arm affectionately. "Please don't worry, Casey. I'm not going down that road again, honest."

Squinting in the dim light, he looked into her eyes. "You're not, eh? I see you watchin' him out there with Remus, stayin' out of sight, but I caught you. And I see how you look at him. Then you start ridin' out to meet him."

"I didn't ride out to meet him. I rode out alone and he happened by."

"Happened by, my aunt Matilda. Worst thing you can do is lie to yourself, you know."

Abby released a shaky breath. "I know."

"You remember how it was, how I found you cryin' and scared in the hayloft? Remember how we worked hard to come up with a story your folks and everyone else would believe, especially that nosy sister of yours?"

Chagrined, she just nodded. "Yes, I remember how we invented Tom Price, then said he drowned. You helped me so much, Casey. I don't know what I'd have done without you."

"Because then, like now, I watch out for you. And here you go again, invitin' trouble. You're fallin' for him again, right?"

Abby stared at the ground, kicking a stone with one foot, unable to answer him. Was she falling for Jesse again? she asked herself.

Casey knew her silence spoke loud and clear. "Honey, don't you ever learn?"

"I guess not." She gazed into the good eye of the man who wasn't quite a father but more than an uncle ever since she was born. "Please understand. I didn't want this to happen. I know he's going to leave again. But I can't help the way I feel, Casey. I've loved him practically from the first time I saw him. But I'm not going to let him get to me this time."

"Uh-huh." His worry lines deepened because he didn't believe her.

"At least I'm going to try." She reached over and kissed his creased and tan cheek. "Don't worry. I'm older and wiser this time around." Leaving him, she hurried toward the big house.

Casey removed his hat and scratched his nearly bald head. Older and wiser. That was a laugh. Older maybe, not much wiser. He'd seen a lot in his fifty-eight years and knew one thing was for sure: when it came to love, age and even experience weren't much help.

Walking slowly to his cabin, he couldn't help wondering what it would be like to be loved like that, so strong it lasted through the years when there was little hope for happiness.

* * *

The last week in June was hotter than ever. Jesse unrolled barbed wire with his thick gloves before stretching it to the fence post he'd just replaced. Slim and Kelly were the two men working with him, both down the fence line a ways. He'd volunteered to help out to keep his body limber and because they could use two more hands.

He'd spent the early morning with Remus and this time, he'd had Abby in the round pen with him. Since he was her horse, Jesse figured he'd have less to fear from her than anyone else. She'd been gentle but firm with him, following Jesse's lead. They'd had a good hour with the stallion, actually getting him to accept the bridle once more. They'd left him contentedly chewing the bit.

And in late morning, they'd had another session with Charley and Sam, who'd both progressed nicely. Jesse had placed Charley in the saddle on Dolly in front of him and Abby had ridden with her arms around Sam on Jasmine. They'd gone slowly around the pen half a dozen times, letting the children get used to the sensation, answering all their questions. They both took to riding quickly and didn't want their sessions to end. Jesse had also spent some time in the tack room of the barn with them, explaining all the equipment. Their parents were surprised and pleased when Abby told them that the boys were more responsive in class, more confident, telling the others about their experiences on horseback.

Abby had been very professional and somewhat distant during both sessions, her conversations with Jesse almost formal. When the sessions ended, she hurried back to her schoolhouse with merely a quick wave.

Had it been the memory of that stunning kiss that had her

pulling back? Jesse wondered as he wound wire around the post. If the kiss had had the same effect on her as it had on him, she'd have been able to think of little else. He kept remembering how she'd opened to him, how her slender body had molded itself to the long, lean length of him, how her special tastes had exploded on his tongue.

Since she'd studiously avoided personal contact with him all day, he'd have to think of a way to get her alone so they could explore these feelings. He'd have to…

Thundering hooves heading his way drew Jesse's attention. A gray stallion was running hell-bent past the men lazily watching over the cattle. He recognized Tex in the saddle and saw that he'd somehow lost the reins and the horse was running wild and out of control.

Without a second's hesitation, knowing how badly a rider on a runaway horse could end up, Jesse ran to Domino, leaped up and was moving after Tex before several of the men even figured out what was happening. Jesse was an excellent horseman, but the gray had a good head start and he had been spooked for some reason, giving him an adrenaline rush. Jesse could hear Tex yelling as he drew closer.

At one point, Jesse thought the gray would run right into several cows grazing in a cluster, but he managed to whip on past them. Jesse had Domino follow, urging him to more speed. He was five lengths behind, then four. Up ahead were some trees that posed a bigger danger. Jesse leaned in, pressing on. Behind him, he heard a couple of others on horseback following.

Finally, just two lengths behind, Jesse and Domino moved closer and he could see the gray frothing at the mouth. The usually insolent Tex was almost prone over the horse's neck, a look of fear on his face. Jesse was alongside but he saw that he couldn't reach over and grab the reins for they were hanging down the other side.

Closer and closer he rode, then yelled to Tex, "Get your feet out of the stirrups and lean your body toward me."

But the frightened cowboy seemed frozen in place. There was only one other way to slow them, Jesse knew. Shifting his weight, he spoke softly to Domino, then urged him as close to the stallion as he dared. When he figured the moment was right, he leaped onto the gray's back behind Tex. The stallion kept on going, not letting a second rider slow him. The frightened man kept his position as Jesse leaned to the right. It took him several precious seconds to grab the reins. Straightening, he saw that they were very near the trees.

Reining in the horse, pulling him back, his knees pressing hard into his flanks, he tried to aim him away from the trees. Finally the gray let him turn them to the left and as he did, Jesse pulled hard, slowing the animal. In a couple of moments, they were slowed to a manageable gait. Finally, Jesse brought them to a stop and saw that Domino had followed right behind. Moving up fast were the two riders who'd tagged along.

Jesse slipped off, still holding the reins, and helped Tex down. But the cowboy's shaky legs wouldn't hold him and he sat down hard. Jesse walked to the horse's head, trying to see if anything was out of order. He talked softly to the stallion, calming him.

"You okay?" he asked Tex as the other two rode up.

"Yeah." Tex rolled his shoulders and massaged the back of his neck. "Damn horse. Saw a gopher and took off like the devil."

But Jesse thought differently. There were bloody marks

on both sides of the horse. He turned again to look at Tex. "You always wear spurs?" he asked.

"When I have a difficult horse, yeah." Slowly, Tex got to his feet. He glanced at Slim and Kelly as they walked over, both looking unfriendly. "What?"

"You've been warned repeatedly not to use spurs, Tex," Slim told him.

"I think we should bring Casey in on this," Kelly added.

"Damn horse nearly kills me and all you can think of is telling on me. Well, go ahead. Casey said it was all right."

Looking doubtful, Slim walked over to where Jesse stood and took the gray's reins. "Hell of a job. Thanks. I'll take him back."

Jesse handed the reins over and walked to where Domino waited, unable to hide the limp this time. That jump had done him in.

"What about me?" Tex asked.

"You climb on with Kelly. This horse isn't going to let you on his back again." Mounting his own horse, Slim let the gray follow behind as he started off.

"Hell of a way to treat a man," Tex grumbled as he went over to Kelly.

"Why don't you shut up and get on," Kelly told him.

Jesse waited until they'd ridden off, then climbed on Domino. Time to call it a day, he told himself. Glancing up at the gray clouds, he thought it looked like rain. Maybe it would cool things off.

Abby lay in bed listening to the rain pound against the window, and the thunder rumble. Lightning slashed in the distance, lighting the sky momentarily. This storm was a beaut.

Rising, she went to gaze out the window and saw that the walkway between the big house and the two cabins on the other side was like a small stream, water rolling downhill. With no underground drains, the area often flooded during a heavy rain. The upside of that was that by mid-morning, the hot Arizona sun usually dried up most of the runoff.

Turning her head, she tried to see the horse barn, but could only catch the corner. She knew how frightened Remus was of the thunder, a throwback to the bully who'd owned him before and left him outside in storms. She couldn't sleep anyhow so she might as well go see him, and hopefully reassure him.

Hurriedly, she tugged off her nightshirt, pulled on jeans, a T-shirt and socks before gathering her hair into a ponytail and tying it. Quietly, she went downstairs, not wanting to wake her parents. In the kitchen, she grabbed a couple of apples and stuffed one in each pocket. Stepping into the mudroom, she slid her feet into a pair of boots her mother used when gardening. Then she took her father's big yellow slicker off the hook, placed the hood over her head and with one hand held the raincoat closed over her front.

Opening the side door, she saw a flash of lightning quickly followed by a thunderous rumble. Pulling in a bracing breath, she hurried across the walkway, her head down. The water surged and swirled, slowing her down. Finally, she reached the barn door, taking her two hands to slide it open. Once inside, she left the door slightly ajar.

The animal smell was heightened by the heat and the high humidity, Abby thought as she shed the slicker and hung it on a hook by the counter. Turning the dim night lights up would probably spook the horses, she decided. Starting down the center aisle, she noticed that the horses were awake and a few were snuffling, but none seemed terribly nervous. She walked on toward the older end of the barn where Remus was housed. Hearing his high-pitched whinny, she hurried along.

Standing on his front porch wearing only jeans and watching the rain with Jughead, Jesse wondered if he was imagining things or if someone had really run from the big house to the horse barn moments ago. He'd been outside for about ten minutes, trying to calm the restless dog, both of them unable to sleep due to the noise of the storm, when he'd seen the side door open in a flash of light, then close. Peering through the rain with the help of the low wattage lights left on all night around the compound, he couldn't make out who had left the dry comfort of the big house to venture out in a downpour.

Too short to be Vern, he decided. Hard to believe that Joyce would be going to the barn, day or night. Lindsay hadn't the smallest interest in the horses, so that ruled her out.

The person all but swallowed up in the yellow slicker had to be Abby. Only what was she doing in the horse barn at midnight?

Jesse went back inside, taking the dog with him. He grabbed a T-shirt and pulled it on while he thrust his feet into his thick-soled shoes.

"You stay put, Jughead," he told the trembling dog. As unpredictable as the animal was, he'd spook the horses.

Outside, he remembered that it didn't rain often in Arizona, but when it did, it really poured. Ducking down his head, he splashed his way past Casey's cabin to the horse barn. He noticed that the door was ajar so he scooted inside, stopping to brush rainwater from his beard and hair. In the short time he'd been outside, his shirt had gotten soaked and was sticking to him but he ignored it as he noticed the yellow slicker, wet and dripping, hanging near the door.

Looking around, he didn't see or hear anyone. Remus. She had to have gone to Remus to make sure the storm wasn't upsetting him too much. He hurried down the center walkway toward the partition at the far end. Passing that, entering the old section of the barn, he heard low murmuring coming from the direction of Remus's stall. He walked closer.

What he saw didn't shock him, but it did surprise him a little. Abby was standing outside the stall, the big horse inside with his head extended toward her. She was stroking his neck and between his eyes along his nose, whispering to him. Remus shuffled his feet once, then was still, letting her pet him. He knew that for a horse to allow someone to touch his face was a sign of trust; at least the beginnings of trust. Maybe Remus was remembering that Abby was the one who'd rescued him from the man who'd abused him. In the pen, working with the stallion, he'd yet to allow Jesse to stroke his nose. This was a great breakthrough.

Sensing more than seeing someone else there, Abby turned her head and noticed Jesse. She, too, was aware of the hurdle they'd just gotten past, and she smiled at him. Her hand on Remus's neck, the scarred side, she spoke softly. "Hi. We've just been talking about you."

Using the same low tone, Jesse slowly walked closer. "Really? And what have you two been saying?"

So elated was Abby at this tangible progress that she was glad to share it with him. "Well, first we talked about the storm, how there's no reason to be afraid, that he's safe here.

Then we decided that you've made him feel more confident, less frightened of people."

"Is that so? You've become a horse whisperer, then?" He was alongside Abby now and raised a hand to stroke the other side of Remus's neck, moving slowly, being gentle.

"Mmm, not exactly. I'm no competition, if that's what you mean. I'm contented just whispering to one horse." She ran a loving hand over the big stallion who looked as if he could stand there all night if she'd continue stroking him.

"You've worked your magic on him. Maybe tomorrow, we can try getting a saddle on him and then soon, see if he'll let someone ride him again." Another sharp crack of thunder all but shook the barn, but Remus's only reaction was a shudder.

"That would be nice, but even if he doesn't want to be ridden, he's still come a long way. Thank you." The smile she gave him lit up her eyes.

Jesse admitted to himself that he didn't want to go home to California and leave her. "Yes, but we need to finish the job, to get him to let me and then you ride him, to get him to interact with the other horses." He nodded to the newer section of the barn. "I'd like to see him in a stall over there. This section should be torn down."

"I agree, as soon as Remus is socially able again." She reached into her pocket and handed Jesse her last apple. "Here, give him this. I'm not above bribery. He was upset by the storm but when I gave him a treat and talked to him, he quieted down."

He smiled. "Yeah, bribery works wonders with horses. And men." He took the apple and held it toward Remus who'd been sniffing ever since he'd spotted the second treat. The big mouth opened and he took the apple, chewing noisily.

Abby stepped back. "I think he's going to be all right now." Noticing that despite the raincoat, her T-shirt was wet and clinging, she crossed her arms over her chest.

"Did storms upset him before the fire?" Jesse asked, moving back also.

"Yes. His previous owner often left him and his other horses out in storms. He didn't even have a shelter for the hottest summer days, just this makeshift ramada. It's a wonder Remus is as good as he is." She started walking toward the newer section of barn.

"So now you come out to comfort him every time it rains?" He realized it was just the sort of thing Abby would do with her soft heart for children and animals.

"Only when there's thunder and lightning." She paused to look up at him. "I understand you saved Tex's life today."

He shrugged. "I wouldn't go that far. Tex has some problems, most he brought on himself."

"You mean the spurs. I agree. Casey told me he was going to talk with Dad about Tex tomorrow and give him some ultimatums. He's done the same thing before, but you'd think the runaway horse experience would scare him."

"I'm not surprised. A lot of cowboys think pain is the way to control horses. Actually, it's just the opposite."

Though the lighting was dim, Abby was very aware that she hadn't stopped to put on a bra, thinking she'd be alone in the barn, and her wet shirt was making her self-conscious. "I'd better get back before Grace wakes up and needs me." The little white lie had her averting her gaze. Grace slept like the dead and never woke during storms.

"Has she asked again about riding lessons?" He wanted to stall her, to keep her with him.

"Oh, sure. Regularly. But you haven't won the bet until I

can ride Red, remember?" And by then, he'll be heading home, Abby reminded herself. She began edging toward the door.

Now or never, Jesse thought as he stepped closer, taking her arm and turning her toward him. "Don't go. Stay with me." He let his eyes say the rest, the look between them holding for long, sizzling seconds.

Abby's breath backed up in her throat as her heart started pounding faster. But a frisson of fear raced up her spine, fear that if she let him touch her again, she wouldn't be able to turn away. "I...this isn't a good idea, Jesse."

"It's the very *best* idea." Before she could react, he tugged her up hard against his chest and pressed his mouth to hers.

Jesse was not a man who'd ever force a woman. He'd never had to. If she had protested, by word or action, he would have backed off in an instant. He waited, but surprisingly, she didn't.

Abby wanted to protest, had thought she should, but every nerve cell in her body celebrated his touch and reached out for more. And still more. He held her close, her breasts pressing to his hard chest through the damp material of their shirts. Close, but she could easily have broken free and they both knew it. They also both knew that deep inside she had no desire to be free of him.

Jesse Calder was a hard man who'd worked every job his ranch had to offer, but his mouth was surprisingly soft, Abby thought, just as she'd been remembering. There was raw heat in the way he kissed her, causing pleasure to whirl throughout her entire system. Who could resist such temptation?

During the long restless nights since he'd come to Arizona and before, Jesse had imagined this, dreamed this, yet even those vivid pictures couldn't match the real thing. The special flavors his tongue sampled on her lips were the ones he'd been seeking to duplicate with others, and never found. As if in generous welcome, she opened to him and he drank deeply from her.

He'd forgotten how small she was, how delicate her bone structure. Yet the breasts that were crushed against his chest reminded him that she was every inch a woman. Despite her slender frame, there was strength here in the arms that wound about his neck and the hands that thrust wildly into his damp hair. Outside, he heard a deep peal of thunder that lent a primitive feel to their embrace. Like jungle drums, the sound came again and then the rain took up the beat, slamming against the aluminum sides of the barn, isolating them in their small world.

Abby heard him murmur her name as he backed her up against an empty stall door, his hard body shoving closer while his greedy fingers raced over her aroused flesh. His rough hands grazed her soft skin, and still she welcomed his touch. Her heated blood churned as a moan she couldn't prevent came from her throat. Needs clamored inside her, needs she always kept so carefully leashed, now bursting free. The one man who could satisfy them was raining kisses on her face and her upraised throat while outside, the torrent picked up momentum.

She was scarcely aware when he dipped his head in a feverish rush to press his mouth to the swollen tips of her straining breasts through the wet shirt. Eyes closed to hold in the feeling, she buried her hands in his hair as he took possession.

He wanted her more than his next breath, Jesse thought, more than a desert walker wants water. It was more than wanting, more like an elemental need that no one else could fulfill, that no other woman could assuage, that had lain dormant during their years apart but had never gone away. He had to have her, to make her his once more, to never let her go again. Moving up, he took her mouth in a kiss that stole her breath away.

Abby arched her back, feeling the solid stall door behind her as he deepened the kiss. If he let go of her now, she'd surely sink to her knees, for they were already trembling. It had been so long since she'd let her senses rule and the devil take the hind road.

Then she felt his hands slip under her shirt and slowly move around front.

The sudden realization that she was acting like the eager teenager she'd been six years ago was like a splash of cold water. Hadn't she done that back then? Look where it had gotten her.

"No!" she cried out.

It took but two seconds for the word to penetrate Jesse's foggy brain. He dropped his hands and took a step back, breathing hard. It was a full minute before he could speak. "What's wrong?" he asked in a voice still thick with passion.

"I can't walk down this bumpy road again, Jesse." Her shaky fingers could scarcely straighten her T-shirt over her damp breasts. She needed to leave, to get to the safety of her bedroom. Gingerly, she touched her face tingling from contact with his beard. She prayed that for some unknown reason Casey wouldn't be skulking around and catch her now with her face red and her mouth swollen.

What was wrong with her? Abby asked herself. Hadn't she learned her lesson the first time around, as Casey had asked? Didn't she remember the high cost of loving Jesse?

Leaning her head into her open hand, she closed her eyes, waiting for her heart to stop pounding.

The undeniable truth was she'd never gotten over him. That much was painfully clear. She had loved in secret, a love she would have denied had it been discovered back then. Love was a dance; music she moved to without conscious thought, with unconscious desire. How could she put herself through all that again?

Jesse was honestly confused. There was no mistaking her response, her desire, every bit as strong as his. He knew she wasn't involved with another, nor was he. They were both adults, more mature than before. Why, then, did she go just so far, then slam on the brakes?

Wearily, he ran a hand over his face. "I don't understand. I know that wasn't a faked reaction just now. I believe you want me and I sure as hell want you. What's the problem?"

Tears trailed down Abby's cheeks like the raindrops sliding down the windows outside. Her emotions were in a jumble, sadness at what could never be and regrets over what might have been weighing her down. Brushing a hand across her cheeks, she reached for the yellow slicker. "I've got to go. I can't talk anymore right now."

Jesse moved to her, touched her arm. "Please don't go like this. I need you to believe that I mean what I say. I'm not after a simple roll in the hay. I'm sorry I wasn't up front with you about my real identity. I'm sorry I didn't tell you everything before I left. Things might have turned out differently if I had. I made some mistakes, but my feelings for you are stronger than before. All those years, I kept seeing your face even when I closed my eyes. You were seldom out of my thoughts."

She put her hand on the door, unable to look at him, unwilling to confess her own lies of omission. "I think we both have some thinking to do, Jesse."

"You're probably right."

Without turning around, Abby nodded, then stepped out into the rain.

Jughead slipped in after her, soaked and panting. "How did you get out?" Jesse asked the dog as he gave a wet shake. Pushed the screen door open, probably.

He saw that the storm was passing over, leaving them with a steady rain. Watching Abby splash her way through the water still streaming down the walkway, he noticed lights suddenly beam on her, then heard the sound of a powerful engine above the noise of the rainfall. The car paused and he recognized Lindsay's red Corvette. Just as Abby ducked in through the side door, Lindsay turned sharply to the right and parked alongside her family's Lincoln.

Holding the barn door only slightly ajar, Jesse saw the Corvette door swing open and a large black umbrella pop open followed by Lindsay. She walked toward the big house, then stopped and stared at the barn then his cabin for long moments. Apparently satisfied, she hurried onto the porch and went inside.

He wondered if Lindsay would go to Abby's room and start a fight, as confrontational as she was. It would only fuel her jealousy if she saw him leave shortly after Abby went out, so Jesse lingered in the barn for a full ten minutes. Finally, he left, calling for Jughead to come with him, both hurrying onto his porch, getting wet all over again, thinking they'd dodged a bullet tonight.

But when he opened his cabin door, he glanced to the big house and saw the unmistakable glow of a cigarette on the porch.

Chapter Eight

Jesse carried his lunch tray to the table nearest the buffet where Casey was eating. "Mind if I join you?"

"Sit yourself down." Casey spread butter on a slab of corn bread. "Heard you rode Red this mornin'. Wish I'd have seen that."

"She's still a little frisky, but afterward, Kelly rode her and then Slim. She settled down nice and easy." Jesse stirred his iced tea.

"Got to thank you for that. I know it wasn't part of your deal. Vern'll pay you extra, I'm sure." The older man cut another piece of chicken-fried steak and speared it with his fork.

"I already told him I don't want anything extra. I volunteered. I hope some of the guys watching will be able to use those methods in the future." Jesse took a bite and chewed appreciatively.

"Yeah, me, too."

"Do you think Carmalita would give me the recipe for this to take back to our cook? It sure is good."

"Don't know. Catch her on a good day and she might."

They ate in companionable silence for several minutes before Casey spoke again, turning to look at Jesse. "That was some storm last night, eh?"

"Sure was. We don't get that many electrical storms in northern California. It's amazing, but most of the downpour has already dried up."

"You weren't out in it, were you?"

Jesse faced Casey, wondering if *he'd* been out in it and seen Abby and him in the barn. There were several narrow vertical windows. "I was out on my porch for a while. As I said, we don't see Mother Nature put on such a show back home."

"Uh-huh. Reason I ask is I went out on my porch, too. Didn't see you on yours, but I saw Jughead at the barn door, whining and scratching. He follows you around everywhere so I thought maybe you'd gone into the barn, maybe to check on Remus."

The shrewd old man caught him. He'd have to wiggle out of this one so as not to involve Abby. Eyes on his plate, he picked up a couple of French fries and kept his tone matter-of-fact. "I did run over once to check on him. I'd heard he hates storms and I didn't want him acting up. I stayed awhile and he quieted down. The rest of the horses were fine."

Casey returned to eating. "Remus damn near kicked his stall door open once in a storm. Mean cuss."

"Not anymore. I figure he'll let me ride him in a day or two."

Finished, Casey stood up to his full five-six height. "Lucky he's got you lookin' after him, ain't it?" He ambled over to the table where the used trays and plates were stacked and added his to the pile.

Jesse debated staying where he was or walking out with Casey, who seemed to want to say more. Curiosity won and he followed the man outside where the bright sun had him blinking. They paused near the doorway, Jesse searching his mind for a subject that might get Casey talking.

"I'm almost finished with my surprise for Grace. Would you like to see it?"

Squinting, Casey looked up at him. "I saw you working on it, but I didn't know you were making it for Grace. I thought it was for all the schoolhouse kids." When Jesse didn't comment, Casey noticed that he was staring across the road where two people were leaning against the barn.

Casey recognized Lindsay talking to one of the cowboys in a hushed tone. "Wonder what that gal's lookin' for."

Jesse watched Lindsay remove her sunglasses and angle her body toward the tall, husky man, who wore his hat tipped back at a jaunty angle. "Who's the guy?" he asked Casey.

"Name's Owens. Hails from Tennessee and that's what everyone calls him. Don't know his first name."

Tennessee stepped closer to Lindsay, placing a hand on her arm in an intimate way. "What business do you suppose Lindsay has with him?" Jesse asked.

"Can't say. Never thought she even knew him. She's not one to talk much with the men."

There had to be a reason she was having a chat with the cowboy, Jesse thought. He looked to be a maverick, like her, so maybe that was his appeal. Lindsay could also have an ulterior motive, taking advantage of the man's obvious interest in her. "What's he do around here?"

Casey shrugged. "Little of this, little of that. Mends tools, sees to the tack room, oversees the stall muckers. He's a good mechanic. Keeps the tractors and cars shipshape."

"So he's worked here awhile." It wasn't that he was a big fan of Lindsay's, but that cowboy looked like trouble.

"Six, eight months, maybe." He turned to Jesse. "Why do you want to know?"

It was Jesse's turn to shrug. "Just curious. He doesn't seem like Lindsay's type."

"Most men are her type, you ask me. She probably needs him to work on her car." Casey adjusted his suspenders. "Gotta get back to work. See you around."

"Right." Jesse stood back a ways, watching the eldest Martin daughter.

Tennessee nodded to whatever Lindsay was saying, his eyes never leaving her face. He moved closer, crowding her so she had to back up. She looked up and spotted Jesse watching her. Almost defiantly, she beamed a smile at Tennessee and put on her sunglasses before briefly squeezing his arm. Without looking right or left, she hurried down the walkway to her Corvette. Once inside, she revved the powerful engine before zooming out through the arches, tires screeching. Tennessee watched until her car was out of sight, then straightened his hat and went into the barn.

Jesse decided he'd give a goodly sum to know what that conversation had been about.

Abby waved goodbye to the last child of the day. Only three o'clock but she was more tired than usual. Probably because she wasn't sleeping well. And when she did fall asleep, dreams disturbed her rest. Dreams where she was with Jesse and she didn't stop him, but instead made love with him as she so desperately wanted to do.

She was truly torn, she admitted to herself as she went into the schoolhouse to straighten up the toys. On the one hand, she wanted Jesse to leave so temptation didn't entice her at every turn. On the other hand, she *didn't* want him to leave, hoping for a miracle.

Sure, like that would happen.

With a final glance around the room, Abby strolled outside. Her mother's flowers looked a little soggy after yesterday's rain, but it was a beautiful day with the sky so blue and not a cloud in sight. The grass was thick and green, making her wish she was a kid again, running barefoot through it.

It was quiet this afternoon. Dad was out somewhere on the range, Lindsay was heaven-only-knew-where since her car was gone and her mother had taken Grace shopping for a new bathing suit. Abby removed the clip from her hair and shook it out. It would be a good day for a swim, but she didn't feel like saddling up and riding out.

Walking toward Jesse's cabin, she wondered if he was inside. She heard he'd managed to ride Red this morning, leaving the men who watched awestruck since the mare had been unusually spirited before Jesse's whispers and gentle touch had mastered her. He was good at that, taming females, human and equine.

Stepping onto his porch, she saw that the door was open, the screen letting in the summer air. She knocked twice, waited and knocked again. No sound from within. Very trusting of him to leave his cabin with only the screen door between his quarters and the outside world. She hadn't been inside this cabin since Dad had had it fixed up. Through the screen, she saw a big, comfortable-looking couch, an easy chair, a couple of tables and a reading lamp. Jesse had added no personal items to make the place homey, but most likely that was because he hadn't planned on staying long.

Back to that again, Abby thought, leaving the porch. She was about to cross the walkway and go home when she heard pounding coming from behind Jesse's cabin. Curious, she followed the sound and found him nailing a board in place to what looked to be a miniature house. He was stripped to the waist, the strong muscles of his back rippling as he hammered away, absorbed in what he was doing.

He was a fantastic specimen of male, she thought, not for the first time, as she studied him. His skin was tan and smooth, damp from his exertions in the heat of the sun. Her fingers itched to touch his thick, dark hair. Just above the waistband of his jeans, she noticed a scar perhaps four inches long, probably a souvenir from his accident, like the one on his left leg.

Jughead was asleep in the sun in a patch of grass, but when Jesse stopped hammering, the dog opened his eyes and noticed Abby. He came rushing over eagerly, all but knocking her over.

Jesse turned and saw her trying to cope with the exuberant yet clumsy dog and smiled. "Well, hello."

Hunkering down to pet the frantic pooch, she tried to fend off his wet kisses. "Hello, yourself. Jug, enough, okay?"

"Jug, leave her alone," Jesse said, motioning toward the grass. "Go back to your spot."

Brushing dog hair from her shirt and shorts, Abby watched the dog quietly return to the grassy area. "He listens to you. Do you whisper to dogs, too?"

"Dogs and horses, yes. It's just women I can't get to first base with." He softened his words with a smile, then gestured to the dollhouse. "What do you think? Will Grace like it?"

Surprised that the dollhouse was for Grace and not her entire class, Abby took a moment to answer. "You made it for Grace?"

"Mm-hmm. We were talking one day when we walked with Grandpa." He thought she knew that Vern and Grace walked with him nearly every day before dinner. "She said she had lots of little dollies but no house for them and no furniture. There was this scrap lumber in the barn and Casey said I could use it." He pointed to several small cans of paint. "I got those at Curly's. Red, green, blue and yellow. It's going to be a colorful house."

Trying to warm to the idea, Abby nodded. "It sure is. She'll love it. I'm just surprised you went to all that trouble." Was he beginning to suspect that Grace was his child? No, that couldn't be.

"Why not? She's a great kid and I've got the time." He picked up a piece of sandpaper and began smoothing the rough edges. "Do you know where I could get some small furniture?"

"I think there's a toy store in Springerville. If not, I'm sure there is in Holbrook."

"Great. Maybe you'd come with me and help me choose."

"Maybe." It was really a lovely little house, Abby thought. There was a veranda and the first level had four rooms, presumably the living space, and up a staircase were four bedrooms, one large and three smaller, plus what she guessed were two bathrooms. "Do you do woodworking as a hobby?"

"Nah. This is the first thing I've ever made. I've got a magazine inside with a picture of one. It wasn't that hard to make." He paused to gaze at her. She had her hair down, falling to her shoulders, looking soft and golden in the sun. She wore a black sleeveless top, khaki shorts and white athletic shoes. Just last night, he'd held her, kissed her and stroked her full breasts, and now, he struggled with the overpowering urge to touch her again.

Under his intense scrutiny, Abby felt a warmth that had nothing to do with the sun spread through her. She broke eye contact and stepped back. "I came over to extend an invitation. The Walkers, who own that big ranch down the road, are having their annual Fourth of July potluck dinner tonight. Remember, I mentioned that they have this big arena? They put on a huge spread. The men play horseshoes outside and the younger ones play touch football. And there's a small band for dancing or just listening. Everyone's invited."

"You're going, then?"

"Sure. It's a lot of fun."

"What about Grace? Is she going to be there?"

A fleeting frown came and went on her face as she wondered briefly why her daughter interested him. "No, Mom's going to stay with her. She doesn't care for these gatherings. Most people don't take children younger than ten or twelve." She found a teasing smile. "You do dance, don't you?" She'd seen his limp, noticeable mostly when he was tired, and wondered if it kept him from dancing.

"Oh, yeah. My brother and I went to Miss Sadie Crenshaw's School of Dance for five years, attending a formal cotillion at the end of each season. Dad wanted us to be well-rounded men." He saw surprise move into her eyes as she tried to picture that.

Abby was at a loss for words. Five years of dance lessons? Unbelievable.

"You should have seen the outfits we wore. White satin shirt with an embroidered bolero jacket and black velvet pants plus patent leather dancing shoes. I guess because we were twins, we were the hit of the class, pictures in the paper, the whole nine yards."

"Really?" She could scarcely imagine this tall, rugged

man, even at a younger age, in the outfit he'd just described. Would wonders never cease?

Finally, the grin he'd been struggling with broke free and he laughed out loud. "No, not really, but I had you going there."

Smiling at last, she swatted his arm. "Oh, you!"

Jesse laughed again. "I'll have to tell Jake." He moved closer to her, chuckling. "Didn't have dance classes but I can hold my own. How about you?"

"The same. I learned mostly from watching others. As I mentioned, the Walkers have had this party every year as far back as I can remember."

"Are you asking me to be your date?" He sat down on a large tree stump at the edge of the cement patio.

"Not exactly. No one takes dates to this. Everyone just goes and dances with anyone they feel like. They have several group dances where you can get to know people because you're changing partners often."

"Are there a lot of singles in the area?"

"Some." Abby picked up a small discarded piece of wood, turning it over in her hands. "Are you looking?"

He kept his gaze on her face until she raised her eyes. "I'm looking at the loveliest woman on the planet. Why would I need anyone else?"

"Jesse, I…"

"Listen to me." He took her hand, tugged her closer. "How long do you want to keep up this charade? Why can't we let everyone see that we're interested in each other and let the chips fall where they may? Who will that upset?"

"Interested in each other," she repeated. "Is that what we are?"

Jesse shifted and pulled her down onto his lap. "Haven't you gotten the message yet? I care about you deeply. I want to explore these feelings, see where they take us. I want you to trust me again, to make love with me again. You're the reason I could never be happy with another woman. I think we have a future together, Abby. The question is, do you feel the same?"

She chose her words carefully. "I care about you, Jesse, you know I do. I have for years. But I just don't want my folks to know, not yet. I have my reasons. Please understand."

He studied her beautiful green eyes and he thought she was being sincere. But there was something more, something she wasn't telling him. He still had some time on the Martin ranch. He'd wait her out, but when he was ready to leave, she'd have to come to a decision.

He let out a frustrated sigh. "All right, Abby. We'll do it your way. For now." He saw the relief on her face and wondered about the seriousness of whatever she hadn't told him.

Abby touched her lips to his, softly, gently. Instantly, she felt the heat and knew he did, too. His arms tightened around her as he angled his head and took over. The kiss went on and on, yet wasn't nearly long enough. When he released her, she saw the haze of desire still on his face.

"Soon," she whispered. "Very soon." Then, with another quick kiss, she left, rushing off home.

Jesse closed his eyes and shook his head in frustration. He hoped Abby wasn't playing a game, stringing him out only to push him away, getting even for his long absence. She didn't seem to be that kind of woman.

But, like most men, he had a hell of a time figuring out females.

* * *

"Oh, Jesse! For me? Honest? To keep?" Grace was dancing around in her excitement as she looked at the finished
dollhouse that he'd carried over and placed under the tree in
front of the big house.

"Of course, it's for you and yes, to keep." Her smile lit
up her entire face and her blue eyes sparkled. That was reward enough for him, he thought. "Do you like it?"

"I *love* it. And it's not even my birthday." She knelt in
front of the colorful little house, checking out all the rooms.
"Omigosh! There's furniture inside. Wait till my dollies see
this."

Jesse sat down in the grass next to her, enjoying her pleasure. He'd gone shopping for some things, but he was sure
she'd want more. "Maybe one day soon, I can take you and
Mommy to the toy store and you can pick out more furniture."

Already rearranging the couch and chair, the tiny table
and lamps, Grace just beamed. Suddenly, she jumped up and
threw her arms around him, giving him a big hug. "Oh,
thank you, thank you so much."

"You're very welcome."

Moving back to the house, she began planning. "We need
more beds, 'cause I have lots of little dollies. And clothes to
put in the closet." She opened and closed the closet door with
one small finger. "Look! It works."

Coming out onto the porch of the big house, Abby paused,
gazing at her daughter and the man who didn't know he was
her father. Even so, he'd lovingly made her a dollhouse and
she could see how pleased he was that Grace was so happy.

Abby felt her heart turn over, just once, silently. If she
hadn't already been in love with him, this scene would surely

have done it. Dabbing at her suddenly moist eyes, she un-
abashedly listened to the two of them chatting away. How
many grown men would sit cross-legged on the grass and discuss dollhouse furniture with an excited little girl? She'd witnessed the hug, too, and had seen Jesse close his eyes and hug
her back.

Something was happening here, something beautiful.
Swallowing around a lump in her throat, she walked over to
join them.

At precisely seven, Jesse stood in front of the mirror in
the cabin's bedroom and inspected himself. Pale blue shirt
with pearl buttons, clean, almost new jeans, his boots polished. He'd gone all the way to Springerville for a haircut,
taken his shower, trimmed his beard, dabbed on a little af-
tershave.

"That's as good as it gets, folks," he told the mirror as he
picked up his keys. Walking outside, he saw that the Martins' Lincoln was gone. Apparently someone had fixed it.
Maybe that fellow, Tennessee. Lindsay's car was in its usual
parking space so she must have ridden over with the family.
Or maybe some guy picked her up.

In the mess hall today, Jesse heard the men talk about the
outing to the Walkers' as if it were the biggest event of the
year. He supposed it was, for guys who had little time off
and very few recreation choices. He hadn't hurried, though
he'd been told the festivities began around five o'clock, not
wanting to be among the first to arrive. Going to his Bronco,
he decided that if it was really hokey, he could always leave.

Driving over, he saw several cars, trucks and a couple of
Jeeps heading toward the big aluminum barn. As he neared,
he noticed that some people were walking over, probably

families who lived nearby. The grassy area to the right of the barn had been turned into a parking lot. Jesse found a space halfway down one of the rows.

He got out and pocketed his keys, wondering if Abby was already inside. He spotted a makeshift game of baseball quite a ways to the left and, just as Abby had predicted, several older men were tossing horseshoes along one side of the barn. Strolling over toward the double doors propped open, he noticed that someone had strung colored lights along the roofline. There were half a dozen guys playing cards at an outside table that sat under the beam of a bright light attached to the building.

A couple of men he recognized from the Martin ranch were lingering near the doors, smoking thin cigars as they greeted Jesse. After the rescue incident of the runaway horse, the hands all knew him, but he didn't know all their names. Nodding to them, he strolled inside.

A grandmotherly woman sat at a small table accepting donations toward the food. Jesse dug a ten from his wallet and earned a generous smile from the lady.

To the left were two long tables laden with food, everything from barbecued beef to corn on the cob, covered casseroles, baked beans, potato salad, jello and several large sheet cakes. Card tables for four or six covered in oilcloth were set all around the concrete floor. Longneck beer and soft drinks were chilling in tin washtubs alongside the buffet table. To the left was a large wooden dance floor and the band, consisting of banjo, guitar and zither, was warming up.

Jesse wasn't hungry but he decided to have a beer. He bent down and chose a frosty bottle, twisted off the top and took a refreshing swallow. The small band had a good sound and plenty of enthusiasm as they swung into a fast tune. In moments, the dance floor was crowded with smiling men and women of all ages, sizes and shapes. Never having seen anything quite like this in California, Jesse found himself smiling as he watched.

"Hey, cowboy," said a short brunette, coming up to Jesse and grabbing his hand. "C'mon. Let's have some fun."

"No, I..." But before he could say more, Jesse was out on the floor, dancing with a flirtatious young woman who had to reach way up to put her hand on his shoulder as they twirled about.

"Where have you been hiding, honey?" she asked, her smile a thousand watts.

"Here and there," he answered, then let go of her hand as another woman traded places with her. This one was a little taller and had strawberry-blond hair, a kewpie-doll mouth and a generous supply of freckles. "What's your name?" he asked.

"Tricia. What's yours?" She twisted under his arm, then back around.

"Jesse."

"Like Jesse James?" She laughed at her own joke, then gave him a quick wave as she handed him over to a young girl of about twelve with pigtails and braces on her teeth.

"Hi, I'm Rachel." Concentrating on her dance steps, she counted under her breath.

The interminable dance went on like that until Jesse was certain he'd danced with every female in the place except the one in diapers and a pink dress in the playpen in the corner. Finally, mercifully, the set ended. He thanked his last partner and scooted to the sidelines, reclaiming the beer he'd had to abandon. Taking several large sips, he leaned against the wall, letting his eyes roam the big building, looking for the one woman he wanted to dance with.

The next number was a slow one and he wished he could find Abby. He saw Vern at a far table and started toward him. But again, he was intercepted, this time by Lindsay. She was wearing a hot pink low-cut shirt and white slacks that were so tight he wondered if she could sit down in them.

"Hey, there," she drawled, which just happened to be the name of the song the band was playing. Capturing his arm, she all but dragged him toward the couples swaying to the old tune. "I think this is our dance."

Seeing no graceful way out, Jesse took hold of her. Immediately she plastered herself against him and tucked her head into his shoulder. But he wasn't having any.

Deliberately, he moved back and held her at a comfortable distance, the way you would dance with your maiden aunt. Her eyes flashed as she gazed up at him.

"Not much of a dancer, are you? Let me show you some moves." And again, she yanked him close.

Her heavy perfume made Jesse sneeze. "Excuse me. I think I'm catching a cold." Noticing that he was near the table where several Martin men were gathered, he set her back and shook his head. "I can't do this right now, Lindsay." Pulling out his handkerchief, he blew his nose loudly. "Sorry." And he walked away, dropping into an empty chair next to Slim.

"I saw that," Slim told him. "Not bad maneuvering. Usually when that barracuda gets her claws in a guy, takes hours to pry her loose." He saw that Jesse's hands were empty. "You want a beer?"

"I had one, but I put it down when Lindsay grabbed me."

"Not to worry." Long-legged and wiry, Slim loped over to the nearest washtub, snatched a cold brew and put it down in front of Jesse.

"Thanks, Slim." Jesse bent his head back and took a thirsty swallow. He listened to the other guys talking while his eyes wandered from table to table, from the buffet to the dance floor. The band ended another rousing tune and segued into "Cowboy, Take Me Away," made popular by the Dixie Chicks. Finally, he spotted Abby by the door. He stood up and watched her look around. At last, her eyes landed on him. He started walking toward her and at the same time, she moved toward him, never taking her eyes from his. People walked in front of them and around them, and still they glided toward each other.

They met on the dance floor. Abby's arms reached up to encircle him as his wound around her, their eyes still locked. Slowly they moved to the music.

"I've been waiting for you," Jesse said softly, for her ears only.

"Grace picked tonight to be fussy. She insisted I read not one but two stories to her before she settled down. I didn't want to leave Mom with a cranky child."

"She's okay?"

"Yes, fast asleep at last."

His hand at her back nudged her fractionally closer. She didn't pull away, instead she rose on tiptoe so her cheek would touch his. She released a small sigh of contentment as her fingers found their way into the hair at the nape of his neck. "You got a haircut."

"I was beginning to look a little shaggy."

"I like your hair a bit longer."

"I'll let it grow." He felt her smile.

"I was thinking of cutting my hair. It gets so hot in the summer on my neck."

He eased back, gazing at the golden cloud of hair that touched her shoulders. "Don't cut it. I love it long."

Abby cocked her head. "Why is it that men like long hair?"

Jesse gave a little shrug. "Makes a woman more feminine, I guess." He pulled her close again, burying his nose in the fragrance of her hair. "You smell so good."

"You smell like beer."

"Does that mean I can't kiss you until I brush my teeth and use mouthwash?"

"Not necessarily. I like beer."

Smiling, he kissed her hair and wished they were alone. He wondered how long they'd have to stay and just when it would be okay to sneak away. And would she come home with him?

Pulling back, Abby gazed across the dance floor and frowned. "Did you have words with my sister today? She's looking daggers at us and I haven't talked to her since yesterday."

Jesse angled his head and saw Lindsay standing by a pole looking right at him, her brown eyes furious. "Yeah, I did. She pulled me onto the dance floor and I wasn't in the mood. Her cologne made me sneeze so I told her I had a cold and needed to sit down."

"Oh, and here you are dancing with me."

"Does that bother you? I suppose I shouldn't have…"

"No, no. Don't be silly. She shouldn't have forced you to dance with her. Listen, if it wasn't that, it'd be something else. With Lindsay, it's always something."

The song ended but Jesse didn't want to let her out of his arms. He held her loosely, gently swaying while the band decided what they were going to play next. When he looked again in the direction where Lindsay had been, he saw she was seated at a table deep in conversation with Tennessee. "I didn't want to hurt her feelings, but she simply won't take no for an answer."

Jesse didn't realize he'd spoken aloud until Abby looked up at him. "Don't blame yourself."

"Rejection's hard to take, I'm sure. I told her I simply wasn't interested, but she keeps coming back."

"When did you tell her that?"

His big hands stroked her back through her soft white blouse. She had on a floral skirt that swirled around her slender legs and strappy white shoes. She was so damn beautiful that he almost lost his train of thought.

"A couple of days ago. She came to my cabin."

Abby had suspected as much. "She'd been drinking?" He nodded his head. "And she came on to you?"

"Yeah, but I'm sure I'm not the first or the last. The truth is that Lindsay wants whatever you have."

Her hands on his chest, she felt his strong heartbeat. "And she thinks I have you." It wasn't a question. "Do I?"

Jesse bent his face close to hers. "In every way that matters."

Abby tensed, afraid to ask the next question, afraid not to. "What are you trying to say?"

"That I love you. That I probably have all along but I was too wrapped up in myself, too angry about your fast marriage, to admit it even to myself."

Her eyes searched his, wanting desperately to see the truth there. At last, she spoke. "I love you, too, Jesse," she whispered.

A spirited couple breezed by and bumped them. Jesse realized that another dance number had begun and they hadn't noticed.

He spoke into her ear. "Let's get out of here."

"Yes," she said quietly.

Without a word to anyone, they made their way to the door and hurried out.

Casey noticed them leaving together and began to worry.

Vern noticed them leaving and decided that Abby could do worse than to marry a man who was a successful rancher.

Lindsay noticed them leaving and the anger inside her built and built.

Chapter Nine

The ride in the Bronco on the bumpy grass of the Walker compound had Abby and Jesse bouncing.

"Sorry," Jesse commented as the top of his head grazed the ceiling, "but the late arrivals have parked all over the place. I have to go out of our way and maneuver around them to reach the road."

"It's all right," Abby answered. She could use the time to settle the argument she'd been having with herself. Her nerves had been on edge since kissing him yesterday behind the cabin. She had the feeling that they'd come to a point in their relationship where she'd have to decide either to stay with him or send him away.

She'd looked around at the dance tonight, checking out various couples, some married, some not, mostly people she'd known all her life. She'd seen Josie Freemont who'd fallen in love with a man who wanted to marry her, but he was a fisherman from New England and Josie had been afraid to take a chance on the unknown. That had been four years ago and Josie, who worked at the drugstore in town, still had that lost and lonely look.

There was Bret Wilson, who'd wanted to join the Marines but his father had said he was needed on the ranch so he'd given up his dream. Only two out of several who'd been afraid to take a chance, to stand up for what they wanted. She didn't have to look any further than her sister. Lindsay was bitter about her broken wedding plans, jealous of other women who had men in their lives, unhappily drinking herself silly night after night.

Abby swayed as Jesse eased around a long white truck with huge wheels and knew she should add her own name to the list. She'd given up on men, marriage, a home of her own and settled for living with her parents and working with children. True, it was work she enjoyed, but she had no personal life beyond her daughter, the kids and her horses. Her disillusionment with being abandoned had left her too afraid to try a new relationship; not that many men had shown interest. Or perhaps she'd been so busy pining away for Jesse that she hadn't noticed anyone else.

Looking around tonight, she'd been reminded that time was short and second chances didn't come along too often. Perhaps it would be a mistake to give in to her feelings for Jesse a second time. Perhaps she'd be hurt again.

But the truth was that she'd been living her life in a sort of vacuum, waiting for she knew not what. She knew that Grace would love having a father, but she couldn't be untrue to her feelings and marry someone she didn't love. Because her feelings about love always revolved around Jesse Calder.

The Bronco surged over a small ditch and finally made it

out onto the road. As Jesse straightened the vehicle, Abby turned to look at him. He was here, hers for the taking. She knew exactly what he had in mind when he suggested they get out of there. Giving in to her feelings for Jesse would be a risk, but then, life was full of risks. If she didn't reach out for him now, if she didn't allow herself the chance to know that kind of love again, she'd surely regret it the rest of her life.

Dancing with him, close in his embrace, feeling his heartbeat against hers, she knew only that she wanted him desperately. In that moment, the downside of being with him melted away. She could feel how much he wanted her, cared for her.

"So where do you want to go, home?" Jesse asked, slowing down. He'd been watching her as a profusion of emotions played across her expressive face. She was struggling with a decision, he knew, which was why he gave her a choice. If she were to stay with him, he needed to hear her say it out loud.

Her eyes in the dim light of the dash were luminous. "No. I want to be with you." She'd made her decision and there'd be no going back.

His soft blue eyes reflected pleasure and anticipation. "Are you sure?" he asked, for the final time.

"Very sure."

Smiling, he stepped on the gas and reached over to take her hand in his. He noticed that nerves had her fingers damp and trembling. Now that she'd agreed, he was a bit nervous, too. "What about Grace? And your mother?"

"Once asleep, Grace rarely awakens during the night and if she should, my mother is there. As to her, I'll deal with Mom when the time comes."

Jesse wished there was a five-star luxury hotel nearby and

he could take her into a lovely suite. Always before when they'd been together, it had been under the trees near the stream or up in the hayloft. Abby deserved better. But all he had to offer was his cabin.

"If we go to my place, will your folks be upset?" Again, he wished they could tell Vern and Joyce about their relationship, be open and up front. "Your dad might have seen us leave together or someone may have told him."

"I'm nearly twenty-six, Jesse. I'm entitled to a personal life without asking their approval." Joyce, she knew, would wonder and perhaps worry. Still, her mother wouldn't question her. It wasn't her way. "I don't plan to stay too long. They may suspect I was with you, but they won't really know."

The nearly full moon was high in the sky as Jesse parked the Bronco in his usual space. Abby stepped down and glanced toward the big house. It was dark except for a light in the living room. Joyce was likely sitting and reading or watching television. She always waited up for Vern on the rare nights he went out.

The compound was eerily quiet. No one was about as Jesse took her hand and led her up the porch steps of his cabin. Inside, he locked the door, something he seldom did. He wanted no unexpected surprises tonight. Without turning on any lights and still holding her hand, he walked her to the bedroom at the back of the house. Lucky for him that Flora, the young woman who did the Martins' laundry, had been there today to change the sheets and towels, and to take his personal laundry. He turned the lamp on the nightstand on low.

Abby glanced around at the walnut-paneled walls, the pine dresser and four-poster bed and a maple rocker by the lone window. Her mother had decorated the cabin with a navy-and-tan striped area rug over plank flooring, beige cov-erlet and white wood blinds that Jesse closed, wrapping them in their own private world.

She noticed a connecting bath with the door slightly ajar and saw Jesse close the bedroom door as well. "Locking us in, are you?" she asked, her voice teasing.

What worried him was a possible invasion from Lindsay, but he didn't mention that as he walked close to her. "I just want you all to myself."

"You have me." Abby pressed her lips together nervously.

He studied her face. "You're a little scared, aren't you? I remember that you used to do that with your mouth when you got scared."

She couldn't lie or brush him off, not with him gazing into her eyes. "Yes." Her voice was whisper soft.

"That makes two of us."

Her brows shot up. "You, scared? Hard to believe." The Jesse she'd known before and the one now seemed unafraid of anything. Yet she relaxed a little knowing he might have a case of nerves also. "Certainly not of me."

"Yes, of you." His hands rested on her forearms, his thumbs caressing the sensitive skin there. "You always scared me. You were so young, still a teenager, and so very beautiful. I felt I had no business touching you."

She smiled at that. "Ah, but I wanted you to touch me." She shifted slightly closer. "Actually, you were the one out of reach. I'd been warned repeatedly to stay away from the cow-boys, and here was this handsome guy with this swaggering walk…"

"Swaggering? I never swaggered."

"Yes, you did." She placed her hands at his waist. "I used to find excuses to watch you work in the barn or I'd ride out when you were repairing fences. You used to take off your shirt." Lazily, she began unbuttoning his shirt. "And sometimes you'd tie this red bandanna around your forehead to keep your hair out of your eyes. You were hot and sweaty and enormously appealing."

"Is that so?"

"Mm-hmm." She tugged his shirt from the waistband of his jeans and slipped it off his shoulders. "My mouth would go dry watching you." Running her fingers through the hair on his chest, she licked her lips. "Like it is now. But back then, I was afraid to speak to you, even though I'd seen you watching me. I was sure you could read everything on my face, my every thought."

Jesse drew her nearer until their lower bodies were slightly touching, lightly teasing. "And if I could have read those thoughts, what would I have learned?"

No turning back, Abby told herself. She'd wanted to be alone like this with him, to have uninterrupted hours together like they'd never had before. She'd wanted to love him, but also to talk, to close the gap and bridge six long years. *All or nothing,* she decided.

She swallowed and reached for her nebulous courage. "You'd have learned that I was crazy about you."

His smile was warm, his eyes heavy-lidded. "I wish I'd known. I'd have grabbed you up onto my horse and ridden off, then had my way with you." He raised a hand to trail along one silken cheek.

"As I recall, you did get around to that." Then she turned serious. "After you left, heaven knows I tried to forget you."

"Was that why you got married, another effort to forget me?"

On shaky ground here, Abby thought. "I told myself I was

over you, that you no longer mattered. It didn't work. You were always there, in the back of my mind."

If Jesse thought her answer evasive, he didn't let on.

"It was the same for me. It was always you." Fiercely he gathered her close, his anger aimed at himself. "I shouldn't have gone away without giving you my real name, but I had no way of knowing what would happen. Everything would be so different now." Grace would be his daughter instead of another man's child. And the woman he was holding would be his wife.

Abby kissed his bearded cheek, trying to soothe his troubled thoughts, to comfort, to kiss away the lingering bitterness. "Let's not do this, Jesse. What's done is done and can't be changed. We both made mistakes, we both have regrets we have to live with."

Jesse held her away so he could look deeply into her eyes. "I need you to know that I never stopped wanting you, even when I knew you were another man's wife. I pretended I was over you, but I wasn't."

Abby slid her arms around him as something stirred inside her. Was it the release of the resentment she'd built up over the years? Was it the reaffirmation of a love too strong to die? And then there was the guilt she felt for the terrible secret she'd kept from him, and was still keeping from him. That, too, she'd have to get rid of, and soon. She was tired of the subterfuge.

But she could be honest about one thing. "There must have been at least an hour or so during those six years when I didn't think of you at all, but I can't remember it." However, she wanted him to know the downside as well. "To be honest, many times I thought of you with disappointment, with anger."

Jesse nodded. "I know that, and I'm sorry I let you down,

sorry I hurt you. If I had it to do over…but then, hindsight is twenty-twenty, right?" He hoped he'd learned, hoped he was a better man now then back then. "We all have some baggage we bring to a relationship, Abby. Most of mine is packed away for good, but occasionally something slips out."

Abby thought of the dark secret she'd kept from him, the one thing that could blow this tenuous reunion sky-high, and knew she had her own fair share of baggage. She would have to deal with that one day, but not this day. "Mine, too. None of us can live several decades and not have some past problems. But let's not go there tonight. Let's not think about any of that. Let's enjoy our time together."

He was glad she'd said that since he was more than ready. He couldn't take his eyes off her face, her beautiful face. The need for her was growing huge. "Do you know how very much I want you this minute? But I need you to be very, very sure. Tell me now if you've changed your mind, before we go any further. I don't want to hurt you again."

Slowly, with a smile forming, Abby shook her head. "I haven't changed my mind." Her breath whispered out of her parted lips. "I never had any pride where you're concerned." Rising on tiptoe, she brought her lips within a hairbreadth of his. "Make love with me, Jesse."

The invitation he'd imagined in his restive dreams, the fantasy that had played over and over in his tortured mind, was here at last. He walked her over to the bed, took her hand and saw that it was trembling. "It's all right," he said, cradling her face. "Don't be nervous and don't be scared. We'll go slowly, take our time."

To Abby, they weren't just two people who'd been without for too long, reaching out to the first available partner.

It wasn't that she wanted a man to satisfy this incessant craving. She wanted *this* man because only he seemed able to awaken her. "Yes, we have lots of time." They had unresolved differences between them and a secret she'd need to reveal to Jesse before long, but at least here in the bedroom, she knew they were very compatible.

"I've thought about this so often, wanted this so badly," he whispered to her. The first kiss was a tender meeting of lips, a gentle exploration. There was hesitancy and rebirth and finally an acknowledgement of the familiar. The gloriously familiar. Then his hands moved to unzip the skirt she was wearing. "I want to see you. I want to watch your face when I touch you." He remembered how her eyes used to go hazy with passion as his hands had roamed over her flesh.

Ever a match for him, Abby fumbled with his belt. "I want to see you, too."

They were down to the bare essentials in a matter of seconds, then Jesse pulled back the coverlet on the bed. Standing very still, they took their time looking, remembering, noting changes.

"I can't believe you had a child," he told her. "You're as slender as ever."

She noticed a scar low on his chest, raised but no longer red, and traced it with a finger. "Does this hurt still?"

"Not anymore." Then he eased her onto the bed crosswise and followed to lean over her. His heart was hammering in his chest, but he forced himself to take a deep breath, to slow down. For her sake as well as his.

For if ever there was a woman made to savor, he was looking at her. Jesse sent his hands threading through Abby's long, thick hair, letting the blond strands fall back in a cloud to frame her lovely face. Like a blind man might, his fingers traced the features of her face, as if memorizing them. They skimmed along a silken eyebrow, across the bridge of her small nose, along her cheeks and circled her stubborn chin. Then his lips followed the same path, pausing to plant warm, moist kisses on her closed eyelids and the corners of her mouth.

He heard a soft sigh escape from her, her body no longer able to lie still. He felt her fingers slide into his hair and grip his head, guiding his mouth back to hers. The kiss was slow and easy at first, but heated rapidly as he stroked along her shoulders, slipping off her bra. Breaking the kiss, he bent to flick his tongue over nipples hardening under his tender attention.

Everything was new, Abby thought, yet achingly familiar. The feel of his callused hands on her skin brought back a rush of memories, yet thrilled her even more than before. It was so easy to fall back into the ways of the past, as if they'd shared all the nights since, as if intimacy so intense was theirs alone. It was so thrilling to let him explore places untouched since the last time they'd been together. It was so wonderful to again feel her body come alive, her heart beat furiously, her breath catching in her throat as he worked his magic on her.

Her skin quivered as he took his mouth on a journey of her, taking his time, ignoring the impatient sounds she made. She felt his clever hands remove the last silken barrier and toss it aside, then she arched as his fingers moved inside her. So ready was she that in seconds she cried out as the first powerful wave took her. She forgot her own name as her eyes closed in acute pleasure.

Watching her eloquent face as she let go, Jesse fought back the need to bury himself deep inside her. Aroused beyond belief just looking at her, with monumental effort he held on to his control, needing to make this wondrous night perfect for Abby.

The softness of a woman had for too long been missing from his life—the silken hair, the gentle female touch, the soothing voice, the lightly floral fragrance, the moist welcome of her body. He needed this, needed her, more than he could put into words.

She was a small woman with exquisitely fragile bones and a delicate build. She was tough when she needed to be, he knew, yet there was a fragility to her that slowed his moves and made him more tender. She'd always been so openly responsive, so trusting that he felt awed at the gift she gave him. He watched her blink to clear her vision, her every emotion visible on her lovely face.

She never held back, and that humbled him. There was a generosity to her that he'd never known in anyone else. That alone had him wanting to please her, to pleasure her in every way possible. And he would, but for now, his control was rapidly slipping as he yanked off his briefs. When her seeking hands closed around him, he knew he had very little time left.

Shifting to the side, he paused to protect them both, then turned back to her. An expectant smile played on her lips, lips slightly swollen from his kisses. Their eyes locked as at last he slipped into her. He heard her sharp intake of breath as she adjusted to the shape and feel of him. Then her arms encircled him as she shifted to allow him to go deeper.

Home. Finally, he'd come home, Jesse thought as he began an easy rhythm. Slowly, savoring the feel of her, he didn't rush, not for long minutes. Not until he heard her breath catch and knew she was about to tumble over the edge. Only then did he give in and allow himself to follow her.

From somewhere on the ranch, the sharp whinny of a horse could be heard, carried on the still summer air. Inside, two lovers peaked and collapsed, still in each other's arms.

Wearing one of Jesse's white T-shirts that skimmed her knees, Abby sat cross-legged on his bed, munching on an apple. Opposite her, wearing gray cotton boxers, Jesse devoured a pear. They hadn't eaten at the dance and realized moments ago that they were famished.

"Sorry I don't have anything but fruit and beer or wine," he told her. "I picked up a few things at Curly's, but mostly I eat at the mess hall." He topped off both glasses of chilled chardonnay.

"Mmm, this hits the spot." She sipped the cool wine, feeling contented.

Had she always been this agreeable? he asked himself, then decided that the answer was yes. He curled a hand along her jaw, caressing her cheek. "I can't remember ever feeling this good."

Heat pinked her cheeks as she pictured them making love in this very bed an hour ago, then showering together, something she'd never done before. And there in the steamy room with water pouring over them, he'd reached for her again. She'd been just as ready, just as eager. "Nor I," she said, smiling.

"I don't want this to end," Jesse said. "Will you spend the night?"

A whole night in his arms, something she'd longed for, for what seemed like forever. To wake in his embrace, to be free to touch him, to love him, whenever she pleased. It was a dream come true.

Only she had responsibilities, obligations. The kids for

her school arrived early, depending on their parents' schedules. She usually spent an hour or more preparing their meals, planning the day with Susie.

And there was Grace. Joyce had watched her all evening, but she didn't want to take advantage of her mother, especially since her back pain had worsened and the frequency of her migraines had increased. Glancing at the bedside clock, she saw that it was nearly midnight. Joyce would still be up, but she hated to call.

"Let me think about it, okay?"

"Maybe I can persuade you," Jesse murmured, kissing the soft spot on her throat where her pulse throbbed.

"I think you could probably persuade the Eskimos to buy ice cubes," she told him, smiling.

They heard several carloads of cowboys returning from the dance, a couple of the guys loudly singing off-key. But not Vern Martin's Lincoln or Lindsay's Corvette. "I didn't picture your dad as a party animal staying until the very end."

The very thought had her smiling. "He doesn't, usually." Abby finished her apple and wiped her mouth, feeling good, feeling glorious.

Just then, they heard the unmistakable hum of the Lincoln and the roar of the Corvette. By unspoken agreement, they got up and walked out into the dark living room. Huddled together, they peeked through the slanted blinds. They saw Vern get out of the car and look over toward Jesse's cabin, probably noting that his Bronco was in its usual parking spot. Without a word to Lindsay, who was staring at the cabin, Vern went inside.

But not Lindsay. She stood looking at the cabin, one hand propped on her hip, her elbow bent. She scrutinized the area for some time, then started walking over. Jesse dropped the slat and whispered to Abby to follow him into the bedroom. Closing the door, he put a finger up to his lips as he turned out the lamp. Sitting on the bed, they waited.

They heard Lindsay march up the porch steps, then knock loudly on the front door. She rattled the screen door, but it wouldn't give. Next she called out Jesse's name twice, quite loudly.

"Does she have a key?" Abby asked, keeping her voice low.

"Not that I know of," Jesse answered.

Moments later, they heard her footsteps leaving the porch. But Jesse indicated that they should stay put. He'd guessed right for suddenly, there was a sharp banging on the bedroom window. Neither one of them spoke or moved.

Again, Lindsay pounded. "Jesse, I know you're in there," she shouted.

"You don't suppose she's going to do something stupid, do you?" Abby whispered.

"You mean, like burn the place down? I don't think so. I think she's had too much to drink, probably saw us leave together and she's mad as a wet hen."

Some minutes later, Jesse got up and went into the living room to peek outside. He came back and reported that an angry Lindsay had stormed inside the big house.

Abby breathed a sigh of relief. "I can't believe her. What did she hope to accomplish by rousting you?"

"Who knows?" Jesse shrugged. "And who cares? You know her better than I do. Why does she do the things she does?"

"I wish I knew."

"My guess would be jealousy, feelings of inadequacy, frustration, low self-esteem, mostly stemming from her disappointment in the two men she'd wanted to marry. You know, she told me that *she* called off the wedding."

"Sort of, I suppose. She wanted to live in San Francisco because she loves the social life there. Adam wanted a simple life, even considered working the ranch with Dad. When Lindsay told him she hated the ranch, that she wanted out, he told her that that was too bad because he didn't think she'd fit in with his family and friends in California." Abby sighed. "That's a lot to deal with. I feel bad for her. I wish she'd find someone who'd love her unconditionally."

Always the compassionate one, Jesse thought as he turned the lamp on low. Abby was filled with empathy for children, animals and grown-ups who'd lost their way. It would be nice if Lindsay had some of those virtues. "She won't until she stops putting herself first in everything. I don't think she cares much about anyone."

Abby shifted so she was facing him. "She cares for Grace. I think she envies me for having such a beautiful child. She forgets her selfish ways when she's with Grace. She takes her shopping, buys her fun toys and she's teaching her chess."

Jesse was surprised. "At five? Is Grace catching on?"

"She sure is. She beat Dad one evening last week, and he claims he didn't *let* her win, that she won fairly."

"Well, look at the bright mother she has. Was her father smart?" He wished she'd talk more about the man who'd won her over so quickly.

"Yes, her father's very intelligent." She couldn't help herself on that one. Maybe he wouldn't catch it.

No such luck. "You mean *was* smart?"

The ringing of the phone saved Abby from having to answer his question.

Frowning, Jesse reached for the bedside phone. "Who could that be at this hour?" He picked it up. "Hello?"

"Mr. Calder? This is Joyce Martin."

Surprised, Jesse sat up. "Yes, Mrs. Martin." He saw Abby's eyes widen. "Is there a problem?"

"Is…is Abby there with you?" Her voice was hesitant, cool.

"Yes, she is. Just a moment." He pressed the phone against his side, covering the mouthpiece. "She guessed that you're here," he whispered. "You want to talk with her?" He wanted to tell Abby that they should just quit all the sneaking around. But they were her parents and it should be her call.

Abby held out a slightly trembling hand for the phone, hoping nothing was wrong with Grace. "Hello, Mom. Is Grace all right?"

"She's fine, still asleep." There was a pause while Joyce collected her thoughts. "Your father said that you left the dance early with Jesse Calder."

"Yes, that's right."

"I see. How long are you planning to stay with him?"

"I'm not sure. I…" This was silly. She was a grown woman who shouldn't have to get permission from her parents nor be obligated to give explanations. "Mom, I'll be home in time to get Grace's breakfast."

A longer pause this time. "Well, all right, if you're sure you know what you're doing."

"I am. Thanks, Mom. I'll see you in the morning." Not waiting for a reply, Abby hung up the phone, then let out a whoosh of air as she fell back on the bed. "I should be relieved and instead I feel guilty. Mothers have a way of doing that without saying much."

"Don't let her make you feel guilty. You're not doing anything wrong."

"Yes, I know, but nevertheless…" She remembered that he had not known his mother. "Didn't your father ever make you feel guilty about something?"

"Mmm, not really. If anything, I feel guilty that I wasn't there when he had his heart attack."

"But he's the one who sent you away, so how could you have been?"

"I know. Guilt isn't always logical." He stretched out beside her, one hand playing with her hair. "Your mother should be proud of you, not critical. Does she expect you to live like a nun the rest of your days? It can't be easy, raising a child without a father, being responsible for a dozen and a half youngsters in preschool, working with physically challenged kids in the riding program. You do it all and you don't complain. You should be proud of yourself, too."

She let down her guard just a little. "It's not the path I would have chosen, but I wouldn't trade a moment with Grace for any other life."

Jesse stared off into the distance for several seconds. "I wonder how many of us ever wind up on a path of our own choosing, or if circumstances dictate what happens to us." He brought his gaze back to hers. "Things happen and we cope to the best of our ability, I suppose."

Abby thought of his accident, the pain and suffering he'd endured, and none of it had been his fault. "They say it's not what happens to us that matters, but how we handle the things that happen to us. I admire you tremendously for the way you forced your body to rehabilitate and heal. That couldn't have been easy."

"Hey, I think we're getting too serious. Let's not talk about parents or the past. It's too crowded in this room. We don't need them in here with us. We came here to be alone, just the two of us." He pressed his lips to her open palm, a soft, tender kiss.

There was a great deal unsettled between them, Abby thought again. But oh, Lord, how she loved this man. Loved his dark head that she now caressed, his hard body, his strong face. "You know, I never kissed a man with a beard until you," she told him, tracing the outline of his chin.

"And look at your face, all red from rubbing against my beard. I should shave it off."

"No, don't. I like it." She guessed he'd grown it to camouflage small scars on his face from the flying glass of the windshield. "I don't mind a little red skin." She kissed him, slowly, sweetly. "Mmm, that's definitely worth it."

Jesse urged her to sit up while he pulled off the T-shirt, freeing her beautiful breasts for his eyes to devour. He looked his fill, then touched with tender fingertips and finally tasted.

Closing her eyes, Abby forgot about everyone and everything else but the wondrous feelings he was stirring up inside her again.

Chapter Ten

Nearly a dozen men were gathered near the round pen to see if Jesse could get Remus to allow a rider on his back. This was the moment everyone had been waiting for, the reason he'd been hired.

Jesse had been rehearsing in his mind exactly how he was going to accomplish this, because every horse was different. He'd gotten Remus used to his voice so he could explain to the onlookers what he was doing and why.

Warned that they had to be quiet, Vern and Casey waited near the fence while Abby stayed by the gate. The others sat on the grass or leaned against the barn. It was ten o'clock in the morning and the hot July sun was high in the sky.

Already accustomed to the bridle, Remus stood at the far side, chewing at the bit that sat across his mouth, familiarizing himself with it all over again.

Jesse came out of the barn carrying a saddle and saddle pad. Abby opened the gate and he walked in, motioning her to step inside with him. He positioned the equipment in the middle of the round pen, then strolled over to stand alongside Abby.

Speaking softly to the men, Jesse kept his eyes on the stallion. "We're treating Remus as if he'd never had a saddle on his back, much less a rider. The traumas he endured might well have caused him to block out memories of that part of his past life. I want him to get used to the saddle before putting it on him. Horses don't like surprises any more than we do."

Concentrating on Remus, Jesse nevertheless heard a couple of the men mumbling aloud their doubts. Most hadn't had the time to watch the stallion's progress and still thought of him as wild and out of control when approached.

Jesse glanced at Abby as she sat on the top rung, looking fresh in jeans and a bright green shirt that matched her eyes. Her fair skin still showed a slight redness around her mouth and chin from his beard, but she didn't seem to mind. After last night, her mother knew they were a couple. Next they'd have to tell them about his deception. They'd get past that, he thought. Together, they could do anything.

Abby noticed his look and smiled, then placed a hand on his shoulder. No more hiding, she seemed to say.

His attention was drawn back to Remus, who was snorting and blowing at the saddle, wandering around it and finally coming to terms with it as his big head lowered and he sniffed. Moving back, he stood a short distance from the saddle and looked at Jesse as if to say, "I'm ready."

Slowly, Jesse moved toward Remus. "This horse, from our long sessions together, trusts me. I've been patient with him and he finally believes I won't hurt him. That's very important because a man hurt him in the past, which made him understandably skittish. He took to Abby, sensing that as a female, she was gentle and kind. Then came the fire and again, he felt trapped, the way he had on that other ranch where he'd been abandoned with no food or water, no means of escape until Abby came along and rescued him."

He walked closer and ran his hand along the stallion's strong neck. "He's ready now for the next step." Jesse put the saddle blanket in place, then slowly lifted the saddle onto Remus's back, quietly whispering to Remus as his big head turned to check things out. Jesse took the girth under his belly and buckled it up the other side. Using hand signals he'd worked out with the horse, he set him going in the opposite direction from where he stood, allowing him to get familiar with the saddle, with the weight on his back, all over again.

"Now I could get up into the saddle and there'd be no question that he'd let me ride him. But he's Abby's horse and he needs to remember that, to get used to her again." He signaled and Abby got down and walked slowly toward Remus.

Vern's face showed his concern. "Are you sure Abby will be safe?" he asked Jesse, using a low voice so he wouldn't startle the stallion.

"Absolutely. I wouldn't let anything happen to her."

Standing at his head, holding the reins, Jesse spoke to the men again. "I've explained to Abby how we're going to accomplish this so she knows what to expect. Vern, again I assure you, she's not in any danger."

He saw Vern nod, but he still wore a skeptical look.

Jesse nodded to Abby and she stroked the stallion's neck along with Jesse, then rubbed his flank and moved to the front to caress along the nose line between his eyes. When Jesse thought that the horse was happy with Abby's presence, he lifted Abby onto Remus's back and lay her across the saddle. With the reins, he turned the big horse's head this way and that, to make sure he saw her and knew who was climbing on. He took a moment to tell the men what he was doing and why, speaking softly in a nonthreatening voice. "This is the same method we used with Red."

Again he nodded to Abby and moving carefully, she lifted a leg over Remus's back and was upright in the saddle. Placing her booted feet firmly in the stirrups, she took the reins from Jesse.

When he'd first explained this to her, Abby had been hesitant. But he'd said that this would be the best way to regain Remus's trust. Besides that, she trusted Jesse when he said he'd never allow her to get hurt.

Abby walked the stallion around the ring, not bothering to change him to a trot or anything else. The object was simply to let him take stock of what was happening on his back, and to again get familiar with Abby.

After five minutes or so, Jesse went to them and took the reins while Abby dismounted and left the ring. "You don't want to overdo the first time. Tomorrow, she can ride him longer and soon, he'll look forward to those times. Then she can trust him out of the ring. Tomorrow, I'll saddle up Red, too. If anyone wants to volunteer to ride her, let me know. We do this all without restraints, harsh words or whips."

As Jesse led Remus toward the barn, Slim had a question.

"How many horses would you say you've broken this way?"

"I never use the term broken. It's a join up, where the horse and trainer join together to accomplish a goal. As to how many, well over a thousand by now, I'd guess." He saw the men wander away, shaking their heads in disbelief.

They'd seen his methods with their own eyes, yet they couldn't quite believe what they'd just witnessed. He heard Tex mumble something undoubtedly derogatory. Confident of the methods he'd learned, Jesse didn't react.

Abby, opening the gate, had overheard the men's doubts. "They'll come around." Though aware that her father was a short distance away, she reached up and hugged Jesse. "You were wonderful."

Surprised, he took her hand in his free one. "Do you have time to come into the barn with me while I put him in his stall or do you have to hurry back to the kids?"

Squeezing his hand, she smiled. "I'll *make* time. Susie's got the kids finger painting. That should keep them busy awhile."

Watching them disappear inside, Casey was more than a little worried. He glanced up at Vern, who was still staring at the open barn door.

"What's going on with those two?" Vern asked.

"Damned if I know," Casey answered, since it was the truth, and it worried him no end.

In his stall, Jesse removed Remus's equipment and gave him a carrot as reward. "You did just fine, big guy," he told the stallion.

"You're a miracle worker," Abby commented as Remus stood chewing his treat, docile once more.

Jesse came out and closed the stall door. "That's me." Not even checking to make sure they were alone, he took her in his arms and kissed her. It was long and loving and had him wanting more.

He glanced up toward the hayloft. "Want to take a break?" he asked, remembering another time when they'd climbed up and spent hours in the sweet-smelling hay.

"Is that why you asked me to come with you?" Still in the

circle of his arms, Abby smiled. "No, I really can't. I've got to get back to the kids."

"Actually, I was wondering how things went after you left last night." Abby had stayed, but not the whole night. Around four o'clock, they'd shared a long goodbye and she'd hurried back to the big house.

"Not bad. I took a shower, got a couple of hours' sleep, then went down to the kitchen to face the inquisition. Mom wanted to know if I knew what I was doing, the same question she'd asked me last night on the phone."

Jesse brought her up close so they were touching from the waist down, and locked his hands behind her back. "*Do* you know what you're doing?"

She gazed into his warm blue eyes. "I think so."

"Is that what you told your mother?"

"Not exactly. I reminded her that I was nearly twenty-six and that I was entitled to a personal life without asking her permission."

"And she was okay with that?"

Abby sighed. "Oh, probably not, but my mother doesn't reveal her emotions freely. However, she's crazy about Grace."

"So why don't we just have a family powwow, tell them that I was here before, explain the name thing and tell them how we feel, all of it?" Jesse wondered if she knew what a big step he'd taken with that question. Admitting that he cared for Abby would inevitably bring about questions like, Do you love her? Are you planning to marry? Where would you live?

Were love and marriage and a home together with Abby and Grace what he really wanted? Jesse asked himself, not for the first time. As always, when he thought along those lines, he remembered growing up with the bitterness of a father who'd loved and trusted a woman, yet she'd walked away anyhow. He didn't think Abby was like that, but how could he really be sure? Yet wasn't he the one who always said guarantees came with toasters, not people and not even horses?

"We will tell them," Abby said, finally answering his question. "When the time is right."

The ringing of the bell over the schoolhouse had her stepping back. "That's Susie, calling me. I'd better go." She gave him a light kiss. "I'll see you later."

Strolling back, Abby wondered why she was so reluctant to bring the past out into the open and step into the future. For six long years, she'd managed without a man in her life, convincing herself that she really didn't need anyone, that she was perfectly happy with the status quo. She'd raised Grace without a father and they'd done very nicely, thank you.

Until Jesse had come back.

Now here he was, handsome and charismatic, winning her over with his soulful kisses, his tender embraces, his passionate lovemaking, reminding her of what she'd been missing. And he'd charmed Grace until she sought him out whenever possible, though neither knew they were father and daughter. She felt a pang of guilt for keeping that information from them.

Head bent, Abby moved along the short path to the schoolhouse. She'd built a life for herself and Grace here. Where would loving Jesse take them? To California, to the unfamiliar, to his turf? She'd have to be very sure of her feelings and Jesse's before she'd uproot her daughter from all she'd known.

Sighing, she ducked into the schoolhouse, putting on a happy face for the children.

* * *

Late afternoon and Jesse was bored. He probably should have ridden out to one of the pastures and asked if anyone needed his help. But he hadn't and now it was too late to start a job.

Yawning, he got up out of the wicker chair he'd carried out onto the porch and decided to go to Curly's, buy a paper and some cold drinks.

Plus he had a special errand to run.

Climbing into the Bronco, he saw that Abby and Susie were in the process of herding the children outside for some games before they were picked up by their parents. He had another lesson with Charley and Sam tomorrow, plus he'd promised to oversee the men who'd volunteered to ride Red. There was a lot he could do, but basically, the thing he'd been called to the Martin ranch to do, help Remus, he'd pretty well accomplished. He'd been here just over a month and he could tell by his last phone call with Jake that his brother was anxious to have him get home. But there was something he had to do first.

Driving through the arches, Jesse stopped, saw there was no traffic and swung out, headed for the highway. But at the ramp, Jesse decided to take the side road rather than the highway since he was in no hurry. Despite the simmering heat, he had the windows down, enjoying a mild breeze.

Tonight, he'd ask Abby to marry him. He knew Grace liked him and he could see himself loving her, being a good father, having more children one day. The Martins, well, they'd get used to the idea of having him in the family. They probably wouldn't like it that he'd take Abby and Grace to California, but he thought mother and daughter would adjust to his ranch easily.

Curly knew the area well. He'd ask the storekeeper for directions to the nearest jeweler and he'd buy Abby a ring. An emerald to match her eyes surrounded by small diamonds. If he couldn't find that, he'd have to special order it.

Lazily ambling along, Jesse approached a curve in the road, feeling good at having come to a decision. A large old eucalyptus tree, one of many along this drive, was just ahead. He turned the wheel to follow the curve around to the right, only it seemed locked. Sitting up straighter, he put both hands on the steering wheel and tried to force it to the right. But the Bronco kept going straight.

"What the hell!" Jesse stepped on the brakes, but the Bronco didn't slow down. He was only going about forty, yet he couldn't slow it down. The big tree was directly in front of him now and he was aiming right for it. Quickly, he tried the wheel again, then the brakes. Nothing.

Finally, he yanked at the emergency brake only to have the lever come off in his hand. Panicky now, Jesse thought to open the door and jump out, but the seat belt held him firmly in place. By the time he got the belt unlocked, it was too late.

At forty miles an hour, the Bronco crashed into the eucalyptus tree with a rumbling, shrieking sound of mangled metal. Jesse's tight grip on the wheel loosened, his head fell forward and he lost consciousness.

"Oh, Mommy, she's so soft," Grace said as she gently stroked the newborn kitten's fur. The mother cat, Chester, watched the little girl suspiciously.

Crouching down with her daughter in the corner of the barn, Abby ran a finger along the tiny kitten's back. "Yes, she is."

"Why won't she open her eyes?" Grace wanted to know.

"That's how they're born. They'll open soon enough." Abby reached to caress the top of the watchful mother's head. "I think we're going to have to change Chester's name."

Sitting down on the hay-covered floor, Grace put the kitten back alongside Chester and the relieved cat began licking her baby. "'Cause boys can't have babies and Chester's a boy's name, right?"

"That's right, sweetie. What name would you like to call her?"

Grace wrinkled her forehead, thinking. "How about Ariel like in *The Little Mermaid?*"

"Mmm, let's think about that."

"Chester never comes when you call him anyway. I mean her. Not like Jughead. He comes running when I yell his name."

"Well, cats are more independent than dogs."

"What's *inpendent* mean?"

"In-*de*-pen-dent. And it means they don't like to be told what to do and they like to take care of themselves, do things their own way."

"Oh, you mean like Jesse. I asked him why he wasn't staying in the bunkhouse with the men 'cause I thought he was lonely, but he said he likes to do things his own way."

"Did he, now?" Grace loved her talks with Jesse and her walks with Grandpa nearly every evening. Abby rose. "Listen, sweetie, we need to get going if we're going to go grocery shopping for Grandma."

"Okay." Grace gave the kitten a pat on its tiny head, then reluctantly got up. "Can we come back later?"

"We'll see." Hand in hand, they left the barn.

Abby drove under the arches and parked the Lincoln in its usual parking space. Though she was wearing shorts and a cool cotton top, she was still hot. She needed to remind Dad to have the Lincoln's air conditioning repaired. Though Vern kept the ranch equipment in top shape, he didn't get around to his own car, often letting it sit idle for weeks.

Popping the trunk, Abby got out, then helped Grace out of her car seat in the back.

"I want to help, Mommy," Grace said as she looked into the trunk at the overflowing brown paper bags.

"Here, sweetie, you can carry this one," she said, giving her a light sack. Hoisting a full bag in each arm, Abby glanced over to Jesse's cabin. His Bronco still wasn't where it should be and she found that odd. It had been gone when she and Grace had gone to look at the kittens and that had been easily two hours ago. Since his arrival, Jesse rarely left the compound except to go to Curly's, which was a ten-minute drive. Frowning, she wondered where he was and if anything was wrong.

She left the groceries on the kitchen table and went back for more. Jesse's cabin was as usual, the heavy door propped open, only the screen visible.

Abby deposited the last load on the table and settled Grace in front of the television with a small bowl of popcorn and her cartoons before helping her mother put away the groceries. "Where's Lindsay?" she asked, having noticed her car gone, too.

Joyce brushed back a lock of auburn hair as she stirred a large pot on the stove. "She left about two. Said she had something important to do in town. I thought she'd be back by now."

Funny how Lindsay always managed to have something important to do when any household chore needed doing, Abby thought, then chastised herself. Her sister had her own problems, she supposed.

Putting the folded bags away, Abby noticed the big pot of soup her mother was stirring. "You're making soup, Mom? On such a hot day?"

"Casey came by earlier and asked me to make my chicken soup for Jesse. Maybe you can take some over later." Joyce tossed in a generous sprinkling of dill weed and parsley.

Abby stopped in her tracks. "Why does Jesse want chicken soup?" She'd thought he usually ate in the mess hall.

Joyce turned, an apologetic look on her face. "I'm sorry. I guess you were gone. It all happened so fast."

The frisson of fear turned into a full-blown dread. "What happened so fast?"

"Jesse's accident. It seems he was on his way to Curly's when somehow he lost control of his vehicle and hit a tree. A retired farmer, Evan Finch, heard the crash and went over."

It was difficult to talk with her heart in her throat. "How badly is Jesse hurt? Where is he?"

Picking up the saltshaker and adding some to the soup, Joyce seemed unaware of her daughter's agitation. She also had to tell her story in her own way, in her own time. "Evan called for an ambulance and they took him to the hospital. They found his wallet and called Casey."

Abby was gritting her teeth so hard she was surprised her jaw didn't snap. "Mom! How badly is Jesse hurt?"

Joyce swung about at the harsh tone of Abby's voice. "Not so bad. A mild concussion, a dislocated shoulder and some bruises is all, I believe Casey said. The hospital was running more tests."

She wouldn't believe it until she saw Jesse with her own eyes. She hurried to call Casey, praying he was on the ranch near one of the six phones they had scattered around the compound. She doubted he'd have stayed long at the hospital.

It was several moments before she heard his gruff greeting. "Casey, it's Abby. How is Jesse?"

He heard the worry in her voice. "Take it easy, honey. He's going to be fine." Casey rattled off Jesse's injuries, the same ones her mother had just mentioned.

"Nothing else? Are you sure?"

"Yup. Saw him with my own two eyes."

"Where is he?"

"Hospital, the one between here and Springerville. East Arizona General. But I…"

"Thanks," Abby said, hanging up on whatever Casey was saying. She grabbed the telephone book from the kitchen drawer and sat down at the table to look up the number, noticing that her hands were shaking.

"Didn't I tell you he'd be all right?" Joyce asked, checking out her daughter's sudden pallor. "Abby, just how involved with this man are you?"

Finding the number, Abby reached for the phone. "Mom, I don't have time to go into that right now." Impatiently, she dialed the number and leaned forward as the phone rang again and again.

Finally, the operator answered. "Yes, hello. I'm calling to inquire about a patient's condition. Jesse Calder."

"Are you a relative?" the somewhat bored voice asked.

"Yes, his sister," she said quickly, hoping the operator didn't have a list of Jesse's relatives handy.

"Just a moment, please."

Fingers drumming on the table, Abby waited. How could Jesse have lost control of the Bronco? She looked up and saw her mother watching her anxiously. She didn't care. Explanations could come later when she was certain Jesse was all right.

The bored voice returned. "I'm sorry, Miss, but Mr. Calder's checked himself out."

"What! But I thought he had some serious injuries?"

"Yes, ma'am, but against his doctor's orders, he checked out. We can't hold a patient against his will."

"Thank you." Wasn't that just like Jesse, impatient to be out of there. She supposed he'd had enough of hospitals when he'd had the other accident.

Frustrated, Abby asked herself where he'd go. Most likely to the cabin.

"Mom, Grace is in the living room watching cartoons. Please keep an eye on her. I'll be right back." Rushing, she was outside and running across the street, thinking that he'd been here all this time while she'd wasted precious minutes on phone calls.

She flew up the steps and yanked open the screen door, finding it unlocked as usual. "Jesse!" she called out. But the house was silent. On the kitchen counter, she spotted a medicine bottle. Pain pills. Had he taken any?

If so, he'd be asleep, Abby thought, heading for the bedroom. But no, he wasn't there, nor anywhere else in the small house.

She went out on the porch and stood with her hands on her hips, trying to think where Jesse might be. She heard a sound and turned to see Casey walking toward her. She raced down to meet him.

"Where is he, Casey?"

"If you wouldn't have hung up on me, I'd have told you." Casey removed his hat and swiped a kerchief over his damp head. "I brought him back to the cabin and told him to lay down, but he wouldn't hear of it. Asked me if I knew where the police had taken his Bronco 'cause he wanted a look at it."

"So did you take him there?" Why was everyone so slow in telling her anything?

"Nope. I told him I had to get back to work. We started inseminating and I couldn't be gone that long." Carefully, he replaced his hat. "Darn fool found Slim, who had some time off, and he agreed to take him."

The news wasn't all bad. If Jesse was well enough to take off like that, he couldn't be too badly hurt. *Could he?* "I don't suppose you know what garage the police use?"

"Don't know if the Bronco's at a garage yet or at the impound lot until the accident is investigated." He took his tobacco pouch out of his pocket, pulled off a plug and stuck it in his mouth.

Chewing thoughtfully, Casey studied the girl he wished was his own. "You got to calm down, Abby. First, he's not hurt real bad, like I said. Second, Slim'll bring him back as soon as Jesse gets some answers."

Her agitated mind finally registered what she'd just heard. "Investigated? The accident is being investigated? Why? What kind of answers does Jesse want?" Then it hit her. "Are you saying that he didn't just lose control and drive into a tree?"

"Jesse doesn't think so."

"If not an accident, then what?" Her mind racing through possibilities, she wrinkled her brow. "If you're thinking someone here tried to harm Jesse, that can't be. He's been nothing but helpful around here. He rescued Tex from a runaway horse, he helped out with the fencing when he didn't have to, worked with that filly, made swings for the kids. Why would anyone want to harm him? I…" She struggled with a sob wanting to break free.

Casey studied her for a long moment. "You've gone and done it again, haven't you, Abby? You've fallen for him."

Blinking back tears, she met his gaze and spoke in a low, emotional voice. "I never stopped loving him, Casey. He's the one, the only one I've ever wanted."

Casey scraped a hand over his unshaven face. "Did you tell him about Grace?"

"Not yet, but I plan to, as soon as possible." She saw the worry in his expression.

"Then what? You think the three of you will live happily ever after? What if he doesn't take the news too well?"

"I don't know. But I've got to believe we'll work it out. I love him, Casey." As if suddenly remembering the present situation, she jumped up. "I'm going to call the police, see what I can find out and…"

The rumble of a somewhat battered black truck turning in through the arches caught their attention. Slowing down, it stopped in front of them.

Abby recognized Slim as the driver, but it was the passenger she was interested in as she hurried around to the other side. She noticed a white bandage on Jesse's forehead and a grimace on his face.

Jesse opened the truck door and sat a moment, getting his bearings. His head hurt like hell and his left shoulder was still painful from when they'd wrenched it back in place at the hospital. But more than anything, he was angry at what he'd learned at the police impound lot.

"Let me help you," Abby said, extending a hand toward him.

"You better let me, Abby," Slim said. "He needs a strong shoulder to lean on."

She hadn't even noticed that Slim had gotten out of the truck and come around. "I have a strong shoulder," she said emphatically. "Which side did you injure?" she asked Jesse.

"The left. I can make it on my own." He swung his legs out and braced his right arm on the door as he maneuvered his body out of the truck. Each movement cost him, but he was standing alone.

Abby quickly moved to his right side and slipped an arm around his waist. "I know you can make it on your own, but I'd feel better if you'd let me help."

Pride was pushing him to go it alone, but he was light-headed, probably from the shot they'd given him. Or maybe it was all catching up to him. The pain medication was wearing off and he didn't want to fall on his face out here in front of everyone.

Okay, so if she'd feel better, he'd let her help him. Taking slow, careful steps, they moved toward the cabin. Halfway there, he turned his head and looked over his shoulder at Slim. "Thanks, buddy. I owe you."

Slim waved away his thanks. "You owe me nothing." Climbing into his truck, he drove toward the rear of the compound.

Casey stood by the bottom stair, scowling. "You shoulda listened to me when I told you to stay put."

"Yeah, I know." With Abby's guidance, they moved up the steps.

Casey spoke to Abby. "You make sure he rests, and if you need anything, call me, you hear?"

"Yes, Casey, I hear you. And thanks." Abby tightened her grip on Jesse, but suddenly he stopped to stare down at the space where his Bronco was usually parked, staring at the yellowish stuff on the ground and next to it an oily stain.

After a long moment, he turned to Abby. "I think someone wanted to kill me."

Chapter Eleven

She couldn't have heard right, Abby decided. Who would want to kill Jesse? Obviously he was somewhat delirious, either from medication they'd given him at the hospital or from pain because he'd refused the medication.

"Let's keep going," she said, urging him up the steps. There'd be plenty of time to talk about the accident after he'd rested.

He was tired and achy, his eyes grainy and his limbs heavy, but Jesse finally reached the bedroom, half supported by Abby. Maybe he had pushed himself a bit hard, but he'd had to know before all the evidence disappeared. He sat down on the bed, his grateful legs stretching out as Abby removed his stained and torn shirt. A shower would feel good, Jesse thought, but he knew he couldn't stand up that long.

"I'm going to get a basin of water and cool you off a little," Abby said, noticing how hot and sweaty he was. "Then

I'll get you a cold drink." And she'd make sure he took one of the pain pills.

Too exhausted to argue, Jesse lay back on the sheets, thankful the room was dim. If only he could get rid of this blasted headache.

In minutes, Abby was back, gently sponging his battered body. She'd turned on the overhead fan, which felt wonderful. He needed to take off his jeans so he unfastened his belt, only to have his fingers brushed aside by hers. He opened his eyes. "Lady, are you going to ravish me in this helpless condition?"

"In your dreams." Gingerly, she unzipped his jeans and when he raised his hips, she pulled them down and off, placing them on a nearby chair. A packet of M&M'S fell out of his pocket and landed on the floor.

"Still a kid at heart, I see," she said, tossing the package on the nightstand and remembering how he used to take a candy break when the other men stopped for a smoke.

"Hey, that's my last package. Take it easy."

"I'll get you some more." She saw that he was wearing sexy black knit briefs, but for once, that wasn't what drew her attention. There was a new dark bruise along his left rib cage. "Does this hurt?" she asked, touching it lightly, her expression somber.

"Not much. They X-rayed it at the hospital. No ribs broken." Blinking to clear his vision, he saw that her normally cheerful expression was gone and instead she was frowning, her eyes filled with concern. "Hey, don't look so serious. I've survived worse than this."

Sitting down on the edge of the bed, Abby brushed a lock of dark hair off his forehead, then trailed her fingers down his bearded cheek, loving the feel of the soft hair. Besides the cut on his forehead, there were several nicks on his face, probably from flying glass shards. She wouldn't give in to tears, she simply wouldn't.

Jesse knew he wasn't operating on all cylinders, but even in his condition, he saw that she was about to cry. "What is it?"

She leaned down closer, stroking his hair. "Nothing. It's just that…you could have been killed today. I almost lost you again, now when I've just found you." Her voice ended on a sob.

With his good arm, he encircled her, drawing her to him. "But you didn't. I'm right here and I'll be fine after a little shut-eye."

She had to let him rest, Abby knew. But first, she leaned in to kiss him softly, tenderly, because she needed the contact. "I'm going to get that drink."

She was back in minutes with iced tea and a slice of lemon. She helped him sit up somewhat unsteadily and held the glass for him.

"Take this pain pill."

He made a face. "I don't need a pain pill."

"Yes, you do. Now take it or I'll shove it down your throat." At his surprised expression, she nodded. "Don't think I won't."

Like a dutiful little boy, he drank it, pill and all, then sank back into the pillows and took her hand. "I can't believe I've got this beautiful woman here at my bedside and I can barely lift my hand. Rain check?"

"You bet. I've got to run an errand, then I'll be back and I'll bring some of Mom's chicken soup. It can cure things even penicillin can't."

Jesse smiled, his eyes already closing as she got up. Abby

stood in the doorway for several minutes, just watching him sleep. He looked so defenseless that she wished she could lie down beside him and hold him close. He lay on his side, one hand tucked under his cheek, the other curled at his chest, just the way Grace often slept. She would tell him about Grace just as soon as he was back on his feet. It was time. Her heart finally settled to a slower pace, she sent a prayer of thanks heavenward.

She hurried home to tell her mother she had an errand to run, hoping she would watch Grace for her.

Brian Kelly, a tall, blond man with freckles spotting his round Irish face, was in charge of the sheriff's department impoundment lot. "Are you sure you want to go under?" he asked Abby as they stood alongside the Bronco up on the rack.

"Yes. I want to see, Brian." She'd been two years behind Brian in high school, but she'd known him and his family for years. "It's pretty banged up, isn't it?" she commented, looking at the bashed-in front, the broken windshield.

"Yeah. The driver was lucky to walk away from this." He grabbed his large flashlight and ducked under, guiding her with his free hand. "Okay, look over here." He shone the light up at a section of oily machinery. "This is the steering column and right here is a puncture. Fairly small so the fluid would drain out slowly. Now over here," he went on, moving the light, "is the brake line. It, too, has a puncture, about the same size." He shifted to look at her. "Can you see them both?"

"Yes. Could those punctures have been made by the Bronco traveling over gravel, the stones bouncing up?"

"Not a chance. First, you can see that each one is a perfectly round hole. Gravel might leave an indent, but no stone could penetrate that metal, and even if it could, the hole wouldn't be perfectly round. I'd say someone used a punch or a Phillips screwdriver or maybe an ice pick, something like that."

Ducking back out, Abby felt a shiver race up her spine despite the heat in the garage. "So then someone deliberately damaged this vehicle?"

Following her out, Brian nodded. "Absolutely." He walked to a long bench along one wall where tools of all sorts were piled in no special order and picked up a long metal piece. "Then there's this. It's the shaft, the inside control that you pull back on to engage the emergency brake." He turned it over so she could see the end. "This is bolted into a track where it stays until needed. The track was damaged somehow, the shaft disengaged and was just resting there so that when the driver pulled on it to try to stop the vehicle, it came loose in his hand."

Heart pounding, Abby didn't know what to say. Unnerved, she walked outside and sat down on a bench by the big doors. It was one thing to hear about what happened and another to see the evidence.

Wiping his hands on a rag, Brian joined her. "Is Jesse Calder a good friend of yours?"

"Yes. He's staying with us for a while, working with a traumatized stallion."

"Oh, yeah. I heard a while back that he was coming. He was here a couple of hours ago to check out the Bronco. Nice guy. He's damn mad and I don't blame him."

She turned to look at him. "Brian, could just anyone have done this, or would it have to be someone who's a mechanic?"

"Most likely it would be someone with some knowledge of how a vehicle's put together. I mean, would you have known how to disable that Bronco before I showed you?"

"No. Would it take someone strong?"

"Not necessarily. Puncturing through that metal with a sharp object wouldn't be hard, but you'd have to get under and know where to hit." Sitting back, he gazed up at the clouds marching across a blue sky. "You know anyone who'd want to hurt this guy?"

"That's what I'm trying to figure out. Do you think their intention was to frighten him, maybe hurt him a little, or was it to kill him?" Speaking the words out loud put a quiver in her voice.

"Depends on how long the Bronco was parked after the hit while the fluids were slowly dripping out. Obviously, Calder was able to drive a ways without noticing a problem, so it had to have been done shortly before. I'd guess that someone's been watching and knew his schedule, knew that he drives to Curly's every day about the same time, like he told me he does. Lucky for him that he took the side road instead of the highway. Speed could have made it worse. My guess is that someone wanted to send a message, to scare the hell out of him or maybe get even for something, not necessarily to kill him."

Brian stood up. "You know what they say—means, opportunity and motive. That's all it takes."

Abby rose also. "It's that last one that worries me. I know you have to get back to work. Thanks, Brian, for explaining all this to me." The phone by the bench rang.

"Glad to be of help." He turned to answer the phone.

Abby closed the lid on the plastic container of chicken soup with a snap. She reached up to the top shelf of the cupboard for the crackers as her mother came into the kitchen.

"I imagine Jesse Calder's had better soup than mine," Joyce said, pouring herself a cup of coffee from the ever-present pot.

"Now, Mom, you know your chicken soup is outstanding." Abby slipped several crackers into a plastic bag and zipped it closed.

"So you're playing nursemaid, eh?" Joyce's voice was troubled as she sat down at the maple table.

"Yes. I stopped in to check on Jesse when I returned and he was sleeping soundly, but I imagine he'll wake soon and be hungry." She glanced around the kitchen, wondering what else to take when she spotted the fruit bowl. Placing an apple and a pear in the picnic basket, she decided she had more than Jesse would probably eat.

"Abby, sit down with me a minute, please?" Joyce folded her hands together on the tabletop.

Abby sighed inwardly. She did not want to take the time right now to have a heart-to-heart with her mother. But Joyce so seldom asked that she couldn't refuse her.

Pouring herself a cup of coffee as well, she sat down opposite Joyce. "Something wrong?"

"What did you find out at the sheriff's impoundment lot?"

Taking a sip, Abby was surprised her mother had either guessed where she'd been earlier or someone had told her, perhaps Casey. "It's not good news." Quickly, she explained what she'd seen and Brian's educated guess.

Joyce's pale face registered concern. "Do you have any idea who might have done such a thing?"

Abby shook her head. "Do you?"

"No." She downed a bracing swallow of coffee. "I suppose it's safe to assume, since you've already spent one night with him and the fact that you're now rushing to his sickbed, that you're seriously involved with Jesse Calder, right?"

Abby would have smiled at her mother's almost embarrassed wording if the situation weren't so serious. "Seriously involved? As in, in love with him? Yes, I am."

Intertwining her hands on the table nervously, Joyce kept her eyes down. "I've always thought I should have had sons. I wouldn't have to worry so much about boys and your father would be the one they'd go to for the hard questions. I feel ill-equipped to advise daughters."

Frowning, Abby leaned her elbows on the table. "What are you getting at, Mom?"

"I know you and Lindsay think I don't know what goes on with the two of you, either here or out in the world, but I see more than you think, Abby. I know you didn't meet a man at college, marry him and then have him conveniently drown. You got pregnant and the man left you. Just like it happened with my own mother. I so wanted you to find a good man, get married, settle down and be happy."

Abby truly didn't know what to say because her mother was right, she'd had no idea Joyce hadn't believed her story.

"And Lindsay. I don't believe a word of her story that she sent Adam packing just days before their wedding. I may not be the best judge of character, but that man spent two weeks here pitching-in on the ranch chores, following your father around. I believe he was, and is, a fine, honorable man. Lindsay's troubled about something, but then, sometimes I think she was born unhappy."

Glancing at the wall clock, Abby wished she could end this odd conversation and get going. But how?

"I'm not sure why you're bringing all this up now, Mom."

Joyce looked up and her eyes were bright with unshed tears. "Because I don't want to see you hurt again. Either of you. I just want you both to be happy."

Abby reached over and squeezed her mother's hands.

"Mom, happiness isn't a given, for any of us. Lindsay and I are adults and we have to work out our own problems. Right or wrong, we make decisions and then we have to live with them. You can't shield us or keep worrying about us as if we were still children."

Joyce gave her a tired smile. "You just wait until Grace is older. You'll find out that a mother's worry goes on a long time after her child is grown."

"I probably will. But what I mean is that worrying about us isn't going to change whatever happens."

Joyce reversed their hands, squeezing Abby's hand with her own two. "Promise me you won't do anything rash this time. He's very good-looking, quite nice and I can see why you're attracted. But he's going to go back to California and you're going to be heartbroken again."

Abby wished she could assure her mother that that wasn't going to happen. But she herself wasn't certain.

Rising, she moved to Joyce and hugged her. "I promise to be careful." And that was the best she could offer.

"Mommy," Grace called out as she came running into the kitchen, "can we go see the kittens again?"

Abby smoothed back her daughter's hair. "Not just now, sweetie. I've got an errand to run. You stay here with Grandma and be a good girl." She turned to her mother and saw she was rubbing her forehead. "You're sure you're okay with watching Grace until I get back?"

Drawing in a deep breath, Joyce seemed to get a hold of herself. "Yes, she'll be fine. We've rented *Lady and the Tramp* and we're going to have a fun evening. Aren't we, sweetie?" she asked, pulling the child onto her lap.

"Will you take me to see the kittens, Grandma?" Grace was never one to give up easily.

"Now, Grace," Abby interrupted, "you know Grandma doesn't like going into the barn. Where's Aunt Lindsay? Maybe she'll take you."

"Upstairs," Grace said, moving from her grandmother. "I'll go ask her." She skipped off, heading for the stairs.

"When will you be coming home, so I can tell Grace later, because she's sure to ask?"

"I plan to stay the night, Mom," Abby said, and waited for her mother's reaction.

Joyce sighed wearily. "Have a nice evening, dear."

"Thanks." Impulsively, she leaned down and kissed her mother's cheek, then grabbed the picnic basket and hurried outside, breathing a sigh of relief. So Joyce had guessed about her pregnancy and figured out that Lindsay had lied, which Abby had thought all along. Why did grown daughters have so many problems getting along with their mothers? It wasn't so with their fathers. Would she and Grace experience the same thing one day?

Abby fervently hoped not as she ran across to Jesse's cabin and hurried inside.

He was awake and ravenous. But not for food.

Abby closed the cabin door behind her and found Jesse pacing the living room barefooted, wearing only a clean pair of jeans that she noticed were unbuttoned. "It's good to see you up and looking better." His color had improved and his hair was wet from a recent shower.

"I've got some of my mother's fabulous chicken soup here," she said, walking to the small kitchen and setting the picnic basket on the table. "And crackers and fruit."

"Later," Jesse said from behind her as he slipped his arms around her.

She hadn't heard him follow her, but she certainly felt his

bearded face nuzzle into her neck and his seeking hands wander over her waist, her stomach, moving lower. Turning within his arms she watched his blue eyes darken as he gazed into hers.

"I locked the door," he told her, then bent to taste her ear and her lovely throat.

"Mmm, good. But I thought you were beat, that you needed sleep." His mouth busily roamed her face, depositing kisses at will.

"I've slept enough," he whispered in a voice thick with desire. Jesse's mellow mood brought about by medication had vanished, replaced by an urgency he could scarcely explain, even to himself. His blood thundered through his veins, fueled by the knowledge that yet again, he'd come too damn close to death's doorway.

His eyes darkened as he pulled her hard up against his chest and heard her gasp. There was an intensity about him, a wild predatory gleam that Abby had never seen before. She'd read that harrowing escapes from danger, near misses, often sent men back to elemental basics. It affected women, too.

Jesse couldn't wait another second as he crushed her mouth with his, thrusting his tongue inside, demanding a response as his arms tightened around her.

Abby tasted heat and need and frustration as his hands snaked between them and kneaded her flesh through the cotton blouse she wore. He tugged the thin material free of the waistband of her shorts and burrowed beneath. His fingers were callused, rough, exploring her naked skin, his touch, as always, causing her knees to all but buckle.

Her head was spinning with dazed pleasure as her body movements urged him on. She moaned softly, overcome by the need to get closer to him, and closer still.

Then a sobering thought stopped her. "What about your injuries? Your shoulder and…"

"Forget them. I'm fine and I want you," he whispered huskily against her lips, "like I've never wanted any other woman." He resumed the kiss, slowly walking her backwards out of the kitchen, through the living room and into the bedroom until the backs of her legs touched the bed.

Urgency had her pulling back. "I want you more. Oh, God, Jesse. I saw the Bronco, all mangled and broken. You could have easily died in that wreckage. I could have lost you again." She clung to him, her nails digging into his back. "I can't bear the thought of losing you."

"You never will."

Nearly in a frenzy, she ran her hands over his chest, her fingers tunneling into the dark hair that covered the firm muscles. Then her hands arrowed down to his open waistband and her hands slowly slid down the zipper.

Breathing hard, Jesse fumbled with her blouse's tiny buttons, growing impatient. With one swift yank, he ripped it open. Buttons flew every which way as her breasts were revealed to his eager eyes.

"You're not wearing a bra."

"I was in a hurry to get here." Then she felt his hands cover her sensitive flesh. On a soft sigh, she let her head fall back as he bent to sample, to taste. With unfamiliar abandon, Abby arched against his mouth, inviting him to have his fill. In seconds, she was flying, desire raw and primitive making her ache, making her groan. "Now, Jesse. I want you *now.*"

Her passionate demand had him half-crazy. They tumbled onto the double bed, still wearing too many clothes, struggling to free each other of every annoying hindrance. His mouth returned to hers, needing more as he bucked and strained to be skin to skin with her. Everywhere he touched seemed on fire. He sucked in air, breathing in the womanly scent of her, letting it drive him to the brink.

She responded with such fervor, such wholehearted participation, that she took his breath away. Her hands thrust into his hair, then skimmed down his rib cage only to move lower. He wondered fleetingly how she knew just how to touch, how to make him feel so much. Then he gave himself up to the sensual pleasure of her mouth relearning him.

Abby's body was as hot as the heat of the desert outside the cabin. She searched for words to say, to explain how he moved her, how he was the only one who could, yet no words seemed enough. So instead, she spoke to him with her mouth, with her fingertips, with the gift of herself. She knew she'd never wanted like this, never *been* wanted like this, never loved another so deeply.

Finally, Jesse opened the nightstand drawer and took a moment to protect her, then leaned down to look at her beautiful face. He saw such love reflected there, for him, all for him. Her hands guided him inside her and he watched her eyes grow cloudy as he filled her. This had been all but inevitable since she'd helped him up the porch steps earlier. After she'd left him sleeping, he wasn't sure she'd return, though she'd promised him her mother's soup. Even as the medication tugged him under, he'd wanted her here, right here. At last she was in his arms, his to love.

Abby felt the ache building and building. Her hands circled his back as she tried to keep her gaze on his. He pushed her higher, harder until there was nowhere else to go. At last she called out his name just before he sent her into a shuddering climax. Moments later she felt the peak subside, but he moved just so and sent her spiraling upward again.

In the dim bedside lamplight, Jesse studied her flushed face, the sheen on her satiny skin, the stunned surprise in her eyes. Her golden hair was fanned out on the pillow. The love he'd felt for her for years yet had denied even to himself threatened to overflow his heart. Knowing he could never get enough of this woman, he began to move again.

In seconds, Abby was racing like a runaway train, arching upward just enough to send him catapulting off the edge. Clinging to each other, hot, damp and reaching, they flew together and met in a place only the two of them had ever known.

They'd gone to sleep wrapped in each other's arms, then awakened sometime during the night, hungry for food. They'd shared the soup and crackers, and then eaten the fruit back in bed. They couldn't seem to stop touching, stop looking, stop smiling at little things. They didn't talk about serious stuff. This night was theirs alone, to love and be loved.

They'd made love again, this time slowly, tenderly, gently. They'd smiled and laughed lightheartedly, then taken a shower together and made love under the steaming water. Then they'd gone back to sleep in each other's arms.

Abby woke at first light and saw on the bedside clock that it was not yet six o'clock, her usual time to get up on weekdays. But today was Saturday and the kids wouldn't be coming.

Jesse was up against her spoon fashion so she couldn't see his face, but she could feel his warm breath on her neck. Never in her life had she slept so well as she did wrapped in the arms of the man she loved.

He'd said she wouldn't ever lose him, and she trusted that he meant it. Only one hurdle left, really. She had to tell him about Grace and pray he'd understand. She'd tell him this morning as soon as he awakened, not wanting to put it off now that she'd made up her mind. She finally trusted him and hoped he'd appreciate the reasons why she'd waited to reveal her secret.

If only he would, then all the rest they could work out. Of course, there was still the mystery of who'd tried to hurt Jesse. Maybe they'd never figure that out. Then again, she thought that Jesse was the kind who'd keep digging until he came up with answers.

Abby yawned and settled her hands atop his as they rested on her breasts. She closed her eyes, feeling happier than she ever could remember.

The ringing of the bedside phone woke both of them an hour later. Jesse struggled out of a deep sleep and reached to answer it. "Yes?" he said, his voice fuzzy.

Next to him, Abby stretched lazily and listened to his end of the conversation.

"I see," Jesse said. "Uh-huh…all right…I'll be there in an hour…I understand…no, it's no trouble. Thanks, Sheriff."

He hung up and flipped over, burrowing into Abby's side.

"The sheriff wants you to go in?"

"Yeah. Something about the accident. He wouldn't say what." He kissed his way up her side, settling at a breast. "Damn, just when I was having this great dream."

"Really? Who was in your dream?" Shifting, she gathered him closer.

"You, of course." He lifted his head. "We were on this Pacific island, just the two of us, living in this makeshift hut, subsisting on pineapples and berries and coconuts. And love."

"Mmm, that sounds wonderful. And no phones allowed."

"Right." He kissed her, drawing it out, then propped himself up on one elbow. "Maybe we can honeymoon on one of the Pacific islands."

Abby's heart thumped so loudly she was certain he'd heard it. "Honeymoon? As in, we're getting married?"

"Well, yeah. That's how it usually works." He pulled the sheet down and, using one finger, traced the outline of her nearest breast, noticing how her skin quivered at his touch.

"I don't recall anyone asking me to marry him," she said cautiously.

He frowned at her. "Are you sure?"

"Pretty sure. I'd have remembered something like that."

"You see, I was on my way to get your ring when that tree stopped me. So we'll have to improvise." Getting up from the bed and pulling her into a sitting position, he went down on one knee, oblivious of his nakedness, and took her hand. "Abigail Amelia Martin, will you do me the honor of becoming my wife? Please say yes and make me the happiest guy on the planet."

Eyes moist, Abby could only nod.

"What's that? I didn't hear your answer," Jesse insisted.

"Yes, you fool, yes!" Leaning into him, she pressed her mouth to his while tears flowed down her cheeks. Happy tears.

Rolling back onto the bed with her, he pinned her beneath him and gazed into her damp eyes. "I love you, Abby. I think I always have loved you."

"Me, too," she said, her heart full of love.

He kissed her again, then jumped up. "I've got to run over to the sheriff's office. Do you think I could borrow the black truck?"

"Yes, of course." Arranging the sheet to cover herself while he put on clean underwear, Abby took a deep breath. "Before you go, there's something I want to talk to you about."

"Yes, you can wear one of my shirts home, since I seemed to have ruined your blouse. Try explaining that to your mother." He stepped into his jeans, amazed that he felt much better. "I'll replace the blouse."

"Thanks, but that's not what I want to talk to you about." She patted the bed next to her. "Come sit down a minute."

"Honey, I can't. When I said an hour, the sheriff said he needed me right away, that there was someone there he wanted me to talk to." Jesse grabbed a black T-shirt from a drawer and pulled it on.

All right, Abby decided. This wasn't something to discuss in a hurry. "Okay, I'll catch you when you get back." She rose, gathering her clothes from the chair.

Jesse stepped into his shoes, grabbed his keys and went to her for one more kiss. "Why don't we go to your folks tonight and tell them everything? What do you say?"

Her stomach tumbled queasily at the very thought. "Sure, okay."

"See you later." Whistling, Jesse left.

Abby stood in the sudden silence, wondering why whenever something wonderful happened, following right behind it was something scary. Walking to the bathroom, she squared her shoulders. It would be all right. It just had to be.

"Hi, sweetie," Abby said, leaning down to kiss Grace, who was sitting at the table eating cereal.

"Mommy, you were gone a long time," Grace said around a mouthful of Cheerios.

"I know but I'm home now." She poured herself a cup of

coffee and glanced over at Lindsay lounging against the counter wearing a robe and a knowing smile as she looked her sister over head to toe, lingering on the T-shirt that hung down to her knees.

"Nice shirt," Lindsay drawled. "Did you lose at strip poker?"

"Very funny."

"So, how is he?" Lindsay asked, a sneer on her face.

But Abby missed it as she reached for the cream. "He's better, at least the shoulder is. But you always worry about a concussion and…"

"What concussion?" Lindsay straightened. "Who are you talking about?"

Stirring her coffee, Abby looked up. "Jesse. I assumed you were asking about Jesse. Weren't you?"

A hint of fear jumped into Lindsay's nervous gaze. "What happened to Jesse?"

"He lost control of his Bronco and crashed into a tree yesterday afternoon. I thought you knew."

"No, I was out. How did it happen?"

Abby shrugged, then sipped her coffee. "Brake line punctured. Steering fluid leaked out, too." Watching closely, she saw the blood drain from Lindsay's face and wondered why.

"But he's going to be all right, isn't he?"

"Yes, thank God. The police are investigating and…"

"The police?"

"Well, sure. It's obvious that someone damaged the Bronco deliberately. Fluids don't just suddenly drain away."

The phone rang, causing Lindsay to jump, startled. She answered it, then turned her back for privacy.

Abby walked over to sit across from her daughter. "Want some more cereal?"

"No, thanks, Mommy." Grace polished off her orange juice.

Abby couldn't help overhearing mumbled snatches of Lindsay's conversation. Whoever she was speaking with was getting her visibly agitated. She cleared her daughter's dishes, placing them in the dishwasher as Lindsay finally finished.

"Abby, you have to take Mom to the hospital," Lindsay blurted out, as she came over and poured the rest of her coffee down the drain.

Abby looked at her, startled. "The hospital? What's wrong with her?" Surely that call hadn't been about Mom.

"She has a terrible migraine. I called her doctor about an hour ago. He's going to be at the hospital all day and said we should take her there. I…I was waiting for you to get back." Lindsay stuck her shaky hands into the robe's pockets.

Joyce's migraines didn't always respond to her prescription medication, occasionally requiring an injection. Abby hoped their conversation yesterday hadn't triggered this one. "Can't another doctor in the office see her?"

"Mom doesn't want another doctor. She wants Dr. Peters."

Abby drained the last of her coffee. "Why can't you take her? I've got Grace here and…"

"I would except I'm waiting for a really important phone call." She glanced at the phone almost angrily. "I'll watch Grace. Please, Abby."

Abby nodded. Lindsay wasn't one to ask favors often. "All right. I'll go up and check on Mom and get her ready." She stood as Grace came over and hugged her. "You don't mind staying with Aunt Lindsay, do you? Grandma doesn't feel well, but I'll be back soon."

"Okay. Can we play Old Maid, Aunt Lindsay?"

"Sure thing, babe." She tried a smile, but didn't quite make it.

"What is this important phone call you're waiting for?" Abby asked, putting her cup in the dishwasher.

Lindsay dropped her eyes. "Someone in San Francisco. I may go there. Actually, I'm thinking of moving there. I need to get away from this ranch."

Leaving the kitchen, Abby wondered if Lindsay had talked to Adam and had a change of heart about him.

"Miss Martin, I've given your mother a shot and have her lying down in a dark room," Dr. Peters said as Abby stood in the waiting room, clearly concerned.

"Is this pretty much like last time, Doctor? Will she be all right?" Guilt washed over Abby, thinking her talk with Joyce yesterday might have caused her mother's migraine.

"She'll be just fine in a couple of hours when the drug moves through her system. It is a lot like the last time and the time before. Your mother worries too much over things she can't control and brings these headaches on." A thin man with sandy hair and black-rimmed glasses, Dr. Peters had been Joyce's medical advisor for twenty years. "I'm going to write a prescription for a mild tranquilizer for her, as well."

"Thank you, Doctor."

"You can go home or wait right here, whichever you prefer," he told her.

"I'll wait here."

"Good enough." He hurried off, his unbuttoned white coat flapping as he walked.

Abby sat down on a worn two-seater and idly picked up a magazine. They'd already been here an hour and it would be a couple more before they released Joyce. Wishing she'd brought along a book, she reached for a dog-eared magazine on planting.

Yawning, Abby tried to concentrate on the best time to lay in tulip bulbs, but it was a struggle. She hadn't gotten much sleep last night, but that was all right, she thought with a smile she couldn't prevent. What a glorious night.

And Jesse had said he loved her, asked her to marry him. Could it be possible that for once all her dreams were coming true?

As she absently browsed through the magazine, she heard her name called over the PA system. Leaning forward, she listened harder.

"Will Abby Martin please come to the Emergency Room right away? Abby Martin to the E.R."

The magazine slipped from her lap as she got up and ran toward the elevator.

Chapter Twelve

Fighting the trembling she felt deep inside, Abby concentrated on what the sandy-haired doctor in the E.R. was telling her.

"She's coming around, drifting in and out of consciousness, but that's to be expected," he said, his tan face serious. "When Grace fell on the pitchfork, one of the prongs embedded low in her left shoulder, not exactly next to her heart, but close enough. It also severed an artery and she's lost a lot of blood."

"If only I'd found her sooner," Lindsay wailed, standing alongside Abby, her face as white as the doctor's lab coat.

"Shush, Lindsay," Abby told her. "What do you suggest, Doctor Ames?"

"She'll need surgery to mend the tear. We have an excellent pediatric surgeon on staff. He's been notified and he's on his way. But we may have a problem." He guided the two women to a more private corner of the E.R. waiting room before turning to Abby. "Your daughter has a somewhat rare blood type. AB Negative. I need to test your blood to see if you're a match. If you are, then that's great."

Abby's hopes sank another notch. "I'm not. My medical records are on file here. I'm A Positive."

Trying desperately to hold it together, Abby was stiff-backed, afraid if she relaxed, she'd fall apart. Her heart had nearly stopped when she'd arrived at the E.R. some minutes ago, been directed into the trauma room and seen her daughter's small form on the gurney, the blood-soaked clothes, the medics working on her. Grace had to be all right. She just had to be.

"Test me. I'm her aunt. Maybe I'm a match." Lindsay was nearly hysterical.

Dr. Ames touched her shoulder in an effort to calm her. "Yes, we'll test you and all the members of her family. You see, we keep a fairly adequate blood supply on hand, but AB Negative is so seldom called for."

"I'll call her grandfather and get him here for testing," Lindsay said, looking grateful to be doing something as she hurried to a pay phone.

"What about other hospitals in the area, Doctor?" Abby asked, trying to think of alternatives. "Wouldn't one of them have AB Negative blood?"

"I have my assistant calling. So far the only one we've found is in Tucson. Even by plane, that would take about two hours by the time they get it to the airport, fly it here, drive it to us." He shook his head. "We need to get Grace into surgery right away. The longer we wait, the worse her chances are."

Abby appeared to sway and Dr. Ames reached to steady her. "Here, let's sit down. Do you want me to get you something? A glass of water?"

"No, I'm all right."

"Any other relatives nearby?"

"My mother's upstairs, a patient of Dr. Peters's, being treated for a migraine. But her blood type's the same as mine." Her hand on her forehead, she rubbed to soothe a sudden headache just above her eyes.

"Dad's on his way," Lindsay said, returning.

"Why don't you come with me and we'll test you right now?" Dr. Ames asked Lindsay.

With an anxious look at her sister, Lindsay followed him.

Abby sank back into the chair. This couldn't be happening, not to her beautiful little girl. Oh, God, why had Lindsay let her out of her sight?

She'd been on the damn phone, she'd told Abby when she'd arrived at the E.R. For only a few minutes, Lindsay had insisted. Apparently, Grace had slipped out to the barn to see the kittens. Abby closed her eyes. She should have warned Lindsay about the kittens being a big draw for Grace.

Evidently Grace had heard Lindsay calling for her when she'd finally discovered she'd left the house, so she'd left the kittens and in her rush to get out of the barn, she'd tripped and knocked a pitchfork over, then fallen on it. The mental picture had Abby squeezing her hands into fists.

She prayed harder than she ever had, that one of them would be a match, that the surgery would be a success and Grace would soon be back to her normal, happy self. *Please, God, please,* she prayed. She couldn't lose Grace.

Lindsay wasn't a match. Vern came rushing in, went to be tested, then took the elevator up to check on Joyce after hugging Abby, telling her everything would be all right. Abby sat like a zombie, staring off into space.

"I'm so very, very sorry, Abby," Lindsay said for the hundredth time. "I...I messed up, in a lot of ways."

More to quiet her than anything else, Abby said, "I know you love Grace. I know you wouldn't intentionally hurt her."

"Oh, God, no! But I was careless. I...I need to move away. Start over somewhere. Get my head on straight." Shoving back her heavy hair with both hands, Lindsay looked as anguished as she felt.

When Abby didn't respond further, Lindsay sat next to her, imploring her. "I didn't mean any harm, not any of it. You know I love Grace and I'd never hurt her. The other...well, it was meant to scare him away, not hurt him badly. But I couldn't stop him and...oh, God! I've really made a mess of everything!" Head in her hands, she wept.

Feeling dazed, Abby couldn't make sense of Lindsay's ramblings. She didn't want to hear it. Being sorry didn't help Grace right now. She didn't want to accuse anyone. She just wanted her little girl to be okay. With fear clogging her throat, she waited.

When Dr. Ames came toward her minutes later, Abby could tell by his expression that the news wasn't good.

"I'm sorry, but Mr. Martin's not a match and we've run out of options with the other hospitals. The surgeon's here evaluating Grace and I've phoned Tucson to send the blood. All we can do is pray it arrives in time." He looked distressed and empathetic. Abby wondered how often he had to deliver bad news to families.

"Thank you," she said, her voice sounding pained to her own ears. "Can I go sit with her?"

"After the surgeon's finished evaluating. I'll come get you."

Abby watched him leave, wondering how life could be

so good one minute and so fearful the next. This morning, wrapped in Jesse's arms, she'd been so happy, so…wait!

Jesse! He was a relative, though he didn't know it. Jumping up, Abby hurried to the phone as she searched her handbag for the cell phone number that he'd given her just last week. Lindsay asked where she was going, but she ignored her.

Some minutes later, Abby sat back down, feeling a tiny ray of hope. Jesse had to have Grace's blood type if she didn't. Where else would she have gotten it? She'd only told him on the phone that there was an emergency with Grace and she needed him at the hospital.

This wasn't the way she'd planned to tell him that he was Grace's father. But fate had intervened and she had no choice.

"I got you a cup of coffee," Lindsay said, handing the foam cup to her sister before sitting down. "Who did you call?"

Abby sipped the coffee she didn't want, hoping she could get through the next few hours. "I called Jesse."

"Is he back from the sheriff's office? What did they tell him?"

"I didn't ask. He's on his way here."

"Why? He's not family. He should go back home." There was bitterness in Lindsay's voice and a hint of apprehension.

Abby had had enough of Lindsay and her diatribes, her meaningless ramblings, her careless and selfish ways. "He's coming because he's Grace's father."

"What?" Lindsay was clearly shocked.

"It's a long and involved story," Abby said, then rose and went to stand looking out at the parking lot, needing to be alone as she waited to spot Jesse driving the pickup.

* * *

Abby left the window when she saw Jesse park the pickup and she rushed down the corridor to meet him just outside the double doors. Noticing that she'd been crying, without a word, he took her in his arms and held her tightly. He felt her shudder as he stroked her back and kissed the top of her head.

Finally, he pulled back and looked at her. "What is it? Tell me."

"Grace had an accident. In the barn, she fell onto a pitchfork and lost a lot of blood. The surgeon's with her now. She needs an operation, but she also needs blood." Swallowing hard, she met his eyes. "What blood type are you, do you know?"

"Sure I know. I had to have transfusions when I had my accident. AB Negative. Why?"

On the one hand, she felt relief for she knew Jesse already loved Grace and would save her. On the other, she hated telling him like this. "Because that's Grace's blood type."

Jesse's eyes narrowed. "Are you sure? It's kind of a rare blood type and…and…" The truth finally sank in. "Are you saying that…"

"That she's your daughter, yes."

His mind raced back six years, trying to get a grip on what she'd said. "Grace is my daughter and you wait until there's an emergency to tell me? All right, so you didn't know where to find me before, but I've been here over a month and you didn't say a word, even after we made love? Were you *ever* going to tell me, Abby?" His voice was accusatory, his features set in stone.

"Yes, of course. I tried to this morning, remember. I said I wanted to talk to you, but the sheriff called and you had to leave."

Jesse ran a hand through his already disheveled hair, paced two steps away, then back. "Why did you wait so long to tell me?"

Abby looked down, trying to find the words. "After I recognized you this time, I became afraid you might want to take her from me. After all, you told me that your father had custody of you and your brother and Jake has custody of his son. You have the means and I was afraid to trust you."

Frowning and furious, he stared down at her. "That's what you think of me, that I'd take a child from her mother just like that?"

"I guess I assumed…"

"Yeah, you assumed a hell of a lot."

Abby noticed Dr. Ames at the door and wondered how long he'd been there. She turned to him, swallowing her pride. "Doctor, this is Jesse Calder, Grace's father. He has the same blood type."

"That's wonderful. Please come with me, Mr. Calder."

Without so much as a glance at Abby, Jesse followed the doctor.

Late afternoon and the sunshine was striped as it filtered in through the slatted blinds in the nearly deserted E.R. waiting room. The triage nurse sat behind her wide desk and yawned. A big man in overalls, his craggy face exhausted, slept in a chair in the far corner. Abby and Lindsay sat with a chair between them at the other end.

Lindsay had tried to start a conversation, but Abby had waved her off. She needed to concentrate on Grace, on sending up prayers for her recovery. Dr. Ames had stopped by to tell her that Jesse was a match and that the pediatric surgeon was prepping for the operation. Abby had been allowed in to see Grace for a mere two minutes before they wheeled her to the elevator. She'd looked so small, so pale. Abby blinked back tears.

Absently, she wondered where Jesse had gone since he hadn't returned to the waiting room. Maybe he'd left through another door. She didn't have the energy to look out the window and see if the truck was still in the lot. As angry as he'd been, there was no telling where he'd gone.

Every time the big double doors whooshed open, she looked up hopefully for Dr. Ames, but he hadn't come back and it had now been over an hour. How long could this surgery possibly take? Did they get enough blood? How was Grace's concussion doing? Propping her chin on one fist, she stared at a spot on the tile floor.

The outside door opened as Abby looked up. Jesse came striding toward them, his eyes cool. She braced herself, but he stopped in front of Lindsay.

"The sheriff wants to talk with you. You shouldn't have blown Tennessee off 'cause he's telling them everything." He shook his head disgustedly. "Why, Lindsay? Why'd you want me out of the way?"

Sitting up, Abby felt the shock. "What?"

Lindsay didn't reply, cringing instead. Jesse glanced at Abby. "You didn't know that your sister talked your mechanic into disabling my Bronco? Oh, yeah, and she promised to be real nice to him if he did what she asked, then she went back on her word. Upset him pretty good." His hard look landed back on Lindsay. "Big mistake, Lindsay."

"I told him I'd changed my mind and tried to get him not to do it, but it was too late. He saw his chance and...but I didn't mean for you to get badly hurt. Just to scare you enough so you'd leave."

Staring at her sister openmouthed, Abby was stunned. "Why did you want him to leave so badly you'd resort to that?"

Lindsay's features turned mean. "Because he thinks he's too good for me, but he's all over you. High time someone taught him a lesson. I'm just as good as you." With that, she huffed herself out of the chair and hurried to the door. In moments, they heard her Corvette screeching out of the lot.

Looking suddenly exhausted, his limp more pronounced, Jesse sat down on the other side of the small room, leaned his head back and closed his eyes.

It took a while for everything to sink in to Abby's foggy brain. "Are you pressing charges against Lindsay and Tennessee?" she asked softly.

"Maybe. I don't know yet."

He had every right to be angry and to follow through. It would be hard on Mom and Dad, but Lindsay had brought all this on herself. Why was Lindsay so jealous of her? Abby wondered. Lindsay was beautiful, popular, going out four nights a week with all kinds of guys, whereas Abby hadn't had a date in…oh, at least seven years. Maybe Mom was right, that Lindsay had been born unhappy.

The big doors opened and both of them looked up. But it was two nurses in hospital greens walking out and chatting. Abby slumped back into her chair.

Would this day ever end, and would it end well? She wanted her little girl back in her arms. She wanted Jesse to forgive her, to be as loving as he'd been just hours ago. She wanted her sister to get some help because she obviously needed counseling. She wanted her world to be set right again.

After the wondrous night she'd spent with Jesse, she'd

hoped he'd be thrilled that Grace was his, that they'd get married and live happily ever after. Abby coughed, almost choking now at how naive she'd been to think everything would work out so neatly. She'd heard a saying that if you want to hear God laugh, tell Him your plans. She'd learned that lesson the hard way.

Lost in her troubled thoughts, she didn't hear the doors open until she saw Jesse get up and go meet Dr. Ames. Rushing over, she saw that he wore a small smile.

"You've got a strong little girl there," he told them. "She came through the surgery just fine. We expect a full recovery. Dr. Endicott, the surgeon, will be out to speak with you shortly."

"Thank you, Doctor," Jesse said, his voice thick with emotion.

"Can we see her?" Abby asked.

"Not yet. The surgery team's finishing up and then she'll be in recovery awhile." He flashed her a smile. "But soon."

Thanking him again, Abby went to the window, turning her back to the room, letting the grateful tears fall. She stood there, eyes tightly shut, shoulders shaking as she cried out her relief. She didn't look up until she heard an engine start up and saw the pickup back out of the parking lot and take off.

Without a word or gesture, Jesse was gone.

Jesse sped along the country road, scarcely aware of how fast he was driving, his mind churning. How could Abby keep the fact that Grace was his from him for all these days and weeks? Had she planned to ever tell him? She'd been afraid he'd take Grace from her, Abby had told him. What kind of man did she think he was? Obviously, she didn't know him at all.

Noticing a slow-moving hay wagon just ahead of him, he adjusted his speed, forcing himself to settle down. The whole damn Martin clan had been messing with his head. Joyce hadn't liked him from the start and obviously hadn't changed her mind. She'd invited him to dinner once and scarcely spoken to him since. Vern was using him to work with Remus, to start up that difficult filly, even on the range. His conscience stabbed at him a bit on that last one, but Jesse was too angry to notice.

Then there was Lindsay. Throws herself at him then hires someone to disable his vehicle when he rebuffed her. Nice! Selfish, self-centered, jealous, she'd carelessly allowed Grace—*his daughter*—out of her sight long enough for her to get injured so badly she could have died. Could have died before he'd even known he was her father.

But damn, he should have seen it from the beginning, the resemblance. True, she was blond like her mother but her blue eyes were just like his and she was quite tall for her age, indicating her father was tall since Abby wasn't. And the quick way she'd taken to him, seeking him out, talking endlessly with him. It was as if he'd never been a stranger to Grace.

Impatiently, Jesse honked and passed the hay wagon on the two-lane road. Finally, there was Abby. Sweet, loving, honest Abby. Only not so honest. What if he hadn't fallen in love with her all over again? Would she have let him go back to California, never knowing he had a daughter?

He drew in a deep breath. All right, so some of this was his fault. He was the one who knew where she was all those years. He should have tried harder to reach her, by phone or mail, whatever. But he'd stayed there, longing for her but doing nothing about it. Because of his pride. He'd believed she was married so he'd backed off, never thinking to check even though he'd wondered how she could fall into another man's arms so soon after being with him. That pride thing again.

Jesse ran a hand over his bearded face, feeling weary. What he needed was some perspective. He'd pack up, go home where he felt welcome and comfortable. He'd think things through and then decide what to do. About Grace. About Abby.

About all his jumbled up feelings.

Exhausted, all cried out, shaky with relief and with her emotions close to the surface, Abby drove home. She'd sat with Grace in recovery for as long as the nurses allowed her to, holding her hand, talking softly to her. While machines blipped and beeped and colored monitors raced across small screens.

The pediatric surgeon, Dr. Endicott, had been kind and very reassuring. Grace would be just fine, he'd said, and told Abby to go home and come back in the morning. Finally, on trembling legs, Abby had walked to the car.

Now, she drew in several bracing breaths. She had one more thing she had to do before this endless day was over. She needed to talk to Jesse, whether he wanted to hear what she had to say or not.

It was growing dark and she hoped he hadn't driven off somewhere. She needed to straighten him out on a few things. Then he could leave, if he still wanted to.

She'd forgotten that the Bronco was being repaired and almost panicked when she saw it wasn't in his usual parking space. But a soft light glowed through the living room window and only the screen door was visible.

Quickly, she parked and walked over, calling on her last

bit of strength. Knocking once, she didn't wait for a reply but went inside.

He was sitting in the easy chair at the far end of the room, a bottle of beer in his hand, his expression not particularly welcoming. *That was just fine,* Abby thought. She didn't feel very friendly, either.

Tossing her handbag and keys on the couch, she went over to stand before him. "What right do you have coming back here after six years, thinking I'd just welcome you with open arms and share my daughter with you? Yes, Grace is *my* daughter. You haven't earned the right to call her your own."

He started to speak, but she held up a hand. "No, don't say anything. You said your piece at the hospital. Now it's my turn."

He ignored her. "I don't want to fight with you, Abby. But I think I have a right to the truth. I am her father."

Growing angrier, blinking furiously, she looked at him. "How is it that it never once occurred to you that I might have been pregnant when you left here? Six long years and you never gave it a thought. Never gave *me* a thought."

"That's not true. I…"

"Well, you sure didn't try very hard to find me, did you? My sister tells you on the phone that I got married just weeks after you and I had been passionate lovers, and you believe her! My God! Is that the sort of person you thought I was? Even my mother, the person I concocted that scenario for, didn't really believe it."

Setting down his beer bottle, he straightened. "What do you mean?"

"I mean when I found out I was pregnant, I made up the story of a quick marriage while I was away at college and an even quicker drowning for my mother's sake. She was illegitimate and ashamed of it all her life. I couldn't tell her the truth."

The picture was becoming clearer, but he still had questions. "I still can't see how you got pregnant. I mean, I know I'm Grace's father, the blood type and all, but we were always so careful, always used protection. How did it happen?"

"How?" She all but spat out the one word. "Sure we used protection, *most* of the time. But remember when we rode up into the hills and stayed late? You didn't have anything with you so we…improvised. And another time when we were swimming in the pond." Irritated, she paced away, her hair swaying onto her shoulders with her angry, choppy movements. "Why am I reminding you of this? Obviously you scarcely remember being here much less making love."

Jesse jumped up, grabbed her hand. "I've forgotten *nothing*. All those months and years while I was recuperating, the memory of that summer with you was all that kept me going." He shook his head sadly. "Of course I remember riding up into the hills and swimming, too. I guess I thought that one time, even two, wouldn't matter. You never said anything."

"Because I didn't find out until after you'd left. I was scared, but I believed you when you said you'd be back to explain. I waited for a call, a letter, something. I didn't know what to do. I was nineteen, no money of my own and the man I loved gone."

Abby heard him suck in a breath, but she was in no mood to be sympathetic. "Then one day Casey found me crying in the barn and guessed. He helped me make up the story about the marriage and drowning. The looks I got when I moved back home told me everyone was suspicious, but they couldn't prove anything. Of course, I had to quit college."

Again, he looked pained. "I'm sorry, Abby. I didn't know. If I had…well, I'd have been here for you. I couldn't travel for months after the accident, but I could have made more of an effort afterward. I shouldn't have believed Lindsay." Gently, unsure of her reaction, he urged her closer. "I can't rewrite the past. When I first heard today that Grace was mine and you hadn't told me, I got angry. But I realize now that I didn't make it easy for you to confide in me. I want to fix things, Abby. Please, let me be a part of Grace's life."

A cold shiver ran down Abby's spine. Was he thinking shared custody, taking her daughter to California half the time? No, she wouldn't allow that. "What do you mean?"

Confused at her sudden stiffening, Jesse took both of her cold hands in his. "I mean I want to be a part of your life and our daughter's. Did you forget that I asked you to marry me this morning?"

She relaxed fractionally. "A lot has happened since this morning."

"Yes, but that hasn't changed. I love you and Grace. I want us to be a family."

Abby searched his eyes, wanting desperately to believe yet afraid to trust. "Are you sure?"

"I've never been more sure of anything in my life." Yet he hesitated. "But I guess I should ask, after all I've put you through, do you still care for me?"

Abby felt the tension of the long day slip away. "There were days, too many to count, when I wished I could forget you, when I wanted desperately to stop thinking of you. But nothing worked. And then I'd look at that beautiful little girl and be so very grateful that you'd given her to me. Do I care for you? More than for the next breath I take."

With more tenderness than he'd known he possessed, Jesse took her in his arms and kissed her. It was a slow, smoldering kiss filled with promise.

Epilogue

Arm in arm, Abby and Jesse stood at the site of their new home being built near the Triple C while Grace played tag with her puppy that she'd named Fred.

"Over here is where your room will be," Jesse told Grace, stepping over the green strings marking the various rooms.

"Where, Daddy?" she asked, running over.

"Be careful not to trip," he said, helping her. "Right here. And your bedroom window will look out on those big mountains."

"Can Fred sleep with me, Mommy?" she asked, turning to Abby.

"I don't see why not," Abby said, smiling at them. She smiled a lot these days.

"And over here is where your baby brother's room will be," Jesse went on, stepping farther.

"Or baby sister," Abby reminded him. Only three months

pregnant, too early to tell, yet Jesse was certain the baby would be a boy.

"Brother," Jesse repeated. "Think blue."

They'd been living on the Triple C since their Christmas wedding and they were both crazy about Jake's son, little Jack, who was a busy three-year-old. Abby and Grace had been welcomed with open arms by Cam and Jake.

Her mother and father had grown fond of Jesse's family as well. They'd sold the Martin ranch and with the proceeds, they'd purchased a condo in Red Bluff so they'd be only a short drive from either of their daughters. Joyce was very happy to be off the ranch; she hadn't had a migraine in months. Vern looked healthier without the financial strain of his ranch. He had a good doctor who was monitoring his heart.

Lindsay had moved to San Francisco with a friend after Jesse dropped the charges against her. She'd gotten a job as a buyer of high-end women's clothes in a large department store. Lindsay seemed happier yet she was still in counseling. The last time she'd visited Abby and Jesse, she'd proudly told them that she'd stopped drinking six months ago.

Casey, who was like a member of the family, had moved with them. Too young to just sit and rock on the porch, he was too old to work too hard, but just the right age to help Jesse "start up" a steady stream of troubled horses brought to the Triple C by grateful owners.

So many changes in their lives, Abby thought, yet she'd never been so happy as she was when she watched Grace go back to playing with Fred.

"Madam, would you come over here, please?" Jesse asked, standing in the center of one of the larger rooms.

"Of course, sir." She picked her way over the strings.

He held out his arms. "I believe you owe me a dance." His

eyes filled with love, he took hold of her. They danced slowly on the grass, much as they'd done seven years ago when they'd first met, while Jesse hummed a slow waltz.

"Happy, Mrs. Calder?" he asked.

"Overwhelmingly, Mr. Calder," she whispered.

* * * * *

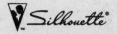

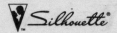

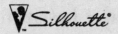

If you enjoyed what you just read,
then we've got an offer you can't resist!

Take 2 bestselling love stories FREE!

Plus get a FREE surprise gift!

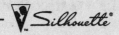

SPECIAL EDITION™

presents
a heartwarming NEW series!

**THE HATHAWAYS
OF MORGAN CREEK:
A DYNASTY
IN THE BAKING...**

NANNY IN HIDING

(SSE #1642, available October 2004)

by

Patricia Kay

On the run from her evil ex-husband, Amy Jordan
accepted blue-eyed Bryce Hathaway's offer to be his
children's nanny. This wealthy single dad was
immediately intrigued by the beautiful runaway, but if
he discovered that this caring, gentle woman was
actually a nanny *in hiding*, would he
help her out—or turn her in?

Available at your favorite retail outlet.

Receive a FREE hardcover book from

H A R L E Q U I N   R O M A N C E ®

in September!

**Harlequin Romance celebrates the launch of
the line's new cover design by offering you
this exclusive offer valid only in September,
only in Harlequin Romance.**

To receive your
FREE HARDCOVER BOOK
written by bestselling author
Emilie Richards, send us four
proofs of purchase from any
September 2004 Harlequin
Romance books. Further details
and proofs of purchase can be
found in all September 2004
Harlequin Romance books.

*Must be postmarked
no later than October 31.*

**Don't forget to be one of the first
to pick up a copy of the new-look
Harlequin Romance novels in September!**

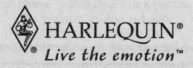

Visit us at www.eHarlequin.com

HRPOP0904